The *Kiss* That COUNTED

Karin Kallmaker

Bella
BOOKS

2008

Writing as Karin Kallmaker:

Christabel	Finders Keepers
Just Like That	Sugar
One Degree of Separation	Maybe Next Time
Substitute for Love	Frosting on the Cake
Unforgettable	Watermark
Making Up for Lost Time	Embrace in Motion
Wild Things	Painted Moon
Car Pool	Paperback Romance
Touchwood	In Every Port

Writing for Bella After Dark:

In Deep Waters 1: Cruising the Seas

18th & Castro

All the Wrong Places

Tall in the Saddle: New Exploits of Western Lesbians

Stake through the Heart: New Exploits of Twilight Lesbians

Bell, Book and Dyke: New Exploits of Magical Lesbians

Once Upon a Dyke: New Exploits of Fairy Tale Lesbians

Writing as Laura Adams:

The Tunnel of Light Trilogy:
Sleight of Hand
Seeds of Fire

Feel free to visit www.kallmaker.com

Bella Books, Inc.
P.O. Box 10543
Tallahassee, FL 32302

First Edition 2008

Printed in the United States of America on acid-free paper

Editor: Katherine V. Forrest
Cover designer: LA Callaghan

ISBN: 10: 1-59493-131-3
ISBN: 13: 978-1-59493-131-4

For Maria, Kelson and Eleanor. Once again, Moogie is done. For now.

Special thanks to the on-the-spot reference sources, especially Lori Lake for the last minute discussion of ballistics. Heartfelt gratitude to the most important people in this writer's creativity—the readers who make the blood, sweat and tears worth it. Finally, my deep appreciation to Katherine Forrest for gently and firmly challenging me to do better.

Twenty. Who knew? Little perennials, where did they come from?

Chapter 1

Gracie's, the fair trade and all-things-organic coffee bar halfway between CJ's office building and Abby's medical center, was crowded with afterwork couples. CJ scanned the room and exits again, then reluctantly brought her focus back to Abby.

"I am not a sexual drive-thru, CJ. You can't just call me up when you want a roll in the hay." Abby licked whipped cream off her stir stick with no sign of her usual pleasure.

But you're here, CJ Roshe wanted to say. Takes two to tango to any tune, she might have added. Given the din of cutlery and conversations, she could have even pretended not to have heard what Abby had said.

Instead, she tried a distraction. "Between your residency schedule and my wall-to-wall meetings, we aren't able to get together that often."

Abby didn't fall for it. With a level look across the steaming cups, she said, "Seven weeks."

Okay, distraction wasn't going to work. Elements of the truth—for instance, that CJ had only realized yesterday how long it had been since they'd gotten together—were not what

1

Abby wanted to hear. Abby's assessment of their relationship was accurate, after all, and CJ wasn't going to pretend otherwise. But she wasn't going to take the whole blame. Abby, deep in the demands of medical residency, hadn't called for a date either. Still, what was the point of hashing over their dysfunctional relationship, especially when the one thing that was more than functional was what they would both be pleased with by morning? Maybe they didn't have to have their usual argument before they adjourned to a more private setting.

"I know." CJ leaned forward to rest her arms lightly on the tiny table. One finger traced the back of Abby's hand. "Seven weeks."

Abby's shiver was palpable. Her problem was that she couldn't admit they *were* about sex. For some reason, that was a bad thing in her book. It wasn't as if either of them was seeing someone else, so what was the big deal? Why was sex supposed to lead down the aisle to ever-after and white picket fences? Regardless, those options weren't available to CJ and she had never told Abby they were.

A clap of thunder announced the arrival of another summer afternoon downpour, and the café's air grew humid and warm in spite of the air-conditioning. CJ watched the ritual of new arrivals shaking off water from their shirts. Denver in August made a raincoat unthinkable; it was drip-dry season.

After another quick visual sweep of the premises, CJ glanced at Abby again. If Abby was truly peeved she would have drawn back from CJ's touch. CJ's pulse stirred as she watched faint mottling creep up the pale throat and chest, enchantingly displayed by a revealing blouse. CJ was almost certain she'd once before unbuttoned that very blouse with her teeth. It was a guarantee that Abby hadn't been wearing a silk blouse on call at the hospital, in the same way that the collar of CJ's tailored shirt hadn't been undone to the top of her cleavage while she'd been at work.

"I'm not—stop that, CJ."

CJ stilled her finger. "Have I ever misled you?"

"No," Abby admitted. A flare of anger marred her lovely face as she tossed back her shoulder-length brown hair. "No, you've been quite honest that I'm in your life to fuck when you feel like it."

"You can call me whenever you like."

"And hear that sexy voice of yours telling me to leave a message."

"Someday you'll find that perfect one you want, Abby. Dearly beloved, diamond ring, the whole deal." Blah, blah, blah, CJ thought. "In the meantime, why not enjoy yourself?"

"You mean why not let you enjoy yourself with me."

"Are you saying you don't enjoy it too?" CJ couldn't help the sardonic lift to one eyebrow and the pointed look at the alluring curves revealed by the clinging silk.

Abby flushed again and CJ was certain Abby could hear the echo of some of the earthy things she had said during their last tryst. "You know that I do. I just wish—"

"That's not going to happen. I'm not made that way." I can't ever *be* that way, CJ added to herself.

Abby regarded her sadly. "I know."

Yet we have to have this conversation every time, CJ wanted to say. "Would you like to get some dinner?"

"No." Abby's little sigh was a mixture of chagrin and resignation. With a glimmer of a smile, she added, "You know what I want."

CJ always tried to be truthful. It made lying easier. "I really want to spend the night with you, too."

"The whole night, huh? Let's go to your place because you make better breakfasts."

CJ squeezed Abby's hand. "Breakfast, and everything leading up to it, will be my pleasure."

Abby picked up her handbag and as CJ rose she surveyed the crowded café to confirm that the route she'd noted earlier was still the best way to exit. No one in her line of sight had a studied nonchalance that set off her internal alarms, but her gaze lighted on an average-looking man in an average-looking suit with his tail so far between his legs that she thought, *Someone just broke his favorite toy.*

She glanced at his companion, then looked away. Looked again, looked away, then stared. Platinum hair hung to her mid-back, straight like sewing silks and catching the light like diamonds. A sleek, shimmering blouse the shade of Kentucky bluegrass set off pale, rose-tinted skin. A nose too long to be conventionally pretty highlighted eyes of crystal-sharp blue. And that wide, curving mouth...

"Are we going?"

"Sure, yes." CJ hid her discomfiture and glanced at the Nordic beauty again. She'd have no trouble at all calling up the woman in her memory. She wouldn't mind if those long legs and vibrant eyes showed up in her dreams. The woman was smiling sweetly at her companion, who looked as if he wanted to crawl under a table to lick his wounds.

As the door closed behind her, CJ resisted the urge to look back one more time. The voice in her head sounded just like Aunt Bitty when she was hunched over her tarot cards. *Dreams*, the voice said, *will be the closest the likes of you will ever get to a fantasy woman like that.*

Abby tended to drive more slowly than CJ did, and they got separated on the way to CJ's apartment. She drowned out her petty annoyances over the traffic with a sweet and sultry Diana Krall CD. She left behind the carefully gridded Victorian streets of the old historic district near the Capitol, and wended her way east, easing onto the long, wide avenues that proclaimed Denver a city of the Limitless West. Her pace increased as she turned onto Colfax. Like most other commuters she was headed for the sprawling network of the multi-lane boulevards.

From there, most drivers would crawl onto the interstates that gave the illusion of all destinations being only a short drive away, that everywhere worth going was connected to Denver. Unlike most of the other commuters, however, she wasn't headed toward a newer bedroom community like Aurora or Centennial, but a small 1950s-era apartment complex, still within the city limits, that had so far escaped the makeovers of its neighbors.

Her gaze moved constantly from the traffic to the speedometer to the rearview mirror as she drove past posh condominium complexes that offered pools and rec rooms, and gentrifying neighborhoods where former small lots were being combined for more opulent homes. She was happy with her nondescript second-floor apartment. It wasn't a place where anyone would look for her. And, giving her the kind of peace of mind she craved, her apartment had a rear exit.

CJ pulled into one of the guest parking spaces so Abby could take the designated spot close to CJ's door. Nearby cars were all familiar, as were the other people arriving home from work. She ran through the rain, which had eased to a misty drizzle, and was up the stairs and inside her door in record time. She quickly went to the tiny second bedroom she used as a home office to plug in her various portable electronics and make sure the phone rang directly to voice mail.

With only a few minutes at most before Abby arrived, CJ opened the unlabeled folder that never left her desk. A faded newspaper clipping floated to the floor and she stuffed it back with the others before running one finger down the handwritten list of a dozen names and amounts. She studied it every night, almost without fail. Once a week she opened the safe in the back of the small closet and added to its contents. Nine of the names now had lines through them and she allowed herself a tight smile. The first person on the list was the reason she'd settled in Denver, and here she was, eight years later, hunkered down, selling commercial real estate like it had always been her career choice, and slowly but surely crossing names off this list.

When she heard the uneven putter of Abby's car, she tucked the folder into the top desk drawer. From the front window she could see Abby's VW disappearing under the covered parking. Everything else below, the little she could see anyway, looked the same as it had earlier.

She selected some sultry Ella on her way to the door, opening it just before Abby knocked. She pulled Abby inside and neither of them seemed to care that a small grocery bag and Abby's purse ended up on the floor in their haste.

"Please, baby," Abby whispered. "Let's go."

"Hold on, sweetie, let me close the door."

CJ ended up with her back against the now locked door with one foot on the groceries, which were probably Abby's favorite sticky rolls.

"What's taking you so long to get me naked?" Abby grinned between kisses.

"Let's at least get to the couch." CJ was relieved to see Abby's sense of humor had returned. Sex ought to be fun, fantastic fun, and with Abby it most certainly was.

Once Abby made up her mind, she was like a racer at Indy with a green flag. The fire of her mouth, the taste of her, always roused a similar urgency in CJ. They fell on the sofa not all that gracefully, clothes still in the way.

Abby laughed, said, "That's my hand," then made that little noise that confirmed that CJ had found a nipple through the blouse. After that, everything was natural and heated, Abby's head tipped back in offering and CJ's mouth nuzzling into one of the most delightfully heaving bosoms she'd ever had the pleasure to know.

Goose bumps dusted Abby's arms, and the texture brought a highly pleasurable tingle to the tips of CJ's fingers. Abby *was* special, and maybe CJ would care more if she wasn't always aware that at any moment she would have to leave without a word. All it would take to get her running for the nearest state line was a glimpse of an old but still familiar face or an authoritative knock at the front door. She wouldn't mind if Abby never forgot her, but she'd feel badly if she left Abby with a broken heart.

"There's nothing better than this," CJ whispered. She took her time dipping into Abby's mouth, then other places that were as wet and welcoming.

Abby's reply was a familiar and pleasing croon, and her hands cupped the back of CJ's head with another rising sound of pleasure. What more did there need to be? It didn't just feel good, it felt wonderful.

Within a few minutes Abby was calling out her name with the abandon that pleased CJ in deep places that didn't seem reachable at any other time. CJ pulled Abby into her arms and kissed away the aftershivers of pleasure, silencing, too, the softly murmured, "CJ" that Abby continued to repeat. Moments like these, when there should only be sweet words and intimate touches, loving caresses and easy smiles, were the only times it ever bothered her that Abby used the name of a woman who didn't exist.

Chapter 2

"So it's not like I want to be an associate forever at such a small law firm. I have aspirations." Brent's earnest expression made his eyes go soft.

He was just like a baby fawn, Karita Hanssen mused. What on earth was she going to say to head him off?

With a fabulous sense of timing, the barista barked out, "Two skinny mochas, Turkish, capped," and Brent gallantly fought the line to secure them, presenting hers with a flourish and courtly bow.

"Thank you, kind sir." Karita got up to doctor her coffee, preferring it sweeter and milkier than Gracie's standard preparation. Stirring in the organic sugar she pondered her options. Brent was going to ask her for an official date and that would be awkward. They worked together and interoffice dating had been declared "the worst thing I ever did" in the three cases she knew about, one very recent. Her job, facilities management and reception in a downtown law firm, was exactly right for her and she wasn't going to jeopardize it.

Her grandmother, watching lovingly from heaven above, no

doubt was thinking that Brent was a lawyer, and that made him good husband material, well worth trading a mere job for. But Gran would also know that Brent's real drawback was his gender, poor fellow. That wasn't his fault, of course, so she'd have to let him down easy. He was very sweet and she didn't want to bruise him. There was no point to bruising people—the world had enough boo-boos without her adding to the total.

Thunder rumbled a warning as she stirred and watched traffic on the congested downtown street outside the bistro. Two years and she was still getting used to summer in Denver. Minnesota had trained her for heat, thunderstorms and humidity. Colorado had the heat, but the air was so dry most of the time that afternoon showers still seemed abnormal.

As if to make a lie of her thoughts, another thunderous warning ushered in a downpour, rapidly filling potholes and sending people scurrying off the street for shelter. She wiggled her toes in the pumps she wore to work, wishing she'd had time to change out of them into her all-purpose clogs before meeting Brent. But wet feet were a small price to pay—the evening skies would clear, the temperatures would fall and the air at home, two thousand feet up from Denver, would be fresh and pure. She laughed quietly to herself as a mixed-breed shepherd paused in the rain to shake off water, much to the vexation of its umbrellaless owner.

Okay, her coffee couldn't get any more stirred and Brent, sweet-as-a-puppy Brent, was still waiting. She turned back to their table with a smile fixed in place.

"Let me get that for you," the man at the condiment station offered as her napkin fluttered to the ground.

"Thank you." Karita accepted the napkin and interpreted the flicker of interest in the man's eyes. He had a wedding ring on his finger and she was willing to bet a picture of two-point-seven children in his pocket.

She was sometimes tempted to tell strange men—as she'd not see them again—the simple truth. How would this fellow react to "I'm a lesbian elf, so run along to your wife."

So she wasn't really an elf, a fact she was still getting used to. She'd believed it with all her heart as a child, and secretly cherished the hope all her life, that it was true, even when part of her knew it simply couldn't be. At twenty-seven she still had lapses of longing to possess just a little bit of magic.

She gave a distant smile to the married man and sidled her way between the tightly spaced tables. At lunch time, Gracie's was always overflowing with coworkers crowded around the little tables to drink coffee and eat muffins. After work, however, each table had a couple. The closest pair seemed about to propose marriage given the looks they exchanged. Just beyond them a swarthy woman with short hair pulled back tightly to a thick twist of curls was definitely making a move—a single finger traced a line across her brunette companion's hand. Even from here Karita could tell both women were flushed. She felt more than a little envious. Men were routinely persistent but women hadn't shown her nearly as much interest.

She hoped she wasn't giving off some kind of "available and ready to breed" vibe that brought the men sniffing but sent the lesbians dashing for cover. The per capita population of lesbians in Denver seemed much lower than in Minneapolis, and the number of women who looked like lesbians, but weren't, complicated the tentative dance of flirtation. She volunteered with several women who laughingly called themselves "false positives" and had told her she was, without a doubt, a "false negative."

The same problem had plagued her in the Peace Corps. She hadn't attracted many dates there initially either. "You're too gorgeous," a friend had declared, adding, "The dykes watch the really hot guys hit on you and get turned down every time. They think they don't stand a chance either."

"That makes no sense whatsoever," Karita had protested vehemently. She was a lesbian so of *course* she turned down one-hundred percent of the guys who asked her out. Half of them accused her of being a lesbian, so why couldn't the lesbians figure it out? She'd finally convinced one or two women she wasn't straight—and proved it satisfactorily in private. After the Peace Corps there had been Mandy, of course. She pushed away a fleeting recollection of loving eyes gone hard as flint, of warm embraces turned stiff and cold.

Since moving to Denver almost two years ago she'd made friends, but hadn't met anyone who made her think beyond tomorrow. She gave the elegant, dark-haired woman one last look. Instead of dark and sexy and ready for love, she thought, as her gaze traveled to the empty seat at her table, she had Brent. Sweet, lovable Brent. The Brents of the world were her penance for deciding initially that the law office was too conservative to comfortably come out. She was no longer sure it wasn't safe to tell her coworkers, most of whom she liked, but other than heading off the Brents, there wasn't really any reason to discuss her love life. No girlfriend to bring to parties, no partner to introduce to her boss.

If she kept standing here her coffee would get cold and Brent would die of old age. She took a deep breath as she faced Brent, her little speech at the ready.

He got up to pull out her chair for her with another courtly bow. He deserved a nice girl, he really did, but it needed to be one who didn't have a vague sense of pity for him at his lack of female anatomy.

She sat, gave him a conspiratorial smile and began. "I can't tell you how relaxing it is to be able to have coffee with a friend. All too often an invitation to coffee leads to a request to date and when you work with someone it can get so awkward. But you're different, Brent, and I really appreciate…"

Brent would get over it, Karita told herself as she left Gracie's alone and without any future date to worry about. Fortunately it was Friday and he'd have the whole weekend to recover. Maybe by Monday all would be well. She really believed he'd be some lucky girl's gallant knight on a white steed soon enough.

She reclaimed her reliable Subaru from the parking garage, emerging from its depths into sunshine streaming between the clouds rushing east toward Kansas. A gap of blue sky was spreading out from the Front Range of the Rockies, which loomed over the entire western horizon. Shafts of gold edged with blue dazzled her eyes—her grandmother would have called it *gylden lyset*, or something equally lyrical. Her lapses into her native Norwegian had often been for poetic purposes, when English was too harsh.

The temperature rose quickly, drying the wet streets. Experience had taught her to avoid the crammed freeways to get from work to the shelter on Friday nights. Surface streets were slower but prettier and she could enjoy the sunlight all the more. The Escort's air-conditioning had given up the ghost last year, so she dangled one arm out the open window and listened to the radio tuned to the public station out of Boulder even though, inexplicably, the signal turned to static whenever she was pointed due north.

Traffic was sluggish near Coors Field, where a Rockies game was in progress. She had no interest in baseball beyond the knowledge that the Rockies were chasing a pennant, which made every game important. Regardless of the outcome, the shelter was always busy after big sporting events, and tonight would be no exception.

She turned onto the quiet residential street where no sign proclaimed what occupied the rambling farm-style house on the corner. Its whitewash and plank exterior was at odds with the cookie cutter stucco covering the tract homes that had overrun an old family farm. She liked the old house, with its sprawling porch, creaking floors and unexpected rooms.

As requested by the shelter director, Karita made a point of trying to park someplace new each time as the chief complaint of their neighbors was loss of the parking spaces in front of their own homes. Emily had enough worries.

She got out of the car, then paused to catch her breath. Even after two years she occasionally forgot about the altitude and didn't breathe in deeply enough. Her head cleared after a few good, deep breaths and she resumed her hurried steps around the old house. She almost knocked Emily over when she opened the back door.

"I'm so glad you're here! You're early, sweetie, bless you." Emily's long arms were full of linens, leaving only her bright green eyes visible over the top of the pile. "Could you make up the Chocolate Factory room?"

Karita shoved her belongings into the nearest locker, made sure it latched and pocketed the key. So much for hoping she'd have time to get out of her work suit and into some comfortable jeans and a cotton top. Maybe there'd be a chance after this client was settled. She'd not only be more comfortable, the clients would be more at ease with her as well. "Absolutely."

"Mom plus two, one can share with mom and one in a crib. I can't get a name out of her, but you give it a try. They're in the common room watching TV."

"I'll show her where the room is and give her the tour," Karita assured her. "How's it been since Tuesday?"

"Business is depressingly brisk. I have been working on the same grant application for two weeks now and we really could use the money."

"I wish I had any talent for it." To Karita, Emily looked more tired than usual. Her round face was pale, and a deep, worried line creased between her brows, making her look at least ten years older than her thirty-eight years. Karita resisted the urge to tuck a few silver hairs behind Emily's ears with the rest of her unruly black hair—they were actually rather endearing. At the moment Emily was the spitting image of the photo of her mother she kept on her office wall. Even though Karita thought mother and daughter were both handsome women, pointing out the likeness was probably not a good idea. She kept her hands to herself.

"You're too good with clients to waste you on paperwork. I don't know what I'd do without you." Emily bustled away to answer the ringing phone, her footsteps heavy.

If there was a way Karita could afford to live on what Emily could afford to pay, she'd have gladly taken any job at the shelter, but economic necessities like food, gas, insurance and home repairs dictated her enjoyable, but not terribly fulfilling day job at the law office. Volunteering for Emily made much more sense, even if it wasn't the total hours Emily really needed. There were other volunteers, too, and the camaraderie was another huge reward for the time she spent, reminding her of the four years in the Peace Corps. She was part of something larger than herself. Between the time here and time at the animal rescue near home, she was well pleased with her life. She had all she needed, didn't she?

She quickly made up the full-size bed for mom and the older child, and slipped faded Pooh and Piglet sheets onto the crib mattress. She set out a few fresh diapers and wipes, toothpaste and brushes, shampoos and tiny soaps all donated from hotel freebies, and went to find the family so she could assess clothing sizes for sleepwear.

Just before entering the common room she took a deep breath and schooled her smile. Even so, it nearly slipped at the purpled swelling around one eye and vivid bruises on the client's slender arms. The girl, with tight red braids halfway down her back, had a vacant expression that tightened Karita's throat. She couldn't be more than five and she'd already seen too much of life's ugliness.

"Hi, I'm Karita. Do you want to see where you and the kids will be sleeping?"

Though Karita kept her distance, the child cowered closer to her mother, who winced as she rocked the baby on her lap. "Yeah, sure, I guess. I don't know…if we'll be staying. If I'm gone all night, it'll be… Maybe I should call his mother…"

Throughout the woman's disjointed comments Karita kept up soothing, easy patter as she led them to the Chocolate Factory room. "It's really no bother, see, everything is all ready, so you can stay the night, and the kids can get a good sleep. They need that. The door locks, see? Your daughter is so polite, and she takes after you, doesn't she? The baby's also got the same red hair, so cute on a little one. I know, maybe he won't be so angry in the morning, but if he is you need to have a plan for the kids. Do you like the sheets? They're my favorite. Most kids love Piglet and Pooh. What's the baby's name?"

She was shameless and she knew it, but she was following the guidelines of Emily's training to the letter. Many women did go back, over and over, to men who beat them, but children were one of the consistent, compelling wedges the shelter workers had. If substance abuse wasn't in the picture, most women responded to the need to do what was best for their kids long before they would think to save themselves.

Pauline, her easy smile not quite overcoming her tired eyes, arrived with another woman and child while Karita was still chatting with her own charge. The two clients ignored each other, and their obvious bruises, which was fairly typical. Their babies were close in age which made for common ground. Both seemed to be the type that took it in silence, but they always had to be on the watch for the rare woman who wanted to pass along the abuse to the first victim she could find.

"It'll be busy tonight," Pauline said, pitching her voice low so the clients wouldn't overhear. She rubbed a hand over her dark face, and Karita wondered how long the shift at the hospital had been before Pauline had arrived here. "There's some big NASCAR event at Bandemere." In jeans and a roomy men's polo shirt, Pauline was one of the biggest false positives Karita had ever met.

"And there's a Rockies game. We might as well make up all the rooms."

"I can stay a couple more hours tonight—Jerry's off to another Interfaith Council meeting. Why don't you go change out of your monkey suit? I have an eye on things in here." Pauline shooed her toward the kitchen. "Start making popcorn or something."

"What a fine idea."

Karita did just that, comfortable that all was well. Anticipatory snacks prepared, there seemed nothing more to do for a few minutes, so she went in search of Emily.

Emily was leaning tiredly on one elbow as she scrawled something on an intake form. The cramped office had once upon a time been a walk-in pantry, and was just large enough for a tiny desk and several file cabinets. "What'd you think?"

"I'd be surprised if she's on something." Karita considered the kinds of comments her client had made. "He sounds like a weekend alcoholic and when he's had a bad week she can't do anything right. The little girl is traumatized but this is nothing new to her. She's been in other shelters."

"I thought so too. Any luck getting a name for Child Welfare when they get here? A friend dropped her off and I didn't see who that was either. Probably someone who has been here before." Emily pushed her wire-rimmed glasses back up her nose, a nose she herself had once described as so pert it ruined her Big Ol' Dyke persona.

"The baby's name is Lila and the little girl is Jenny." Karita grinned. "It might not be her jacket, but Jenny's collar has *Jones* written inside it."

Emily grinned back. "I don't know what I love more, your body or your brain."

Karita flushed slightly and knew it showed. "I learned that kind of detective work from the best there is."

The doorbell rang and their smiles faded. A glance at the closed-circuit monitor showed a uniformed female police officer and a woman crying into a tissue.

Emily sighed. "At least this one, we'll know who she is."

"I'm pretty sure she's been here before." No kids, Karita didn't have to add. No kids, so she'd probably go back to him.

The Rockies had lost badly to their chief rival in the race for a division championship. Karita didn't give a rancid flea for the sport, but the game's importance had been beaten into two more women by the time it was midnight.

"If there weren't any pro sports, we'd have half the business." Pauline poured herself coffee as they all took advantage of a brief respite. She peered into the cup. "When was this made? It's blacker than I am."

"My fault," Karita admitted. "I lost track of how many scoops. It's a bit...strong."

Pauline gave her one of those looks that no doubt quieted unruly patients in an instant. "Do I need to get you some instructional aids for counting? This coffee is like pudding."

"I didn't notice. No wonder I feel wide awake." Emily looked up wearily from her almost empty cup. "If there weren't sporting events, there'd just be a different excuse. We'll only have half the business when half the men stop thinking they can use women for punching bags."

"Not just men." Lucy, who had arrived while Karita was settling in the latest arrival, rinsed her mug and set it in the drainer. She tucked a strand of sandy blond hair behind one ear, and a minute rainbow earring glinted in the light. "I guess it makes me sexist, but when it's a woman beating on her partner I feel ashamed. Dykes are supposed to be...better than that."

Emily got up to drape a sympathetic arm around Lucy's shoulder. They were of a similar height, but Lucy was lean as a cheetah. "I know what you mean. And the one tonight—same old thing. I'm drunk and you're to blame for everything."

Pauline propped her head on her hand. "At least it's rare, by comparison. You'd think I'd have seen enough here to put me off men, but oh well."

"You got a good one to go home to," Karita said. "Given the stats I just read for black women getting married these days—"

"Believe me," Pauline said. "I make sure he knows he's special and all those parishioners know he's *very* married."

Lucy headed out of the kitchen, saying over her shoulder, "He better treat you like a queen, because you are one, sisterfriend. At least you have someone warm to cuddle up to at night."

Emily and Karita raised their mugs in a hear-hear toast. The doorbell rang, and Karita rose to respond. "I'll bring them in, Em."

By two a.m. the night volunteers had arrived and settled. The house was quiet when Emily and Karita slipped out the kitchen door into the garage.

"How far away is your car?" Emily's trim minivan occupied the attached garage, along with extra cribs, rollaways and stacks of household supplies.

"I'm actually a block over. I didn't want Mrs. Carruthers in your face again and that was the only place open."

"You're too good to me," Emily said softly.

In the harsh garage lighting, the stray silver hairs at Emily's temples had a glow of their own, and the urge to tuck them away, to comfort Emily's weariness with a simple gesture, was almost overwhelming. They both knew the healing power of human touch, that a hug or a sympathetic squeeze of the shoulder could do wonders for a person. Stopping at a hug was the problem. Maybe that was because it took more than a hug to counteract what they had seen over the course of the evening.

Karita's heart started to pound and her palms were slick. How often had they agreed that nothing was going to happen, and would tonight be the night they actually stuck to their intentions?

Emily unlocked the passenger door and what might have been an accidental brush of her forearm against Karita's sent a flash of fire all the way to Karita's toes. She hadn't meant the contact and she was pretty sure Emily hadn't either but there was no doubt they meant the sweltering, gasping kiss that they shared seconds later.

"We can't do this anymore," Emily managed between groans. One hand gripped Karita's waist while the other grappled at the van's sliding door and finally shoved it open.

Karita scrambled up onto the bench seat, pulling Emily after her. "Why shouldn't we? It feels so good, after a night like tonight. It feels good to both of us."

Emily groaned again as Karita found the hem of her T-shirt and pulled it up. "I'm your boss."

"If you paid me you'd be my boss."

"Makes no difference—holy Christ." She shuddered as Karita ran her nails up her back. "Honest, I wasn't thinking about this, I didn't—"

"Shut up, Em," Karita said before another near-bruising kiss. "We're not at work now."

"No, we're in the backseat of my van and I want to touch you so bad—"

"It's okay." Karita unhooked Emily's bra before pulling down the zipper on her own jeans. She said truthfully, "If I'd planned this I'd have shaved my legs."

A laugh rumbled in Emily's chest and her hand slipped down to help Karita squirm out of her pants.

"Touch me," Karita breathed.

"Baby, yes."

The shudder was mutual and Emily smothered Karita's little cry with a kiss. Touching was good, and it could be fast, even rough, the way Emily was inside her now. There could be raging emotions behind the need and still be healthy. Karita gave herself to the flush of desire, letting things she knew write themselves again on the surface of her skin. Love didn't have to include pain. Women could be fierce and strong and not hurt each other.

She knew why Emily was like this because she also needed the same thing, and right now. It was dehumanizing to ignore split lips and bruises, and what had been done to the women and children in the shelter wasn't human either. Emily, inside her, kissing her, their matching heartbeats—that was human. Vulnerability without shame. Intimacy and passion that wasn't taken by force. Together, because it was what they both wanted, they reached a moment when nothing but vulnerability could suffice. Karita couldn't hold back a sharp cry and she felt, rather than heard, Emily's low groan of understanding pleasure.

Emily shuddered and shifted on top of her and Karita couldn't help the slow grind she did in response. "Take me back to your place?"

Emily's smile was tired, but already her face had relaxed. "Well, since we already fell over the cliff I don't suppose there's much harm in going the rest of the way."

Karita laughed as she shinnied back into her jeans and wiggled into the passenger seat. Emily pulled down her shirt, slammed the sliding door on her way out and reappeared at the driver's door.

Emily waited for the garage door to open before starting the van. After backing out she glanced at Karita and said, not unexpectedly, "How come I'm not in love with you?"

"Because I'm not the one you need, maybe."

"But you are. Tonight for sure. You're exactly the kind of woman I need in my life."

Karita shook her head. Sometimes she felt older than Emily, though she was a good ten years younger. "If I was what you really needed you'd be in love with me. And since I'm not in love with you, we're square in that department."

"I know. Want to get your car in the morning?"

"Sure, it'll be fine." She knew the drive to Emily's house, just a few blocks, from their previous handful of nights together. If Emily had to leave before Karita woke she could easily walk to her car. In daylight she wouldn't mind at all.

The van glided into Emily's garage and they lost their clothing again on the way to the bedroom. Some time later, with Emily drowsy and both of their bodies melted into the bed, Emily said, "If we didn't do this we'd be dating. We'd be looking for someone. We'd be serious about it. We're enabling laziness in each other."

"Hey," Karita said softly. "You're not a surrogate anything. We both know why Lucy goes to the gym on her way home from volunteering. I'm betting Pauline wakes up her husband most times, too. We all need a little healing magic. This is how you and I find some."

"I worry about you." Emily's eyelids stayed closed longer each time they fluttered shut. "You're so sweet and a natural giver. I'm afraid I take too much. Your time and your energy and even this, when you should be in bed with someone who loves you."

"Silly. I am in bed with someone who loves me." She watched Emily sink toward sleep.

"You know what I mean. I'm so scared you're going to meet up with some psychic vampire who'll suck you dry."

Karita closed her own eyes as Emily's breathing steadied. She had no fear of vampires, evil witches and the like. She whispered the little safety charm her grandmother had taught her and hoped the spell would comfort Emily too. She respected who Emily was, and trusted her.

In the encircling warmth of a good woman's arms, when she ought to be drowsy and at peace, her mind instead picked at still painful places.

Don't start, she warned herself, but it was already too late. Memories of curling up with Mandy, just like this, filled her mind. Mandy had long since found someone else. Someone who would put Mandy at the center of her universe and revolve around her. Someone who would find the arrangement as perfect as Karita had, until she'd made the mistake of thinking that, for just a little while, she could pay more attention to her own life than Mandy's, and that Mandy would wait, for just a little while.

You're not an elf, she reminded herself sleepily. No amount of magic would have changed Mandy's mind. Because of Mandy she did know what love was, however, and she knew that what she felt for Emily wasn't that kind of love. Her feelings for Emily were simpler, and maybe that was better for her, right now. Emily's hand drifted on to her hip to pull her a little closer. She had all she needed, didn't she?

21

Chapter 3

"I was just heading out for lunch. Nate Summerfield is going to sign for the fourteenth floor of the Prospector Building."

Jerry gave CJ his usual bright smile. "Attagirl! Top of the sales chart again this month, I bet." His boyish, sports-buff charm made him a good salesman, but it grated on CJ. Jerry had never had to shake a living out of the world, nor spend a minute of his day looking over his shoulder except to see if anyone from his old boys' network was offering to buy him a drink. He'd been born with connections, and they continually paid off. She had long since decided that he wouldn't have survived life in the Gathering where your connections—your family—didn't give, but instead took.

"I always try, Jerry, you know that." CJ, aware her tone was terse, made a show of putting on her suit jacket and gathering her portfolio and handbag. Unwelcome thoughts of the Gathering had tightened her nerves and put her in a bad mood. It was clear Jerry was hoping she'd invite him along to lunch, but she had no intention of doing so. It wasn't a good idea for people to horn in on business meals—that was Jerry's own edict—but he was notorious for cadging lunch. She didn't want to be the exception to his rule, not today. The contract she hoped to get signed was too valuable to risk interference. "Gotta run, boss."

On her way from her office to the elevator she made a slight detour to Juliya's cubicle. "The LoDo Round Table was pretty dull," she told her, "but I picked up a few business cards for prospective small merchants. None of them seemed particularly hot, but you never know."

"Thanks, CJ. That's really nice of you." Juliya beamed, her pixie features lit up with enthusiasm.

CJ didn't handle small leases so it was no skin off her nose to pass on the contacts. "I also told them I had a colleague I thought knew their district better than I did, and put in your name."

Juliya leapt to her feet to give CJ a hug, and CJ did her best not to stiffen. "Even if they don't invite me, thank you so much!"

"De nada." She gave Juliya's back an awkward pat. "I'm off to lunch."

"The Summerfield deal? Good luck!"

"It's in the bag, but thanks."

Unfortunately by the time CJ got to the elevator Jerry was already there and he still looked hungry. She couldn't think of any small talk that wouldn't end up with him sucking up for some lunch. Fortunately, the rookie, Burnett, provided a distraction. Being the most recent addition to the staff, he had the cubicle closest to the elevator and the least amount of privacy.

Every word he said into his phone was crystal clear: "As I said, this is not my prescription. This is an estrogen prescription for my grandmother who can't call you herself. No, she doesn't have extra prescription coverage. She's not eligible for Medicare yet. Yes." After a pause he said slowly and carefully, "I am her grandson because she is my grandmother..."

A long-dead mother and a father she hoped never to see again spared CJ conversations like that.

"Where you taking the client?" Jerry was doing that bouncing on his toes thing that always made CJ think of bobble-head dolls. His just-a-guy demeanor had always tempted her to take him lightly, but she'd learned he was astute in business—and, at times, unprincipled.

She fiddled with her briefcase. "Where else for an ex-quarterback from U. of C.? Elway's."

"Oh, nice place, nice place." Jerry smiled hopefully but CJ was not giving in.

Burnett joined them at the elevator, heaving a vast sigh of frustration. "Never call an insurance company on an empty stomach. Time for some lunch."

"I'm off to a deal closer," CJ said, caught between appearing rude by not asking him to join her and appearing to boast. He was a nice enough kid—probably not more than seven or eight years younger than she was, which put him at twenty-seven or so. Even in his real estate broker uniform of dark blue suit and patterned tie, he seemed fresh off one of the farms up near Fort Collins. He had a recent business degree from a college known for agriculture but enough personal charm to win a job that paid mostly in tiny commissions to start. She'd heard him canceling his cable a few weeks back, probably hoping to connect up again when the commission checks got steadier. It wasn't easy being the office rookie.

Jerry clapped the kid on the back. "Just the thing, my boy. A great lunch will set you right up. Why don't you join me?"

Burnett was flattered, and why wouldn't he be? Real estate, especially commercial deals, relied heavily on personal relationships. Rapport with the boss meant money in the bank, plain and simple. CJ sketched a good-bye wave in the parking lot and counted herself lucky to have other plans.

Even though Elway's was a little heavy on the leather and dark paneling for her tastes, the food was excellent and many of her clients loved the place. She was pleased to find Nate had arrived only moments before her and they were seated quickly. Even as he agreed to get business out of the way so they could enjoy their meal, a small part of CJ watched with the same disbelief she always felt when a client prepared to sign the lease agreement. He really was going to sign it. She hadn't come to Denver eight years ago thinking to change her luck. Luck wasn't something she'd been raised to believe in. Yet, since settling here, she'd discovered a knack for the business sense behind commercial real estate. The captains of industry that men like Jerry usually dealt with seemed to like the way she did business.

Commercial real estate was fairly stagnant in downtown Denver, and had been even before she'd decided to give selling it a try. Sweet-talking Jerry into a brokering job had led the way to a lucrative living sweet-talking people into signing contracts. There was a certain thrill in overcoming resistance to initial offers and the subsequent negotiation. It took insight and reading clients on both sides of the table. Those skills ran in her family, no doubt about it.

Aunt Bitty's voice was whispering that if Nate only knew who CJ really was, he wouldn't be initialing fifty pages and signing on the final dotted line. But he didn't know who she was, and the deal was a good one, CJ answered back. She tucked the signed sheaf of documents into her portfolio and they toasted their mutual success with a delicious Australian shiraz of Nate's choosing. After that it was no trouble at all enjoying grilled mahimahi on greens and chatting companionably about Nate's family and the upcoming University of Colorado football season.

She stood up to shake hands with Nate as he took leave of her and only then did she realize that Jerry and Burnett were seated on the other side of the dining room. Ouch, the poor kid. She wasn't even sure he was cut out for this kind of business, but one thing was for certain—he was about to get the shock of his young life. She'd found out the hard way about Jerry's tendency to excuse himself before the check came.

She sat down again at the table to finish her glass of wine and make sure all the fields on the accounting data entry form were completed. If it was scanned in today she'd get her initial commission in the next pay period. After this commission it would take only one more medium-sized deal to cross another name off her list. She had three possible contacts in the hopper—one would pay off.

All the data blocks completed, CJ added her flourish and sat back to drain the glass of the very fine shiraz. She wasn't exactly spying when she craned her neck to see how Burnett was faring with Jerry. Sure enough, Jerry was patting his pockets, no doubt saying he'd get the car from the valet. Jerry left and the waiter was on the way with the bill.

She tucked her own credit card into the folio that had been discreetly placed at her elbow a few minutes earlier. She would be able to submit her expense for reimbursement because she had a big contract to show for it. Lunch with the boss was not reimbursable. She peeked over the divider again. Hell, the kid looked like he was going to pass out. Including the wine, her own bill was over a hundred and fifty sans gratuity. Given Jerry's tastes, she bet Burnett was looking at two hundred once he figured in the tip.

Her waiter emptied the last of the wine from the bottle into her glass, then began to pick up the folio. CJ quickly put her hand on his.

"This is going to sound crazy, but I want to pay the check for the gentleman at that table over there. Can you arrange that? Use my credit card instead of his?" She was going to regret this, she just knew it. She wasn't going to get a thing back for it, so why bother?

"I think so, madam, I'll just let the gentleman know—"

"No, I don't want him to know it was me."

She got a look that said she was being strange, but he waylaid the other waiter, who then headed toward her.

"Madam?"

She'd not been madam'd so much in her life. She held out her hand for Burnett's folio. "May I?"

She scanned the bill. Jerry was such a weasel—he'd picked a

reserve cabernet and used it to wash down a starter, a salad, a soup *and* a filet with foie gras. He was a candidate for heart failure, no doubt about it. She didn't know why she was doing this—it made no sense to feel sorry for Burnett, no one had bailed her out when Jerry had stuck her with a lunch bill that size when she'd had next to nothing in the bank after forking out major dollars for the real estate licensing course and exam. Better Burnett should toughen up or quit. It would save him time if he figured out this wasn't the business for him. Really, it would be kinder in the long run to let him pay for it.

With a sigh, she nodded. "Yes, put that one on my card as well. Just make it two separate transactions."

Both waiters intoned a serious "Yes, madam" and went away. Given how much the lunch was now costing her she saw no reason to waste that last half glass of shiraz. She quickly downed it, munched on the crumbs of the tart she'd had for dessert, then signed the two charge slips the moment they were delivered. She packed up her folder of paperwork, tucked everything into her portfolio and went the long way toward the exit, not wanting Burnett to see her leaving.

She waved at Jerry, who was idling in the valet driveway, waiting, and murmured, "You ass," behind her gritted teeth. She had parked on her own, preferring not to hand her keys to a stranger or be prevented from quickly reclaiming her car should that be unpleasantly necessary. By the time she exited the large Cherry Creek parking garage in her all-weather Trailblazer, there was no sign of Jerry or Burnett and she heaved a sigh of relief. With luck, Burnett would thank Jerry for the lunch and Jerry would presume Burnett was pleased to have paid for the pleasure of Jerry's company. That's how big Jerry's ego—

A squeal of brakes and furious honking brought CJ out of her meanderings. She waved an apologetic hand at the other driver, realizing she'd not seen the car as she'd turned out of the side street. Hell, there'd been a stop sign back there, too. She waited for cars to pass, then pulled out into traffic only to realize her reflexes were way off. That last bit of wine…by a miracle there was a spot open at a meter she could pull into. Motionless at the curb, she switched off the engine.

Well, that was idiotic, she scolded herself. She ought to walk it off—she felt like a teenager. How stupid was that, not to have realized that her delicious but light meal hadn't offset the wine? She'd practically chugged the last four ounces.

A knock on her window startled her and her heart went into overdrive at the sight of a blue-uniformed Denver police officer. She belatedly realized a police motorcycle was just behind her car, lights flashing.

"License and proof of insurance, please."

CJ fumbled for her wallet. "I realize I pulled out in front of that other car, Officer. I wasn't concentrating, and it rattled me, so I pulled over." Don't babble, she could hear her father telling her. Don't explain too much. Don't volunteer anything. Don't give them the real ID.

But she didn't have fake ID anymore. And she didn't think she was over the legal limit—shut up, CJ, pay attention.

She watched in the rearview mirror as the officer—burly, white but otherwise indistinguishable behind his sunglasses and visor—checked the small computer display on his bike, then wrote something in his ticket book. Struggling to control her panic, CJ couldn't help but tell herself that law enforcement was more connected today than it had been sixteen years ago. What one traffic cop suspected, marshals could learn in minutes.

That's only in the movies, she told herself, and it was just a stop sign. As the cop started his walk back to her window she hated that her father's advice came back to her after all these years—become the person you have to be to get what you want from the other guy. But CJ didn't want to be anyone but who she was—focus, CJ, for Christ's sake, focus. It's a cop, with handcuffs and a direct path to the nearest jail.

He returned to her window with ticket book and a wrapped object of some kind tucked under his arm. She reminded herself that the slow tread and flex of muscle was meant to scare her. "Would you please step out of the car and join me at the curb, ma'am?"

Moving carefully, but not too slowly, CJ did as requested. The sun had reached its peak for the day and the heat was intense.

"Have you been drinking, ma'am?"

Like she was going to tell him. Eyeing the kit in his hand, she asked, "Are you going to give me a breathalyzer?"

"Yes ma'am." He quickly showed her where to breathe and CJ knew her father would have figured a way out of this by now, including making a run for it. When nothing you have belongs to you it's easy to leave it behind. She was exhaling before she could think of a reason not to.

He showed her the result: .07, under the limit by a hair. She wanted to do a dance but she wasn't out of the woods yet.

"Ma'am, you realize the law isn't just about this number. If you're impaired in any way, I can still arrest you for being under the influence. My judgment is that you were operating your motor vehicle while impaired."

Never tell a lie for no good reason—that was the first rule of running a con. Cops could smell lies, so CJ went for the truth bolstered with some plausible fiction.

"Look, I left the restaurant quickly and yes, obviously, I've had some wine." He'd never believe her if she said she'd ducked out to avoid being identified as the person who had settled someone else's bill. Her pounding heart added an authentic quaver to her voice. "My boss was hitting on me. As soon as I got out into the sun I realized I wasn't thinking clearly and I pulled over. I wasn't going to go on driving. I was just going to walk around for a while and figure out what kind of job I'd rather have."

The face remained impassive. CJ glanced at his wedding ring.

"If I quit I'm going to have to tell my boyfriend why and then I'm going to have to figure out how to keep him out of jail for beating up my ex-boss." The sun was so hot and bright she didn't have to feign tears in her eyes.

After a long moment of studying her, the officer sighed. "If you had any priors, I'd take you in, but you did pull over and stop your vehicle as you say. I'm writing you for the right-of-way violation and the failure to stop at the sign back there. I'm noting on the ticket your breathalyzer result, which will require you to make a court appearance."

"So that means a fine? Points on my license?" Her heart rate declined a little. She didn't want to go into a courtroom ever again, but traffic court, surely, couldn't be that bad.

"There's also the option of traffic school and community service. It depends on the DA, you and the judge. Sign here, ma'am."

She signed her legal name, the name on her license, the name she'd used for so long she sometimes forgot she'd had another. CJ Roshe would pay her fines with a check on a real bank, and with sufficient funds to cover it. CJ Roshe would do traffic school and community service, litter patrol, whatever it took to keep anyone in Colorado from looking further back than the eight years she'd lived here.

She'd left Cassiopeia Juniper Rochambeau in Kentucky, and that was the way it was going to stay. Everything depended on it.

"Skinny mocha, Turkish, capped!" The overworked barista glanced around the small mob waiting for their orders and Karita realized it was probably hers. She moved toward the counter but the barista didn't see her. "Skinny mocha—for Kari–Rita!"

"That's me. Thanks." Karita scooped up the cream-topped cup and headed for the condiments.

"I'm sorry, that might be mine." A woman who'd been lingering nearby gestured at Karita's cup.

Karita paused. "No, it's mine." She pointed to her name. "Karita."

30

"Oh." The other woman, her dark, elegant hair and features vaguely familiar, smiled an apology. "Sorry, I didn't hear what name they called."

"That's okay."

"Skinny mocha, Turkish, capped for CJ!"

After a husky laugh, the woman said, "Now I really apologize. That one's mine."

Karita was more than halfway through her ritual addition of sugar and milk when she realized she might have just been chatted up by that woman. A glance to her right revealed skinny-mocha-Turkish-capped CJ looking far too innocent as she added artificial sweetener and more nonfat milk.

"Very clever," Karita said. "You could have just asked me my name."

"That's not very subtle."

"Subtlety is your specialty?"

"I try."

"Why did you want to know my name?"

"I would have to be three days dead not to want to know your name."

In spite of her better judgment, Karita laughed. "And that's subtle?"

CJ's dark eyes took on a gleam of mischief. "Subtle didn't seem to be working."

She recognized the dark-haired woman from somewhere. The sleek, short hair pulled back with two tight clips allowed a spill of natural black curls over the mandarin collar of a tailored dark plum suit. The button-up blouse of pale blue was undoubtedly silk, and wrapped tightly across a slender torso that filled out nicely in the very best places. Unusual, and very attractive, Karita thought. She went for the obvious. "Come here often?"

"Yes, and so do you."

"How do you know that?" It was a bit of a novelty to look another woman right in the eye. At five-ten, it wasn't often she got that pleasure.

CJ gestured at the condiments. "You know where everything is, and you didn't hesitate in the amounts you wanted." Lips of dusty rose curved in a genuine smile and Karita had a peculiar sense of vertigo.

"Sherlock Holmes in a prior life?"

"Plus I saw you here a few weeks ago."

Oh, that was it, Karita recalled. She'd seen skinny-mocha-Turkish-capped CJ with another woman and it had looked very next-stop-is-the-bedroom cozy. "How was your date?"

"Just fine when I last saw her."

It wasn't egotistical to assume that CJ was hitting on her, not after the three-days-dead remark. She wasn't all that used to flirting from women and the novelty had made her a little slow in discouraging it, but she wasn't going to be another notch for CJ, even if the clothes alone said she was probably more successful than most of the Brents who crossed Karita's path. So what if she was quick-witted, admittedly charming, very nicely put together and—most importantly—female? "Give your girlfriend my regards."

She was in her car and already turning out of the parking lot before she was willing to admit that she was bothered that CJ had let her go so easily. If she didn't count Emily, and she shouldn't since her private relationship with Emily wasn't about romance, she hadn't had a real date in a very long time. Saying yes to dinner or a movie wasn't yes to breakfast, as well.

That the gleaming bedroom eyes, the sultry aura and repartee vividly reminded Karita of Mandy had nothing to do with her rapid exit.

CJ watched the elderly Subaru make its way into traffic before carrying her own coffee out to her car. When she'd realized that the eye-catching platinum blonde she'd noticed before was also waiting for her coffee it had been a bright spot in an otherwise unpleasant day. She'd already been told by a client that he was going with a different deal, and one of the two remaining hot irons was getting cooler every minute. Next up was traffic court.

She knew now what people meant by "long, tall drink of water." It described Karita perfectly. And what had she done with the opportunity to talk to the intriguing Nordic beauty? Blown it, and thoroughly.

It was a bit of an ego stroke that Karita remembered seeing her around, too, but definitely it counted against her that Karita had seen Abby as well. Now she looked like a two-timer, and it wasn't as if she was planning to change anything in her life in any form. Abby and she had the perfect relationship. Flirting with Karita—or anybody else—was pointless. She just hadn't been able to help herself when the opportunity presented. That kind of thinking, she scolded herself severely, was greedy, and greed was dangerous to anyone who had everything to lose.

Maybe it was a good thing that she had gone about meeting Karita entirely the wrong way. Used to flattery and flirting, a woman like that couldn't be rushed and would definitely be choosey. She hadn't batted an eyelash over a woman hitting on her, either, which probably meant that the faint ping on CJ's gaydar hadn't been wrong. The way CJ read her, all cool on the outside, Karita didn't have a thought that didn't show in her face. Behind those ice-blue eyes was a perceptive wit, passionate heat and lots of it. She was a woman who gave without counting the cost.

In the parlance of the Gathering, Karita was the perfect mark.

More than twenty years out of that life and she still couldn't stop herself from thinking of people in the language of theft.

Aunt Bitty's voice, ever the harbinger of doubt, reminded her as it had the last time she'd encountered Karita, that a woman like that would never be interested in a filthy, smart-mouthed little tramp, if only she knew what CJ really was underneath the fancy suit. Karita would never give CJ anything. Like everything in life, if CJ wanted something she had to lie, cheat and steal to get it.

Though she had for the most part learned to ignore Aunt Bitty's lingering voice of doom, one thing was true. A woman like that wasn't worth the effort. Abby was the perfect not-quite girlfriend, and her passions were at the surface, easy to tap. She'd told Abby no lies, whereas a woman like Karita would require a lot of planning, time and, yes, lies to get close to. CJ had other things to focus on besides unattainable treasures. Even if she could capture the prize, no way would she be able to keep it. Treasure attracted thieves, and thieves attracted the law. She couldn't afford the attention of either.

Yet, she told herself, your stupidity over a half-glass of wine and bailing out that kid has you heading into the arms of the justice system.

She parked in the designated courthouse lot, gathered her summons, made sure she had her checkbook and wallet and called up all the confidence she could to quell her shaking hands. She was here for legitimate reasons, going to traffic court like thousands of people did, and there was nothing to be afraid of today. Traffic court used a different entrance than the criminal courts, and no one in sight had "federal" written all over them. The matter was routine and there was no reason to think anyone would attach importance to her case. She was a fine to be collected, and nothing more.

"Citations starting in letters A through F go to the room on your left." The woman in the white shirt and dark slacks of court personnel pointed toward Room 101 and CJ went that way, peeked inside and then read the sign that said to have a seat and wait to be called.

She waited, watched the black-robed, blank-faced judge assign numerous fines to people who had been driving without insurance. She played a game on her BlackBerry, wished she were at the gym or doing useful work, waited some more and was actually relieved when her number was called.

A brisk young woman with a firm handshake introduced herself as a deputy district attorney and they sat down in a cubicle

34

to one side of the courtroom.

"Let me review the citation." The woman's dark skin was sleek and smooth, and her neatly trimmed hair and economical movements suggested she wouldn't be easily swayed from whatever she believed was the correct path. "I see. Are you here because you dispute the breathalyzer result?"

"No, I don't. I want to pay my fine for the moving violations, but the officer said I had to appear."

"I see." Her quick sigh told CJ she had a low opinion of officers who tried to direct the court. "There was no field sobriety test in addition to the breathalyzer?"

"No, there wasn't."

"His reasoning is circular in the citation."

CJ knew when to say nothing.

"This is a first offense?"

"I'm a careful driver, and the moment I realized I wasn't concentrating on my driving I pulled over. Then the officer caught up to me."

"I see." She pursed her lips. "You can pay the fine for both violations, but the fact that you had been drinking, even if under the legal limit, means your choice of treble the fines or community service and online traffic school."

"What's the fine?"

"One hundred seventy-three for each, then times three."

She stopped herself from saying "shit" just in time. The estimated increase in her insurance was already bad enough. "So a little over a thousand dollars?"

"Be thankful you had proof of insurance."

"What does traffic school entail?"

"It's an online course that takes four to six hours and costs about forty dollars in fees."

"That's a no-brainer choice, isn't it? The base fine plus traffic school is okay with me."

"And community service."

"Wait, you said I had a choice between—"

"Online traffic school *and* community service of twenty-one hours is required as well if you don't want to pay the treble fine. The court clerk will provide you with a list of entities that need volunteers for which hours during the week so you can select something that does not require you to miss work. You will need to select one within fourteen days and the entity must forward proof that you fulfilled your obligation within forty days."

Twenty-one hours of her life spent picking up litter instead of paying seven hundred extra dollars? She thought ruefully that it wasn't all that bad a rate of pay for trash patrol. Three Saturdays in the great outdoors, fine, whatever. She wanted out of the courthouse and the matter completely closed.

"I'll take the community service."

Chapter 4

"I don't know what I'd do without you, Karita." Marty Hammer, the sweetest boss on earth, beamed at her from under two of the bushiest eyebrows she'd ever seen. Even after more than a year working for Marty, she still found them adorable. "Are you sure you don't want to take the paralegal training?"

"Quite sure," she answered. "I may not know what I want to be when I grow up, but I'm pretty sure what I don't want to be, which is working eighty hours a week. I'm happy with my schedule as it is."

"You do all that volunteer work, and I admire that." He gave her a fatherly look. "But there's your future to think about, princess."

She patted his hand as he leaned on the counter that framed the reception desk. "Money isn't everything."

"No," he agreed readily. "It's just most things."

Thankfully, a messenger tromped in with another package for one of the attorneys and Marty headed for his office without suggesting she meet yet another of his nephews, cousin's sons or a wealthy client's spare heirs. She appreciated his concern, but the time just hadn't been right to tell him she was looking for a princess, not a prince. She felt bad about that, too. The day she'd interviewed with him she'd sensed he was a good, honest man. Her intuition told her to be truthful, but Colorado was far more conservative than Minnesota. Plus her faith in human beings had been sorely tested by Mandy and she'd erred on the side of caution.

Once she'd not said "I'm gay" to the first blind date he'd offered, how did she suddenly admit it at the offer of the fourth or fifth? *See what happens when you're not honest up front?* The Brents of the world take you out for coffee, and because people think you're attractive enough to catch a man, they presume you don't have one because you don't know how to find and kiss your own frogs.

A pox on the closet. The world ought not be this complicated over the matter of love.

It was just a bit vexing, too, to remember that woman at Gracie's—CJ. She'd seemed charming, but obviously was out for just one kind of experience. In some ways, Emily was right. Their occasional night together did keep her from taking chances on other women. If hit-and-runs like CJ were her alternative, as far as she was concerned, those nights with Emily were keeping her from making big mistakes. Emily, at least, was someone she respected and cared about, someone who believed that one person could make a difference. She would think of CJ as a frog—that would do it. The last thing she needed was another disastrous, soul-crushing experience with a woman for whom money wasn't a means, but an end. She wasn't going to be anyone's accessory, a piece of pretty jewelry for show-and-tell. CJ was a frog that all the kissing in the world wouldn't change.

Her phone chirped and she tapped it.

"Karita, sweetie, there's no air in conference one. Could you be a doll—I never can remember that code."

Speaking of frogs, Karita thought. "Sure, I'll punch it in for you. You should feel it in just a few minutes."

The honeyed tones in her ear went away and Karita quickly keyed in the conference room's HVAC setting from her computer. Brent returned from lunch while she was occupied on a call, but she responded to his distant smile with a cheerful one of her own. He was still not quite over her "thank goodness we can be friends" speech. The messenger arrived on schedule to pick up all the paperwork going to the courthouse so far, and, from her perspective, everything was tidy.

The smile she gave Susan House, who left for the day shortly before three, was not nearly so cheerful as the one she had shared with Brent. If she had her druthers, someone like the grand dame Susan House would feel a great deal of heat, and for a very long time. If Susan weren't Marty's brother's widow she'd have probably been fired over the way she could go off on people, especially her last assistant. Most people seemed to think that insults and invective were part of some kind of necessary hazing to become a lawyer, but Marty didn't behave that way. When he was unhappy he could make it very clear without resorting to foul language and personal attacks.

Nevertheless, Karita was pretty sure she was the only one who knew that Susan had slept with the poor girl, too, and getting seduced by your boss was *not* in the lawyer-training handbook. Pam had been the one person at work to suspect Karita was gay after they'd spotted each other at the Tattered Cover in front of the LGBT books section. A few days later Pam had been summarily dismissed after a classic Susan House tirade. That glance in the bookstore was probably why Pam had told Karita about the affair while Karita helped her carry her things to her car the day she was fired.

"I told her if she wanted to break it off, I could handle it," Pam had said between sobs. "She said she treated me like shit so no one could accuse her of favoritism. Suddenly it's my work *deserved* all that criticism. All I did today was misplace a file for fifteen minutes, and then I found it. It was on her desk the whole time."

Standing at Pam's car, holding one of the two small cartons of her personal items, Karita hadn't known what to say that might comfort. She'd overheard some of the things Susan had called Pam, words that could cut a smart, ambitious woman like real knives. It wasn't fair.

Sighing, Karita tried to stop stewing about Susan House. She made a note to herself to call Pam and see how she was doing, though. It had been a week since she'd been fired, and Pam probably felt like she didn't have a friend left in the world.

Unlike the paralegals, Karita closed up her desk promptly at five thirty, forwarded her switchboard to night greetings voice mail and headed out into the warm night. The heat was receding, however, and at home the temperatures would be comfortable with cool evenings over the weekend.

She avoided the freeway out of habit and stubbornness, instead taking the route into the foothills that was both scenic and fun to drive. A quick stop in Morrison for her favorite gyro and lemonade sherbet filled the empty pit in her stomach, then she resumed her journey toward home and her evening plans. For twenty minutes the gently curving road climbed steadily, passing through thick spruce-fir forests and exposed granite scrub. Her spirits elevated along with the roadway, until the final curve nearest home presented a vista of craggy cliffs above and below the highway. To the west the green-crusted foothills seemed like hundreds of children gathered close to the knees of dozens of strong, white-haired grandmothers who in turn linked their arms in a protective embrace for as far as she could see.

She loved it here, loved everything about the sunshine, the snow, the eons-deep green and rock, and the self-reliant people. Mother Nature expected a lot at this altitude, but gave back unstinting beauty. Yes, she thought, she had all she wanted. By the time she pulled into the parking lot of the animal rescue in Kittredge she was ready for some real puppy love.

"Girl, you are just in time." Nann, her freckles standing out from pale skin in testament to a long, tiring day, handed her a heavy bucket of dry dog food and a scoop. "I think I've found a placement for both of those malamutes before they eat us out of house and home. I've fed the big birds and that mountain lion, but I hadn't gotten around to feeding the back kennel yet."

"I'll do it, no problem. Any new critters today?" Karita's nose twitched from the sharp tang of disinfectant and odor-killer. The converted building had once been a bakery, with a storefront for display and several large rooms in the rear. Karita knew from experience that the calm of the long, narrow reception area didn't begin to reflect the chaos behind the doors to either side of them.

Nann quickly retwisted her brilliant red ponytail. "We got some overflow out of the wildfire north of Golden Gate Canyon, but only three scorched marmots. Lost pets include two cats out of the wildfire zone and a pup discovered at Little Bear that's so filthy I don't know what it is."

"I'll do the bath after the feeding."

Karita went about the basic chores that Nann needed help with, clucking to the kittens and puppies, scratching a proffered head through the cage when she could, and murmuring the simple little charm her grandmother had taught her for hopeful situations. All these creatures deserved a loving home and maybe they'd find one. Animal rescue could be very depressing, but it had its rewards, too. Just like working with people, she thought.

There was also no money in it, so she took her pay in the form of licks, purrs and wagging tails. Some people unwound in front of the television, but she found feeding the critters extremely relaxing—not even conversation was required. The day she had stopped in with a wounded and half-frozen pygmy owl she'd found tangled in a fence had been a very good day indeed. She and Nann had hit it off immediately, and the shelter was only a mile from her little house on Bear Creek.

The new dog looked as if it had been left to die in a pool of oily mud, but it didn't act injured. Had it seemed unwell, Nann would have reluctantly sent it on to Animal Control, where its fate would have been quickly decided. There were gleaming brown eyes underneath the muck and it—she, rather—was very docile. No tags or ear tattoo, but until recently she had obviously worn a collar.

Patience combined with gentle, pest-killing shampoo revealed a brown coat that curled tightly, once dry, and nothing worse physically than malnutrition, worn footpads and general shock. Nann would check ears and nose and so forth, but they looked clean to Karita, and the dog was mercifully free of ticks and fleas. For a large dog, it had a lean, light frame. The right rear leg was shorter than the others, but that was probably a birth defect. She suspected it was a mixed breed, and it obviously wasn't show quality. Someone's well-loved and well-cared-for pet had gone astray, no doubt about it. It happily ate some dry food from her hand and licked her fingers very thoroughly.

She put her nose to the dog's for just a moment and whispered a few phrases of Gran's Elvish, then added, "If you don't have a home you're coming home with me."

Nann leaned in the doorway of the shampoo room. "You've got the girl looking so much better."

"She's an old girl." Karita gently ruffled the soft ears. "Maybe she got dumped because of some big vet bills. She seems too sensible to run away from home."

Nann stooped to join in the petting, eliciting a hearty tail thumping on the wet tile. Animals went euphoric around Nann, and Karita had seen more than one woman do the same. "I'd be surprised if she got dumped, because I think she's a doodle."

"A doodle," Karita echoed. "Okay, you got me. What's a doodle?"

"Specifically, this looks like a cocoadoodle." Nann's fingers explored the dog's chest in the guise of more scratching. "A cross between purebreds—a labrador and a standard poodle. If her coat was more gold, she'd be a standard poodle and golden retriever mix—a goldendoodle. All the positive traits of the people-loving breeds combined with a poodle's low-allergen count. Oh, aren't you sweet, yes, you're a doll," she cooed. The dog's noises of ecstasy grew louder.

"So, she's probably valuable."

"Not in the sense of breeding stock, not with the leg. Doodles aren't accidents, though, and they are great family pets. She's so comfortable with being handled, I'd say this lovely old girl has a wonderful home, and if we hit the local breeder sites with a photo we'll get the word out in time to find her family."

"Oh," Karita said, deeply pleased, "a happy ending."

"Yeah. We get them sometimes. And those malamutes have also gone to their new home. It's a good week." Nann leaned closer to let the doodle lick her face. It did so with such alacrity that Karita was surprised that Nann's abundance of freckles didn't come off. "You are pure love, oh yes you are."

Pure love, Karita thought, as she drove home a few hours later. You could get that from a dog more reliably than from people. Her hands still smelled of the lavender gel she'd applied to the doodle's curls, and she'd left Nann posting notes to the local breeders. Happy endings—it had been another good day indeed.

The Subaru's tires thumped over the bridge shared by the dozen or so small houses on this stretch of Bear Creek. Though it hadn't flooded since she'd moved in, she'd been warned that finding herself trapped on one side of the creek or the other was a possibility in the spring. Douglas fir and blue spruce crowded along the bank, but were more sparse around the homes and outbuildings, leaving room for sunlight to warm the yards. She looped up the driveway to her own little house. The garage door opener didn't work and the doors stuck, but it was all hers, courtesy of her grandmother's will.

Though it was August, the night temperatures up the mountain made evening fires not uncommon, and she loved the hint of wood smoke in the air. She paused for a moment before pulling the garage door down, gazing up at the diamond canopy of stars over her head. Gran would have said that night was a black veil the angels dropped to let God's creatures get some rest from the glory of heaven. The stars, Karita, my little elf, she'd say, were just holes poked in by the angels so nobody worried that heaven had disappeared.

She made her way through the utility room and into the kitchen, pausing to smooch her index finger and press the kiss to a photo of her parents, timelessly caught with baby Karita on their laps. After she'd tossed a load of laundry into the washing machine and brewed a nice cup of peppermint tea, she cuddled on the old divan under a light throw. At this altitude the night air was delightful. A great deal of it came in around the windows, however, which was a source of concern.

She selected solo flute music for her evening, read a little more of a slow but interesting mystery, then made a list of the things she needed to do tomorrow. Replacing the washer on the kitchen faucet was a priority and she was going to try her hand at weather-stripping. The little house wasn't very tight—it had originally been somebody's summer home away from Denver's heat and crowds. Gran's sister had bought it several decades ago, left it to Gran, and Gran had last visited it some ten to twelve years ago, when she'd inherited it. Now people lived in the neighborhood year 'round and Kittredge was considered not a bad commute into Denver. Neglect had taken its toll on the structure, though. Last winter she'd occasionally had to break ice on dishes left in the kitchen sink.

After a quick, hot shower, she pulled on an old soft T-shirt and made one last cup of tea. She liked living here, very much. Maybe they should have moved here when Gran had inherited the place, getting Gran out of the humidity of Minneapolis and into dry air and the three hundred days of sunshine a year. It would have been better for her lungs, maybe.

If they'd moved here so many things would have been different. She might have liked college more here, instead of giving up midway, cashing out with a two-year degree and joining up with the Peace Corps. If she'd been home she might have realized Gran's health was failing, but instead she'd been off teaching basic English in Vietnam. She certainly wouldn't have been on that stretch of crowded freeway when a beautiful, accomplished businesswoman was fiddling with her cell phone instead of keeping her eyes on the road. Had they moved here she'd have never met Mandy over a fender bender. She'd never have mistaken an accident for fate at work.

Well, it just sucked that whenever she was in a quiet place lately, thoughts of Mandy cropped up. What was that about? She chased her tea with a chocolate wafer, brushed her teeth and tumbled into bed, glad of the flannel sheets and down comforter.

She'd gone quite a while without thinking about Mandy, what with the move, finding a new job and the absorption of her time spent at the shelter and the rescue. It had taken a while to get settled, to feel like her life had a rhythm that made sense. She had everything arranged just as she liked. So why was Mandy popping into her head?

Emily would say Karita was classifying memories and letting them go, a useful coping skill. It didn't feel all that useful. At the moment it hurt quite a lot. She'd seen cruelty and viciousness in the world. She'd joined the Corps to try to change some of it. Bad people did bad things. Evil came from hate. Good people did good things, and nothing bad ever came from love. She had loved Mandy. So she hadn't believed Mandy had meant her ultimatum, not at first.

"Gran could die while I'm traveling with you," Karita had explained as they had drifted in the afterglow of passion. The safety and comfort of Mandy's arms had helped ease the ache in her heart after the talk she'd had that morning with Gran's doctor. "She took me in when I was two, and gave me everything she could. I can't leave her now that the doctors say the time is so short." She had been certain Mandy would understand the need to postpone the trip.

But Mandy had gotten out of bed, saying, "If you loved me,

you'd go."

For a moment the words just didn't make sense, as if Mandy had lapsed into a foreign language. Karita had lain there, her face still smelling of Mandy, of lovemaking, and struggled to decipher the words. "Are you saying that I have to choose? Between my love for you and my love for my grandmother?"

"You said I was the most important thing in your life. If you're backing out of our vacation after all that planning, it doesn't sound like I come first to you." Mandy kept her back turned as she pulled on her bathrobe.

Still not sure she understood, Karita had repeated, "Are you asking me to choose between my love for you and my love for my *dying* grandmother? Who has maybe two months to live? Are you saying you won't wait, that you'll go without me? You can't wait two months to see Switzerland so I can take care of something I need to do? I don't understand."

She still didn't understand. Karita played the bitter scene over in her head, trying to figure out where it had all gone wrong. How could love, all that love, have been based on misperceptions? Had they been doomed from the start because they both wanted the other to be someone she wasn't? If Mandy had understood who Karita was, she'd have known without a doubt that Karita would see her grandmother through to the end. If Mandy had been the woman Karita had thought she was, Mandy would have respected no other choice. But the Mandy standing there with that cold, stony look on her face, her hair still mussed from sex, had turned into a stranger.

Mandy had watched Karita get dressed, saying nothing.

"I'm only asking for two months," Karita had finally said. "I love you. But being there for Gran is the only right thing to do."

"I was looking forward to introducing you to so many people. We make such a beautiful couple. And you're not a home health nurse. I don't see how you can help."

"I'm not talking about just nursing her. I'm talking about

reading to her, holding her hand, reminding her of happy times. Being there."

"I need you to be there for me. You've been really distracted lately and I had a feeling you were going to bail on me, just like everybody else."

Pulling the covers up to her chin, Karita tried to turn off the movie in her head before it got to the bitter end. Even now the loss brought tears to her eyes. But her brain wouldn't cooperate and she could hear herself inviting Mandy's final blow.

"If you thought I was going to bail on you, what was tonight about?" She had gestured at the bed.

Mandy had shrugged. "It'll be hard to find someone as enthusiastic as you are. You might be a flake, but you're great in bed."

Even the most casual encounters in the Corps hadn't made Karita feel as cheap as she had at that moment. She had exhaled as if she'd been punched in the stomach and said, without thinking, "Some elf I turned out to be."

Mandy had laughed. Worse even than the broken heart was Karita's broken faith that nothing cruel could ever come from anything offered or received with love, and Mandy had shattered every bit of that faith by saying, "And you know what? That elf thing is really stupid. You need to grow up."

She had numbly gathered her things and believed that in the morning Mandy would have thought it over. Instead, a messenger with a box had arrived, and in it were her pajamas and the contents of the drawer she'd had in Mandy's dresser, her toothbrush, her shampoo.

She dried an errant tear on the pillowcase. She knew in her heart that caring for Gran through her final days had been the grown-up thing to do. She was not a *flake* for thinking so. The last words Gran had spoken that made sense had been, "Karita, my elf, you're a good girl."

It had been a beautiful lie to tell a little girl who badly needed to believe something in her life was special. Even when part of her accepted her elven status was no more real than the Tooth Fairy, little Karita, deep inside, had gone on cherishing the idea that she could do just a little bit of magic. Mandy's derision of that innocent hope tarnished it. Though she was content with her life, was doing the things she loved and thought important, she could still hear *flake*. Truthfully, when Marty fussed at her about her future it felt like he, too, thought she was headed in the wrong direction with her life.

She burrowed her head into the pillow and consciously put Mandy out of her thoughts by thinking about the events of her day. People she'd coaxed a smile from, the animals she'd nurtured. Recollections of the soft fur and liquid eyes adoring every moment with her chased Mandy away, at least for the rest of the night.

If the lovely doodle dog had a family it would be another happy ending. Happy endings were real. It also meant her magic streak would be intact—so far every animal she'd promised to take home had been quickly claimed or adopted out. So maybe she wasn't an elf, but that didn't mean magic couldn't happen. The Mandys and what-was-her-name—the CJs of the world— they were the Assassins of Magic, and she was avoiding them all from now on.

"Now that's a downpour," Burnett said, watching CJ shake water off her umbrella.

"You can say that again. We got through touring the site just in time. Thank goodness for the Trailblazer's four-wheel drive or we'd still be stuck in the mud. It's in the upper eighties out there, too. I'll be glad when September gets here."

"Yeah, but after September comes October. Blizzards, snow, shoveling, that sort of thing."

CJ, looked up from wiping off her handbag to give Burnett a sour look. "And your point is?"

"My point is that I'd really like your advice on a client. Do you have time?"

"Sure." She fished in her handbag for her BlackBerry and pulled out an unfamiliar bundle of papers—damn, the stuff from traffic court, and it was two days later. Tick tock, she thought, she had to get in touch with one of these groups right away. She kept the papers out of sight, though. No reason to advertise her brush with the law. "Jerry's not available?"

"Um, I, well, I want to be lead on this."

"Got it." The kid wanted help, but he didn't want whatever connection he was working to get taken away from him so he ended up with a lowly co-commission again. Jerry would steal the contact. She wasn't sure it was a good thing that the kid thought she wouldn't. She dug in her bag again. "Hang on just a minute."

She hurried out to Tre's desk with a copy of a Vietnamese community newspaper she'd run across coming out of her meeting this morning. "I'm sorry it got wet. I went by color of the masthead. This is the one that's the new start up, isn't it?"

Tre took the paper from her, his eager eyes already scanning the headlines enscribed in his native tongue. "Yes—thank you so much, CJ. I couldn't find it this week."

She gave Tre a friendly wave and went back to Burnett. "What can I do for you?"

He sat down in her office chair with a sigh of relief, loosening his tie. "I was at a networking deal, some college thing, and I overheard someone talking about looking into the old Comstock property for a potential ground floor eatery. Upscale place, new western cuisine, new west decor, all that."

"Why the Comstock? The Prospector is a better location, better parking. Higher tenant upgrade allowance. You could undercut the Comstock by fifteen percent. Our client is dying to get that kind of place in there, if they've got a decent business plan."

"That's what I thought. But how do I approach the guy? He wasn't talking to me and I kind of crashed the event, not like I went to that school, I just knew..." He looked guilty.

"Out with it." CJ gave him a stern look.

"A guy who met with Jerry last week was on his way out of the meeting and I heard him on his cell talking about this get-together, how good it would be to get the alumni together, that sort of thing. And I thought this guy has got to have friends just like him, guys with growing businesses, and maybe I would just pick up a few names and I could cold call them later."

"That was a long shot." But not the worst thinking in the world. Burnett had a brain behind the liquid brown eyes.

"It's all a long shot until you get a couple of deals down. So I showed up in the bar where they were meeting ahead of their dinner, just kind of mingled and listened."

"This possible deal isn't Jerry's, is it?"

"No, no, that's the thing." Burnett leaned forward excitedly. "I just overheard one guy telling another about a friend's restaurant plan. I got the name of the friend—now my potential client—and he's one of the investors and the architect. The Prospector is perfect for them, and just what the owner wants, too. You've filled half that building on your own, so you seemed the person to ask."

No doubt about it, if she were Jerry, she'd steal the lead from the kid because she was going to end up doing a chunk of work advising him and he'd learn a whole lot in the process. She realized, then, why she felt a little protective, maybe. He pinged her gaydar, ever so gently.

"Tell you what. I'll take the co-commission but you have to do the work. I'll give you ideas on approach, proof your proposals, role-play negotiations, sit in if you want. But you're going to earn every penny of the lead's pay."

"I don't expect to do any less. Really." He was all puppy dog, a sweet kid who couldn't help the fact that he wore a sign on his back that said *Wallet's in the left pocket, help yourself.*

"You did a nice job getting the contact. So—don't waste any time. First thing you're going to do is study up on the guy via Intellidome."

"I already did that. Cray Westmore. Up-and-coming architect, he's done a few other restaurants. Finances look clean, no liens or court filings."

"Good. So send out a cold letter and packet on the Prospector. We'll tweak the cover page and aim it right at his flavors-of-the-new-west restaurant. One of our architect designs has a sort of rawhide and Remington feel."

Scarcely thirty minutes later, Burnett set an impressive package and well-written cover letter on her desk. Relieved that she wasn't propping up someone who really ought to consider a different line of work, she made only a few changes. She would have to stop thinking about him as a puppy—he was quietly smart, the kind of guy who walked off with the big prize while the other men were measuring their penises.

With a social dinner on her calendar she dropped the papers off in his cubicle with a cheerful "Well done" and headed out for the day.

She was parking her car when she got a text message that the couple she was meeting was running late, but the restaurant was a casual, popular place that wouldn't hold the table, so she claimed the reservation. After a reassuring scan of the faces of customers who'd entered after her, she followed the server to an out-of-the-way table and ordered a likely-to-please bottle of wine along with a cheese and olives plate.

She'd met Raisa while working on a deal—what else—and had had dinner a couple of times with her and her partner, Devon. Raisa was trying to make partner at the biggest architectural firm in town and a social connection was useful, CJ had told herself. There'd been no reason to refuse the invitations to dinner and both were busy women, so invitations weren't that frequent. She wasn't used to socializing without a purpose beyond conversation and a good time, and it was odd not to be brushing up on notes and reminding herself of the client's spouse's name and favorite hobbies.

They were a pleasantly interesting couple and had always

suggested she bring along a date, but as usual, she'd told Raisa she didn't really have time to be serious about anybody. They'd like Abby, no doubt about it, but bringing her to any kind of event with friends would be a kind of lie. Even if Abby occasionally thought the sex-only truth sucked, at least it was the truth.

She read through the community service information sheets she'd stuffed back into her purse. She had expected litter detail, but the organizations listed were places like Mile High Senior Services, Meals-on-Wheels and the like. She would have preferred trash patrol to real people.

She took a quick look in her compact, marveling that the mirror didn't reflect the cold-hearted bitch she really was. To be sure, she saw the near-black eyes that all the Rochambeau women shared, and if she stared into them too long it was Aunt Bitty staring back. A casual glance, though, merely revealed the façade of an expensively-coiffed businesswoman, which was exactly what she wanted the world to see. The only need she had for people was the money she could make off them. Burnett wasn't so much a nice guy she felt like helping, as he was a potentially useful ally. She dismissed again the memory of the icy fire in Karita's eyes and snapped the compact closed when she heard Devon's voice.

"Hey, girl." Raisa, in a snug, sea foam linen suit, had obviously just come from work.

Devon, a part-time teacher at the university and part-time artist, was splashy in an orange and yellow wrap only someone of her mixed Native American and Polynesian blood could wear so fetchingly. "Sorry we're late. Traffic was awful at the U."

CJ got up for a round of hugs, and wondered at Devon's cat-with-cream smile. She understood when she was introduced to Elaina, a colleague of Devon's from the university. Elaina was lovely in a very nice sweater dress that brought out her green eyes, but wasn't so eye-popping that it announced that she'd fussed. Her darting, shy glance conveyed that she was both nervous and so far not displeased at the sight of CJ. Raisa, of course, wouldn't meet the meaningful look that CJ directed at her.

As they took their seats around the crowded table, Devon said, "Elaina is one of the law professors."

"Correction." Elaina spoke with a clip to her words, reminding CJ of the accents in upstate New York, where she'd gone to college. "I teach business law to undergrads who are *not* going into law as a profession. The curriculum is so set that a monkey could teach it."

"I think you're incredibly modest," Devon said. She gave CJ a nudge under the table.

"I couldn't teach," CJ said quickly. "I admire anyone with the patience." She found herself answering the usual questions about her job, offering the standard evasions about where she'd grown up and urging everyone to please try the wine. She'd forgotten Devon didn't drink, but Raisa and Elaina were both grateful for a glass. By the time they'd settled on entrees, everyone seemed comfortable.

After ordering and surrendering her menu to the waiter, CJ realized that her community service materials were still sitting on the table. She began to gather them with a nonchalant air, but Raisa interrupted her.

"Okay, what did you do to get you community service, huh?"

Thanks for announcing it to the world, Raisa, CJ thought, another thing to appreciate about the evening. "I blew a stop sign, didn't even see it, almost hit somebody. I thought community service meant litter patrol, but these are social welfare groups. I could visit senior citizens." She pointed at the grouping of retirement communities.

Raisa's scan of the list stopped when she excitedly tapped one name with a fingertip. "I know this one—I was the on the board of a group that loaned them startup money. Beginnings Women's Shelter. Incredible woman runs it, totally committed to her cause. Even if it's just a few hours, I know Emily could use someone with a brain to help out. She squeaks a dollar farther than any group I know of, but she's not long on business sense."

Battered women…it was a subject CJ didn't want to know more about. She also didn't want to explain why she didn't want to go there, but Raisa would want an explanation. More wine, and quickly, she thought. Is this what having friends was all about? Suddenly you're accountable for your choices?

"Well," CJ finally said, "I'll have to give them a call then." It was easiest just to do it.

Elaina was nice, another nice woman, the world was full of nice women, CJ concluded. When Raisa excused herself to the restroom, CJ went with her, asking as soon as the door was closed, "What's with the fix up?"

"Devon is an unstoppable force when she decides to match-make. She's got a decent track record, too."

"But I'm not in the market. I'm really not the settling down kind. Elaina is very nice, don't get me wrong."

Raisa's voice rose over the stall separator. "Devon doesn't believe anyone isn't the settling down kind. I wasn't when she met me, after all."

It was hard to picture Raisa as anything but married to Devon. They were like two puzzle pieces with a perfect fit. "You dated a lot before her?"

"Not women. Lots of guys because I was straight and figured sooner or later I'd find a guy who could actually do that stuff I'd read about in Cosmo. Then I met Devon. My first fireworks, if you get my drift, and it's only gotten better."

"I'm really quite capable of acquiring my own fireworks. But I've scarcely the time to go shopping, you know?" She joined Raisa at the sinks, glancing at her in the mirror. "Elaina's very nice and I don't want to hurt her feelings."

"I told Devon this was a bad idea. She wants to go to some bistro after this for dessert."

Thankfully, CJ could tell the truth. "Sorry, but honestly, I need an early night. There's a meeting with a client at their site, before the construction crew arrives. The alarm goes off at six a.m."

They walked back to the table and were reclaiming their seats when Raisa said, "You do work too much."

"I know." CJ seized the opening. "I'm a workaholic. I really enjoy what I do. It's so nice to have a break once in a while, like tonight, with friends. It's a completely client-focused business, so I have days like tomorrow where I have to be up at sunrise and a networking meeting after dinner. That means it'll be nine p.m. before I can even think about the gym. After meals like this, the gym is essential." She smiled brightly, hoping she looked like the antithesis of good girlfriend material.

Her gaze slightly narrowed, Devon said, "I was hoping to convince you to try this new place I know that has a crème brulee to die for."

"I really can't, not tonight."

"I couldn't either." Elaina's smile was just a trifle forced. "I've got a department meeting in the morning too. Perhaps another time." She was looking at Devon when she said it, without a sidelong glance at CJ.

CJ turned a gusty sigh of relief into a cough. No follow-up date was sought by Elaina—*workaholic* or *friends* had done the trick, or Elaina had decided something didn't click, which was okay, too. Devon was easily the most disappointed person at the table.

Her early night was the better for the relaxing meal and a hot shower when she was safely home. She pushed away her concern that Raisa and Devon could get to know more about her over time, and there were questions she couldn't answer. It would be better if she claimed to be busy the next time they called—nothing had changed. She couldn't afford anyone getting close to her, even if it was only close enough to wonder why she might want to avoid a battered women's shelter.

After the highs and lows of the day, the honey of Chet Baker's trumpet in the quiet of her apartment was just what she needed. Out of habit she checked the parking lot from her window, then glanced out the back as she checked the heavy deadbolt. Another lost client annoyed her, especially when she was sure he'd been misled by the other broker.

She finished a cup of coffee as she idly studied her list of names and numbers. If she'd closed that deal she'd have had just about enough to take care of the next name on the list. It would have to wait another month at least. What she really needed to do was work some old clients and see if she could pick up a lead or two.

She hadn't yet asked herself what she would do when the list in her hand was completely marked through. She was good at real estate and maybe she'd stick with it, now that she was licensed. She liked Denver–for what that was worth to someone who might have to run for her life at a moment's notice. So far, she'd not seen a hint of anyone looking for her, but she had to remain vigilant. She might be able to stay here, when she'd finished with the list, but such decisions were two years off, at least. There was nothing in this apartment that she wouldn't easily walk away from, she told herself. That was the point of her lack of a social life, why she couldn't really afford Raisa and Devon as friends, the point of her honesty with Abby. She could leave it all behind. That is, everything but the list. It would go with her until she was done with everybody on it.

She was about to call it a night when she remembered the stupid community service papers. Expecting to get an answering machine or recording that gave the time she should call back in the morning, she was startled when a real person answered the phone with a brisk, "Beginnings. How can I help you?"

"Oh, hi. I'm not sure if this is the right time—"

The voice deepened. "It's okay. Do you need help right now?"

"No, I'm calling because I have to do community service."

"Oh. Cool. Okay, can you be here tomorrow night?"

"I guess. I have a business dinner until about eight."

"Nine is fine. It's Friday night."

Was that supposed to mean something to her? "Nine it is.

Where are you located? It just says Denver Metro area on the paperwork."

"We're in Lakewood."

The voice, taking on a harried quality, quickly related the address and a few general directions. "That's confidential, so I'd appreciate you keeping it to yourself. We do our darnedest to make it hard for batterers to figure out where the women they're beating have disappeared to."

"I get that," CJ said. She spelled her name when asked for it, then added, "Tomorrow night, then."

Strangely agitated by the phone call, she pushed the laundry basket out of the way and got down on her stomach so she could open her safe. Wedged into the back of her closet, it wasn't something anyone could casually pick up and carry away. Spinning the dial with the ease of long practice, she opened the door and caught the bundles that immediately spilled out.

Twenty fifty-dollar bills neatly wrapped. Seven stacks of five bundles each and an eighth stack of four—thirty-nine thousand dollars. Tomorrow when she went to the bank she'd have an even forty. If her checks were what she hoped over the next month, she'd have at least forty-two-five, and that would take care of the third to last name.

It was calming and reassuring to restack the money in the safe. She had to move the gun twice, but finally everything fit. She shoved the door closed and spun the dial several times.

Turning off lights as she headed for bed, she conceded that at that moment it might have been nice to have Abby near, to curl close to the warmth of contact. She shouldn't have let Raisa see the papers, and shouldn't have agreed to any time in a women's shelter. She'd just have to grit her teeth and survive it. It would be a piece of cake compared to other places where she'd been required to spend her time.

She left the music on and willed herself to sleep.

Her dreams were disturbed with the memories of breaking glass, hoarse shouts and grunts of anger and pain.

In the morning the past felt closer than it had in years. She examined the circles under her eyes and considered the long day and even longer night ahead.

"You should have just paid the money," she told her reflection. "Nothing good is going to come of it."

Chapter 5

"Great news, Karita darlin'." Emily beamed at her but something in her smile made Karita nervous.

She secured her locker and turned toward the long kitchen. "Lay it on me."

"We get an extra pair of hands tonight."

"Okay, that's a good thing." Why did Emily look so smug? "Who is it?"

"Some woman who fell afoul of the law."

"Community service refugee? Emily—no, you're not going to stick me with her!" The evening had begun so promisingly, too, with a message from Nann that the lovely cocoadoodle's family had been found, scoring another one for Gran's magic charms.

"If anyone can get some decent work out of someone who really doesn't want to be here, it's you." Emily sipped from her coffee mug, deliberately oblivious to Karita's scowl.

"Plus you've taken the last of the coffee." Karita rolled her eyes as she set about making more. "Can't she just answer the phone for the night? I'll have to show her what I want and then do it myself anyway. The number of grown women who don't know how to make a bed is shocking."

"Maybe this will be the one." Emily patted Karita's cheek on the way past her to her office. "The one who gets as hooked as you on helping out and we'll all get some relief now and again."

"Dream on. What we really need is someone who can patch linoleum and fix those twisted Venetian blinds. And while they're on a ladder, paint the ceilings." Her cheek tingled where Emily had touched it. Not tonight, Karita thought. We shouldn't and we won't. Emily doesn't need my welfare and future on her conscience and she's right, I ought to be dating and having bad sex and awkward third dates, oh joy. "What time should I expect her?"

"Nine. Remember to get her to—"

"Fill out the confidentiality and consent forms, I know."

"Of course you do." Emily disappeared into her office, then leaned back out the narrow doorway, the light teasing gone. "Thank you, Karita."

Without the banter there was only the honesty of her affection and she knew Emily could see it, even from across the kitchen. She was a good woman, and if they would do the sensible thing and fall in love, it would make life easier. "You're welcome, Em."

By the time nine o'clock came and went, Karita had forgotten about her supposed help for the night until the doorbell rang at nine thirty and the monitor revealed a solo woman in a business suit carrying a briefcase. She sighed. The refugee was definitely not the type to put on a ladder with a paintbrush. Emily was in the intake room with a new client and a frightened little boy, so Karita answered the door.

"Please come in." Karita gestured brusquely, not liking to have the door open for long. "I'm Karita and I'll be—oh, it's you!"

"And it's you." Skinny-mocha-Turkish-capped CJ looked as surprised as Karita felt.

They stared at each other, and Karita felt as if the world were taking a long, steadying breath, right along with her. She exhaled as quietly as possible. Her scalp prickled and her palms itched and she didn't know if that was good or bad. Well, given that even though there was little physical resemblance and CJ still reminded her vividly of Mandy, it was bad.

She said the first thing that came into her head. "Do you know how to make chocolate milk?"

"Ever since I was four."

Karita carefully locked the front door again, then led the way to the kitchen. "Milk and syrup are in the fridge. Tumblers in the drainer are clean. Make up about a half a glass and I'll just get some forms for you to fill out."

CJ set down her briefcase and Karita thought that those penetrating eyes hadn't missed the crack in the counter, patches in the linoleum, nor the significance of the monitors displaying the empty front and back porches. Still, there was a wry twist to her mouth as she asked, "Is the chocolate milk for me?"

"No," Karita said as she leaned over Emily's desk. She snagged the folder with the necessary forms, and returned to the kitchen. "It's for a little girl with adorable red braids in the dining room with her mom and baby sister. They were here last week and mom's got a broken arm now. This time maybe she's left for good."

CJ glanced in the direction Karita pointed, but only nodded as she stirred together the milk and a generous tablespoon of chocolate syrup. "Shall I take it in?"

"No, I'll do that. You fill these out—the confidentiality agreement is the most important. I should be right back and then I'll give you a quick tour and we can put your stuff in a locker. Never leave out any personal items, especially your cell phone. The last thing we need is a client calling her batterer to ask to get picked up."

She took the plastic cup out of CJ's hand; their fingers touched briefly. A chill flush spread down her arm. At least at first it seemed cold, but there was a sensation of heat in other parts of her body. Don't let it show, Karita told herself, but she knew her smile had faded completely. CJ wasn't smiling either. Flirting in the coffee bar had been fun, challenging even, but at that moment all Karita could think was that the tension between them felt nothing like flirting.

This is not fate, she told herself, not magic, you're not an elf and the moment she's done her time here she'll be out of your life, and she'll never look back.

She delivered the chocolate milk to the little girl along with a picture book and a soft toy to tuck next to the baby sleeping blissfully in a basket carrier. The book had no interest for the child, but after her mother said it was okay, she sipped at the milk and kept drinking. Color came back into her cheeks almost immediately, and as the child relaxed, so did the mother. Chocolate milk made the world safe again.

CJ looked up from the papers as Karita returned. Her expression was impassive, but Karita thought she knew that look. CJ really did not want to be here, and not because she had a date or better things to do, or thought she was above it or was being treated unfairly by being forced to help other human beings. She doesn't want to experience this kind of place, Karita thought.

A minute flicker of dark light in CJ's eyes made Karita expand her opinion. *She doesn't want to experience this kind of place—again.*

CJ didn't know what she had expected, but an evening of making beds and catching up on a backlog of laundry and dishes wasn't it. She deeply wished she'd brought a change of clothes because going up and down the stairs in her business heels was giving her a blister. The money belt filled with fifties from her trip to the bank earlier would be just as hidden under jeans.

The time, however, passed quickly, but chances to talk to Karita were nonexistent. She took it that the night was busy, and the shelter director spent almost all of it with new arrivals in what had been the old house's dining room. She was welcomed by Emily, who looked as disarming as Winnie-the-Pooh, but CJ knew she was decidedly no pushover. Near midnight she was introduced to Pauline, a registered nurse who volunteered at the shelter just on Friday nights. Overall, she did her best not to cause anyone more work. Karita seemed to be everywhere at once, including carrying both the baby and little girl upstairs while the mother with the broken arm trailed absently in their wake.

Not that CJ wanted to flirt or even just chat. There had been a moment when she'd first arrived when she'd thought, irrationally, "Oh good, another chance with her." But moments later, aware of the way Karita was evaluating her, she'd realized she just wanted to escape. All her instincts told her that Karita, who looked naïve and trusting, saw and understood far too much.

She could hear her father's training: when you suspect you've been found out, run for it. Karita could put a lot of pieces together. Something about her was too perceptive, and yet, everything about her said she couldn't possibly guess at the life CJ had once led. It still wasn't safe to be around anyone like Karita. Being in this house didn't feel safe, either. She'd gone from one like it to detention, and then to four long years free of the Gathering, but also without freedom to do anything but read, exercise and keep her head down.

She didn't go a day when she didn't feel the Gathering reaching for her, trying to pull her back in. Because nobody ever escaped it. It was not a place, but a state of mind, a way of living. She didn't want to go back to a time in her life when ignoring Aunt Bitty's split lip or her own mother's bruised neck was how normal people behaved. By comparison, Karita's obvious kindness and open heart seemed freakish. CJ had worked too hard to leave it all behind and she didn't want to start thinking of Karita as yet another do-gooder to be shown contempt for the stupidity of caring about people.

She didn't want to be Cassiopeia Juniper Rochambeau, not ever again, and this place made Cassie June seem all too real. She did not want to think or behave the way that had been necessary for Cassie June's survival. Even now, living with the possibility that someday the knock on the door would be a marshal, she had more choices than Cassie June had ever had.

She bent over the hot towels just out of the dryer, and realized her hands were shaking.

"Need help with those?"

"No, I've got it." CJ could feel Karita's gaze on her back. She methodically folded the threadbare bath towels. It was just like life in the Gathering. Back then nothing matched—everything was cobbled together. Sheets from an unguarded coin laundry, a jacket left on the back of a chair. Everything a hand-me-down, and they were proud to be free of any need they couldn't fill themselves. If it couldn't be stolen, it wasn't needed.

"Let me show you where to put those."

CJ followed Karita silently down the long central hall that split the old house in two. They left a few of the towels in a downstairs closet, and carried the rest of the stacks upstairs. Karita excused herself to the communal restroom near the top of the stairs as CJ put the linens on the empty shelf in another large closet. The piles needed a little tidying and she took care of that, then stepped back into the hallway. She was startled by a small but sturdy woman right next to the door—for a moment she was staring at Aunt Bitty's face after Uncle Vaughn had gone on a bender.

She knew how to hold her expression, had learned young that a curl of a lip or a blink of the eyes could draw attention. Nothing in her face moved, so it must have been her eyes that betrayed the rush of memory and fear.

The woman snapped, "Don't stare at me."

"I'm sorry."

"No, you're not. You got a problem with me?"

CJ sincerely hoped the woman had no kids, because guaranteed the moment her own beatings stopped, she turned around and passed on the pain. "I have no problem with you."

The woman dropped her voice and got eye-to-eye. "You should see the other guy, bitch."

CJ leaned forward—it was an old reflex. Never give ground to a bully. A scant inch separated their noses. "I am nobody's bitch."

The woman's arm cocked back and CJ saw it coming. The light in the hallway went red and black as her own arm began to rise, then a flash of silver caught her attention.

"Stop it," Karita said sharply.

It broke the spell of the confrontation and CJ relaxed—then realized a moment too late the other woman was still in attack mode. She ducked the punch and had no time to warn Karita. There was a dull thud, a sharp cry and CJ managed to get her shoulder against the other woman's chest. The struggle was dizzying, but one thing was apparent—the other woman was an amateur. She had no sense of weight or momentum, and she left her kidneys wide open. One sharp strike would have put her on the floor, but CJ managed instead to protect her own head while she shoved the woman backward into the closet. She slammed the door and braced herself against it while the woman cussed a blue streak that no doubt everyone in the house could hear.

Karita was sprawled on the floor, one hand on her neck. Footsteps thumped up the stairs toward them and Emily, looking incongruously like an out-of-breath teddy bear in her brown sweats, arrived at a run. A door slammed and Pauline was hurrying toward them from the far end of the upstairs hall. The door behind CJ's back resounded from the trapped woman's blows.

"What in hell happened? Karita, are you okay, sweetie?" Emily rounded on CJ. "*What happened?*"

CJ's vision swam as adrenaline abruptly drained out of her. She couldn't find any words. Her mouth wouldn't work.

"Emily, Em." Still holding her neck, Karita said hoarsely, "It's okay. I'm okay." She glanced at Pauline, who was out of breath. "I'm okay Pauline, just surprised. It's Sonya—she didn't get my face or anything. I'll just have a bruise."

Emily looked back at Karita, then focused again on CJ. "You can move out of the way." CJ did as she was told, and Emily snatched open the closet door and held up an imperious hand. "Sonya! Stop that immediately or I will call the cops."

The woman bellowed, "That bitch started it!"

There were tears in Karita's eyes. I should have let her hit me, CJ thought. I know how to take a punch.

"There's no way Karita started anything with you, and you know it." Emily put her sizeable bulk between Sonya and the rest of them.

"Not that bitch, the other one!"

"I don't care, frankly." Emily said something else, but CJ didn't really have a clue. She did something she'd never done before in her entire life, and had only enough time to think, *So this is what it feels like to faint.*

She came out of unconsciousness with a start, surging upright and nearly knocking Emily in the mouth with her head. Her heart fluttered in her throat with panic—she'd been completely vulnerable, in front of strangers.

"Hey, hold on."

"Is Karita okay?"

"I'm fine," Karita said from behind her.

CJ tried to sit up all the way, wanting off the dusty patched rugs. There was no sign of Sonya or Pauline.

"Don't get up," Emily said sharply. "You were completely out."

"I know. I'm fine, though. It was just adrenaline." It was the truth, well most of it.

"Has this happened before?"

"Actually, no. I was taken by surprise, that's all. She was spoiling to hit someone. She meant to punch me, not Karita. She might have thought I was one of the other vic—clients because she's a smart enough bully not to attack one of the staff."

"You got toe-to-toe with her. That's what that type will do when challenged. Are you sure you're okay?"

CJ proved it by getting carefully to her feet. "I'm fine."

The woman with one arm in a sling passed them in the hall, shying away from getting too close. She gave CJ a look of sympathy, as if she understood they shared some experiences. Again, CJ thought nothing showed in her expression by way of response, but Emily said quietly, "I'm not sure this is the right place for you to be."

She couldn't help it, she turned her head just enough to glance at Karita. When she returned her gaze to Emily she realized that Emily was watching her very, very closely.

Emily's gaze flicked to Karita and back. "Do you two know each other?"

"No," CJ said.

"Not really," Karita said. "We frequent the same coffee place."

Emily's expression became professionally distant. "I think you're very uncomfortable here."

"Look," CJ said, trying not to sound defensive. "I can fold sheets and wash dishes, vacuum, whatever."

"You're still not comfortable." Emily shifted her weight. She was no Winnie-the-Pooh. Social workers liked to look warm and fuzzy but they weren't. "You see our clients as asking for it, don't you?"

"Nobody deserves the first beating, not even the fifth. But when you go back for the tenth, the twentieth…" CJ realized she'd not meant to say any of that. Why was she trying to argue herself into finishing out her time? Emily was right—this place wasn't for her.

"Then you deserve the twentieth beating?"

"Then you have some responsibility for your actions."

"What if you've got no choice, and you're sure that no matter where you hide, he'll find you and then he'll kill you."

"There's always a choice." She tried not to see Aunt Bitty

with that crowbar in her hand.

"Some women no longer believe that. And that makes them stupid, doesn't it?"

"No. Just another permanent victim, soaking up resources and energy that might actually help someone else."

"Our goal here is to get every woman into the recovery system. To show them they have choices that don't include being beaten to death or killing their abusers while they sleep."

CJ blinked and Emily saw it. No doubt Emily thought she knew all about CJ now, but Uncle Vaughn hadn't been asleep. Showers were easier to clean than beds, Aunt Bitty had told her mother. "Does my opinion really matter if I can do the work?"

"I can't afford another scene like that."

"I didn't start it—like I said, she was spoiling to hit someone."

"You don't step toward someone in that mood. You step back."

CJ was certain that had she stepped back, Sonya would have lunged at her. She'd been that ready to fight. She was also certain she'd been in more fistfights than Emily, but it wasn't a credential she wanted to establish. "I'll keep that in mind."

Emily's eyes were a light brown that blended out to purple. Right then the purple was darkening, and CJ could see the attempt being made by Emily to get inside her head. No doubt about it, Emily was good at reading people, and CJ was willing to bet she read men nearly perfectly. Women weren't quite so easy for her, maybe because she was gay and didn't really want to understand how dark a woman's soul could be.

CJ understood women's souls in all their shades of black. "I'm just here to do my time."

For some reason, Emily glanced at Karita. "Well, you're done for the night. I'll have to decide about anything more." Her expression softened slightly. "I'm just not sure this is comfortable for you and above all, this is a safe place for *everybody*. You might… pay more than you owe."

CJ tried to keep an ironic smile off her face. "That's against my principles."

Emily's gaze hardened. Again, it flicked to Karita and back. "What do your principles say about taking more than you're due?"

"I avoid that, too." She added, sure Emily would understand her meaning, "I don't overreach."

Karita, who had been watching their exchange with her arms crossed over her chest, said quietly, "I'd really like some tea."

"You're going home," Emily said. "No arguments."

"Don't be silly." Karita turned toward the stairs. "It's Friday night."

They were nearly back to the kitchen when the doorbell rang. CJ took a moment longer than either of the others to glance at the closed-circuit monitor. A cop and yet another weeping woman stood on the front doorstep.

"I'll go," Karita said.

"No you won't." Emily pointed at the nearest chair. "Sit."

Emily was no sooner out of the kitchen when Karita got up to make tea.

"Let me do that," CJ said.

"I'm not the one who fainted." Karita's voice was still hoarse.

"You're going to have a hell of a bruise tomorrow." CJ watched on the monitor as Emily let the officer and the woman in. After a brief pause, the officer left.

"Tomorrow's Saturday. I can rest my voice."

"Take some anti-inflammatory." CJ couldn't stop staring at the slowly purpling bruise on Karita's throat. Were it not for the rising tide of unwelcome memories she might have offered to kiss it and make it better. But there was nothing flirtatious inside her at the moment, not with the sound of sobbing coming from the dining room.

Karita heard it too. A bleak expression flitted over her expressive face, then it was gone, replaced by something that might have been determination. "I think I'll make tea for everybody."

CJ couldn't think of anything to do but go back to the utility room and resume folding towels. As she creased and stacked she repeated to herself that she was a thousand miles from where she had grown up, and it certainly felt like a thousand years since then, too. She didn't know why she kept thinking about Aunt Bitty, who was probably still alive. Why did she look at these cowed and beaten down women and think of Aunt Bitty? Why didn't they remind her of her mother?

Karita set a steaming mug on the washing machine. "Drink it. I don't care if you don't like sweetened tea."

Karita hurried away before CJ had time to thank her. She loathed sugar in her tea as much as she loved it in her coffee, but she dutifully sipped. She swallowed with great care and realized she was babying her mouth, as if she had a loose tooth or torn inner cheek, or a neck that was sore from being grabbed and shaken. The way she felt inside was like after—she forced her thoughts away from more memories. She was not there, she was here. She was in the here and now and she wasn't hurt. To prove it she took a large gulp and burned the roof of her mouth. Terrific.

She was nearly done with the tea and the towels when Emily said from behind her, "I thought I told you to go home."

"You did. I wanted to finish up at least one chore tonight."

Emily watched CJ work for a moment, then said, "She's off limits."

A bitter laugh escaped CJ before she could catch it back. "I barely know her."

"Good."

"I don't see what you—"

"I don't know you. But I know her. I'll bet that just about no one in your life has any idea that you are a great big open sore. She knows, she can't help but know. God love her, she wants to help the world."

"I don't need help." CJ finished the last towel, then busied her hands making the stacks neater. "And I surely don't need any psychology one-oh-one."

"If that's your choice, that's fine. But don't go sucking empathy out of an amateur when you're ignoring professional advice."

She slowly raised her gaze to meet Emily's and wasn't surprised by the fierce protectiveness she saw there. The pang of envy was sharp and surprising. No one had ever protected her from anything.

She straightened her spine. She didn't need protecting. She was fixing everything all by herself. "All I really need is my twenty-one hours and I've knocked off four of them tonight so far."

Emily began to reply, but Karita's voice cut her off.

"I just heard from Lucy. She was so sorry she forgot to call. Her mom's had another stroke and she's in Cheyenne."

Emily leaned tiredly against the washing machine. "That can't be good news, not after the last one."

"She doesn't know when she'll be back."

"Makes sense—she should take care of family."

CJ didn't say anything, but was aware that Emily was deliberately not looking at her. Right then she couldn't have said if she hoped Emily would still tell her not to come back or if Emily would ask her to finish out her time. The moment felt like a crossroads, but she didn't get to choose the path.

Finally, Emily sighed. "Against my better judgment." She heaved herself toward the utility room door.

Karita let her pass. "Thanks."

Emily grunted a reply. Her grumpiness didn't surprise CJ at all. It wasn't as if Emily had many choices here either. The abruptly brilliant smile that Karita gave CJ—that was unsettling. It burned bright in her mind for a long while, banishing all shadows.

By two a.m. Karita was pleased to see that CJ had sorted and filed the client records for the last week. She worked methodically and quickly, and Karita wasn't sure she could have done it any more quickly herself.

"What line of work are you in?"

"Commercial real estate." CJ looked up from the stack she was alphabetizing. Only her eyes gave away her fatigue. "Is this a job for you, here?"

"I wish—Emily can't afford other paid staff. If she didn't have a small private practice of her own, she couldn't even afford herself. So I spend my days pushing paper around a law office."

"If it pays the bills, can't complain about that."

"Real estate is in a slump, isn't it?"

"Yes and no. Some locations never go out of fashion, no matter the times. I've been lucky in that regard. Not to change the subject, but why does it matter that it's Friday night?"

Karita was pretty sure CJ meant to change the subject. "The incidence of domestic violence goes up on Friday and Saturday nights. Weekend syndrome."

"After a bad week, take it out on the wife and kids?"

"Primarily. But some abusers know just how much damage they can do on Friday night and their victims will still be able to go to work or school on Monday, nobody the wiser. This has actually been kind of quiet."

"This was quiet?" CJ's smile was tight.

Karita put a hand to her throat. The bruise had settled into a dull ache. "Violence here is pretty rare. I've seen and heard more yelling in the law office where I work."

CJ straightened up and rubbed her lower back. "These are done. I have to be honest, I don't have much left in me. My day started about twenty hours ago."

"The next shift arrives shortly, but why don't you go ahead—"

"I'll stay until you get some relief."

There was a clatter of keys at the back door and Karita peeked at the monitor. "Help has arrived, as a matter of fact. Can you find Pauline and let her know?"

Karita greeted the next shift and gave them a quick rundown on the night's events, making only brief mention of the altercation with Sonya. Emily would have to decide about Sonya's eligibility for future stays. When CJ returned she made introductions as she got her things out of her locker. By the time she was ready to go CJ was likewise ready and Karita showed her the back exit. "We're paranoid, but it's not unheard of for some guy to figure out where the shelter is. We try not to leave alone after dark and never by the front door. Where are you parked?"

"Just here." CJ pointed out a late-model Trailblazer under the buzzing streetlight. "How about you?"

"Just across the street. We do try to mix it up, where we park, because the neighbors can get testy about it." Karita was glad of her sweater. Though the sidewalk still radiated warmth the cool air felt as if it had rolled right down off the mountains.

CJ shrugged and unlocked her car. "See you here, again, I guess. I hope."

Karita heard the hint of reluctance in CJ's voice and didn't know quite what to make of it. "Maybe so. If not here, I'm addicted to coffee."

CJ sketched a salute, but Karita just couldn't let her go. "Were you hitting on me, you know, at Gracie's?"

"What happens if I say no?"

With a shrug, Karita said, "I'm not sure I'd believe you."

Something leapt in CJ's eyes as she turned to face Karita. "It's not a plausible lie. So yes, I was hitting on you."

"Why? Is it just the way I look?"

"That would be the obvious answer." CJ slowly raised one hand to touch Karita's hair where it fell forward over one shoulder.

Breathing was abruptly difficult. "But not the whole truth and nothing but the truth."

With a shake of the head, CJ whispered, "The whole truth is that I couldn't help myself, which is very rare for me."

She let strands of Karita's hair slip off the ends of her fingers and the quiet sound reminded Karita of snow falling. She'd never felt so delicate.

"You walked away," CJ said, just as quietly. "Why?"

"You have a girlfriend."

"Not in the way you mean, but...yes, there's someone."

"So this shouldn't happen."

Their gazes locked and Karita fell into dark, deep eyes, lit in the depths with a lining of gold turned silver in the streetlight. There was something there, it could have been a warning, but there was more than that. She couldn't help a little gasp when CJ blinked and the connection was broken.

"No," CJ said. "No, it shouldn't."

It was all the truth that should have been needed for Karita to step back from the luminous glow in CJ's eyes. Her heart was beating like a hummingbird, trying to escape to safety. CJ let the last of her hair trail from the tips of her fingers and there was space between them again. With space there was cooling air that should have brought rational thought with it.

She ought to have remembered her decision that CJ was a frog, no princess, and kisses wouldn't change that. There was no fate at play here, no magic. CJ was another Mandy, all about money. Even if she was looking for more than sex, all she wanted was a girlfriend-cum-tennis bracelet, an adornment. Eventually she would call Karita a flake, twit her about the uselessness of helping other people. There'd always be poor, and there'd always be battered women, so why didn't she just grow up?

CJ was bad news. And telling herself that had no effect whatsoever.

Instead Karita was dizzied by the pulse of the night and the inescapable thought: *I have to know.*

She cupped CJ's face, giving her time to say no, but CJ didn't say no, she didn't say anything, then there couldn't be words with Karita's mouth pressed to hers. They were still and again the world seemed to take a deep breath. The crickets fell silent, the streetlight's buzz faded to nothing.

In the spell of their stillness, Karita first felt their mutual surprise. Kisses before had always brought feelings surging to the fore with a physical drumming that caught Karita in the dance of emotion, of life. This kiss pushed all that into the background, leaving room for something else to pour through her veins and pass between them in the quiet of their kiss. *She doesn't kiss like a frog*, Karita thought and it made her smile against CJ's mouth.

CJ made a small sound, breaking the spell, then kissed her more deeply. Karita was aware, then, of a deep fire, one she had never tapped, and as it swelled the laughter died.

They separated, didn't look at each other. That was magic, Karita thought dazedly, but I didn't make it.

"I'm sorry—"

"It's okay, I shouldn't—"

"Tired, long day…silly."

Karita finally stole a glance at CJ, and those remarkable, deep eyes were mirrors of midnight. A glint of quicksilver might have been the reflection of her hair in the depths.

She offered another kiss. For a moment, she offered everything with her eyes, the curve of her arms, the yearning of her body. That she hardly knew CJ seemed irrelevant.

CJ said, "I can't." Her eyes darkened, and Karita's reflection was gone. "I can't."

She was aware that CJ didn't start her car until she was safely inside hers, motor running. She didn't remember what inanity she spouted as she walked away, but it was surely as stupid as the wave she gave as she pulled away from the curb.

What was that about, Karita? What did you just do?

She could tell that her voices of inner reason wanted to ask why but she had no answer to that. Did she have to know why, right now? The obvious answer was basic animal attraction. That was a good enough reason for just a kiss, wasn't it? No harm done. That's all it was—attraction. Pheromones. Maybe even hormones.

She was an adult, and she knew nothing good would come of

it, and honestly, she told herself sternly, nothing *ought* to come of it. She'd loved Mandy and been left feeling both cheap and used. Nothing *had* to happen. CJ wasn't safe. It had been the kind of night that had first driven her and Emily into bed together, too, the kind of night where they both wanted to pull a veil of very good feelings over things that ached.

Karita put a hand to her still throbbing neck. That's all it was—mutual need. Well, she had Emily if that need got urgent. There was no need to get involved with a near stranger, even one who made Karita feel as if every kiss, every touch before that one had been hollow practice, tepid foreplay. Maybe CJ didn't kiss like a frog, but that didn't mean she wasn't one.

CJ found her apartment too quiet in the dead of night. Dawn wasn't all that far off, but sleep was not going to happen. She sat with her list of names in her hand, consciously thinking about nothing, trying not to relive that moment of disbelief when she'd realized Karita was going to kiss her.

She'd walked out the shelter door with Karita, reminding herself that it would take so many lies, and so much time, that it simply wasn't worth the effort to seduce her. That Karita might take the initiative hadn't occurred to her. She'd been kissed before. She'd been pursued and seduced before, too, yet the kiss had been a surprise. And after that extraordinary kiss, Karita had offered herself, freely, a gift.

Wasn't it ironic, she mused. She had no experience with gifts. She didn't how to accept one and she certainly didn't know how to turn one down. For a moment long enough to quash the tremulous feeling in the pit of her stomach, she had heard Aunt Bitty's sour assessment: *If it's free, it's not worth having*.

You fool, CJ, you should have grabbed on with both hands, and let all the light you could take from her chase away every shadow, every memory. Karita was *clean*, and a kiss from her was purifying. More than that could be redeeming and Lord knows you need redemption.

76

Aunt Bitty wouldn't shut up. So, you take that light into your arms, CJ, and what happens, then? You take the light, you burn away the past and then she finds out who you are. What you were. What you've done.

She drowned out Aunt Bitty's rasp, but her own voice of reason took over. She would only bring pain to a woman like that. Violated trust and a broken heart was the repayment she could guarantee for freely given grace—well, wasn't that a thought? Grace couldn't be a gift and it couldn't be stolen. It could only be earned.

She laughed into the silence of her bedroom. Rochambeaus didn't earn anything but jail time. She got out of the desk chair and unzipped her skirt so she could unsnap the money belt under the waistline. A few moments later she had the safe open and another bundle of twenty fifty-dollar bills stuffed inside.

A hot shower eased the tension in her shoulders, but when she turned out the lights she felt as if she were on a seesaw, teetering between the memory of Karita's kiss and what the shelter had stirred up. With a lost moan, she tipped over the edge. It had only been a kiss, a kiss like no other, but it didn't change the past.

The jailhouse shrink had said that it was okay if memories she'd managed to put out of her mind suddenly resurged. Happenings in her life would remind her of things she'd rather not recall. Of course the shrink, like the rest of the social welfare system, had no real idea what CJ remembered.

Though the recollection was murky, she could see her mother and aunt bent over Uncle Vaughn's body. There was a lot of blood and sounds were muffled. Aunt Bitty had said showers were easier to clean than beds and then she'd seen CJ standing in the doorway. Her face was like a painted ghost's in CJ's memory, no eyes, no expression, a red streak across one cheek. Her mother turned and then just wasn't there. It was her and Aunt Bitty, and Aunt Bitty telling her to ignore Uncle Vaughn and if she needed to pee, to go ahead and do it. The way she said it meant Cassie June had better be fast about it, or else.

It was the finest house CJ could remember them ever living in, and they'd left the next day, before the sun came up, the way they usually left places. It had to have been a fine place because the toilet flushed easily and the bed she shared with a cousin, Daria, was warm. That night she'd been cold, though. Daria had slept through the yelling, the thuds and then the eerie silence broken only by the shower turning on and off, on and off.

The memory wouldn't get any more solid than that—over the last ten years it had, in fact, gotten less vivid. Less intensity was supposedly a good thing, but CJ's racing heart and pounding temples didn't feel less intense. It wasn't the worst memory, either, just one of the oldest.

The cool sheets of her bed made her think of Karita, but she refocused on the deals she had in negotiation, on Burnett's contact, on the list. She wanted all the names crossed off that list. After the last one she'd feel free, wouldn't she? These memories would continue to fade, and the past would be settled, wouldn't it? She didn't need kisses from angels for that.

She thought, then, even though she tried not to, of seeing Karita again, bumping into her at the coffee bar, or going back to the shelter to watch her bring peace to almost everything she touched. CJ closed her eyes and knew that even if the past could be settled, there were futures forever closed to her.

Chapter 6

Karita raced across the building lobby, Marty's briefcase in one hand and a lunch bag in the other. So much for yesterday's resolution to stop cutting court appearance timing so close, she thought. He pulled up to the curb as she burst out of the main doors. She tossed the briefcase in through the open window and the bag after. "I made you peanut butter and banana—you eat that or Minna's gonna have my head about your blood sugar."

"Sorry about this—you're a doll. Get some lunch." Marty pulled out into traffic just as a patrol car turned the corner behind him. "Later, princess!"

Karita caught her breath, then glanced at her watch. She still had time to make it to lunch. She'd never been to the Down the Block Deli, but it was Pam's choice. Far enough from the office not to risk bumping into anyone else who worked with them, but not so far that it would be a long walk in the heat of the day. She was glad she'd had the sense in her mad dash out the door to trade her low-heeled pumps for her comfortable clogs.

Pam was at the counter, paying for her meal, when Karita arrived. "I'll snag us a table," she said as Karita got in line.

"Sorry I'm late," Karita said as soon as she joined Pam at the table. She spread out her sandwich and chips, then popped the cap on a bottle of organic sweet tea.

"Marty had a court date?" Pam smiled up at her, but it was clearly an effort. Her long, brown hair was as dull as the look in her dark-ringed eyes. She blinked in the bright deli light, giving her the look of an owl out unexpectedly in the daytime. The weight of the world seemed to be on her shoulders, making her seem even more petite.

"Nothing changes." Karita was so glad she'd remembered to call Pam—she looked as if she hadn't been outside for a week. Like most of the associates, Pam had worked long hours and probably didn't have much of a network of friends for times like these.

"There are things I could hope would change." After a listless nibble on the crust of her sandwich, Pam put it down. "Thanks for calling. I can't seem to focus on much, but it was nice to have lunch with you to look forward to."

"Have you thought about suing? Susan House fired you after...you know." Karita dropped her voice. "Sleeping with you."

Pam shrugged. "I'd love to tell the world what a heartless shit she is. But lawyers who sue other lawyers, especially associates who sue partners, well...I'd like to have a career. Plus, one of the things we tell clients is that going to court rarely takes care of the emotional distress. I'd lose so much more going to court than I'd gain. All I really need is a recommendation, and yesterday she said she might give me one."

"You're *talking* to her?" Karita glanced around nervously, not meaning for her voice to be quite so loud. The deli was crowded, though, and no one seemed interested in them.

"There was something at my apartment that was hers. She stopped to get it. Hey—I didn't beat in her head with the television, so that's something." Pam's bitterness was slightly eased by something like a genuine smile.

"So what are you going to do?"

"Lick my wounds. I'm going to give up my apartment and move home and regroup. My student loans are huge and I can't afford to be unemployed for long. My folks are disappointed, but I finally came out to them and just admitted that I'd made a really huge mistake—guess what, they still love me."

"Well, that's something good. Not that you have to thank the Evil One because one good thing might have come from the mess." Karita sipped the tea and wished there were some way to make Susan House pay for the pain she'd caused Pam. It was so unfair that she was getting away with it. After another bite of her avocado and jack cheese sandwich, she said, "If I didn't love Marty I'd quit. Do you think he has any clue what Susan is like?"

"Some, yeah, I mean he's heard her blow up at people. But I liked Marty a lot, too. I was learning a ton from him. Nothing flashy, just practical application of law and how to run a practice."

"Do you think you could tell him the truth, at least?"

Pam pushed her half-eaten sandwich away. "That's the problem. The truth."

"She seduced you—"

"No, Karita. I seduced her." She glanced up as if to see if Karita was unduly shocked. "At least...I did more than half the work of getting us into...the situation. I know all about the fact that she was the boss and she had all the power, but I'm not without responsibility. I thought I loved her. I thought, sex, would bring us closer together even if we never pursued a relationship. She was so much older and I didn't care, but she did. Then she started dating what's-his-name and dumped me. It's actually kind of sordid and dull, and I brought it on myself."

"Pam." Karita took a deep breath to get control of her tone, not wanting to sound as irate as she felt. "Okay, yes, opening the door to a sexual relationship with your boss wasn't the smartest thing to do. Taking responsibility for your choices is right, but it doesn't mean she's not responsible, too. She heaped abuse and ridicule on you, had you working sixteen hours a day, and weekends, and told you all that was necessary to keep the relationship secret, right?"

Pam nodded, tears swimming in her eyes.

"She used your emotional attachment to her to work you, and her position as your boss to keep you from complaining about your treatment. Then, when she wanted out, what did she do? She fired you. Why couldn't she just say that it was over? Why did she have to be so cruel about it? Why couldn't she just say she'd made a mistake and tell you that you needed to move on?"

Karita paused when Pam surreptitiously dabbed at her eyes. "Forget the boss/employee stuff for a minute. On the personal side of it, I don't get it—she had a choice, you know. She could have been *kind*. Firm, but kind. She chose not to be. She fabricated that missing file, it was a lie, so she could get rid of you. And that's on her. That's all about her ducking out of responsibility for her choices, and has nothing to do with you. Don't tell yourself you somehow are so bad that you brought out the worst in her. You're not the only person who has ever seen this side of her."

"She yelled at me more than her other two associates put together. I couldn't do anything right."

"So you made her insecure or nervous or anxious or whatever. She still had a *choice* about what to do with those feelings. Her choices are not your fault. She kicked you because you couldn't kick her back and she knew it. That makes her a bully and bullies are cowards." Her voice caught and she took a sip from her tea.

After clearing her throat, she added, more quietly, "I don't understand why people choose to be mean when they have all the power in the world to be nice."

Pam gave a little laugh. "Promise me something."

"What?"

"Whatever you do, don't go into the law. It'll eat you alive."

Karita laughed. "It hasn't exactly treated you better."

"True." Pam picked up her sandwich and took a large bite out of it. "It wasn't just the, you know...the love she rejected. It

82

was me, the person. The lawyer, the human being, the lesbian, the woman. I don't know why she had to do things the way she did and I guess I thought, you know, it had to be me making her do it somehow."

Karita shook her head. "She treated you like that because it made life easier for her. That's what cowards do—they cause other people pain to escape it themselves. If Susan was worth anything, she'd have found you another job, written you an accurate and compelling recommendation, you know, made sure you didn't lose anything. But evidently she had to make sure you lost everything for her to feel secure. As if she could prove she loved the new guy by grinding the woman she'd cared about into the ground. You, at least, have a chance to get your self-respect back. She'll never even know that she lost hers."

"Where were you when I was falling for her? I could have used that speech back then." Pam tore open her bag of chips. "I ignored her temper, and the way she blames everyone else when things go wrong. I tell myself I could have done things differently. That I could have bowed out before she made me go. I tried, you know? I told her all she had to do was say we were done and I'd never speak of it again. Next thing I knew she hadn't ever wanted gay sex, that it was my fault, and she was dating a guy and I was the worst lawyer she'd ever worked with. She had no respect for me at all."

"Closet case," Karita muttered.

Pam let out a chortle. "Can I have lunch with you once or twice a week for a couple of months? I'll even buy."

Karita grinned at her, glad to see real humor in Pam's eyes. "Maybe you should talk to a bona fide therapist. I just have a junior merit badge. Imagine what a pro could do for you."

"You should be a pro. You're a great listener." Pam finished her last chip and stared into the bag. "Wow, that's the first whole meal I've eaten since it happened."

"Good for you." Karita reached into her purse for a little box. "I remembered these were your favorites and thought a few might be medicinal."

"Oh, you're so sweet." Pam took the box of truffles. "Mochas and caramels, you're right, my favorites. Have one with me."

"No, those are for you. For the dark of night."

Pam blinked back tears, then gave her a broad smile. "Okay. Karita, be honest. Why are you single?"

Karita knew she blushed. Her answer felt like it might be a lie—she didn't think of any particular set of very dark, intense eyes, or of a kiss that had suggested she didn't know the first thing about passion or love—but she said it anyway. "Because I haven't met the right woman yet."

CJ watched Karita and her date leave the deli, glad not to have been noticed. She'd not even realized Karita was there until she'd heard the unmistakable, engaging laugh. From where she sat she could see the other woman saying something Karita found very amusing, then in another flurry of laughter, the much shorter woman scooped up a lavish bouquet from the flower vendor on the corner and presented it to Karita with a bow. They disappeared from CJ's sight, Karita's cheeks stained red with delight.

The beauty of Karita's smile lingered behind her eyes like the afterlight of staring at the sun. Butterflies flitted in her stomach until Aunt Bitty whispered, "She won't ever be smiling for the likes of you."

It took her a moment to realize that Burnett had stopped talking.

"Sorry. I saw someone I knew. I didn't realize she worked close to me is all."

Burnett looked mildly speculative, as if he was wondering the significance of a woman who could distract CJ from business. Those puppy dog eyes saw more than CJ had initially thought. "It's okay, I was blathering."

"No," CJ corrected. "You were giving me all the details you know about your potential client. He took your call which means the package was right on. What's your next move?"

"I can't decide." He chomped thoughtfully on his BLT. "More information, detailed first floor plan, tenant improvement budget, all that of course. I could hand deliver it on the hope of getting a brief face-to-face."

"How about this?" CJ tipped a little more white balsamic vinaigrette on the last of her shrimp salad. "Leave him a voice mail saying that you're getting together more material but it would be ultimately time-saving for him to just see the space. He's on the architect association's environmental subcommittee, right? If he walks the space and it's obviously unworkable you save a lot of trees and time. You're happy to pick him up at his convenience, tour the site and have him back in his office in under an hour. Or, if he prefers, you can send over the material first, that's really no bother. Whatever is most convenient for him."

"If I time it right I might get to talk to him live. Jerry is big on always catching the client for a live chat—he doesn't like voice mail."

CJ took her time chewing and swallowing, then she said, "Think about what you want and which communication will get you what you need. You don't know Cray and have no rapport that will make him want to listen to you for long. I personally would go for a practiced and succinct, highly professional voice mail. If you talk to him live he'll tell you to send the package first to get you off the phone. If he gets a chance to think about doing a quick tour and has to call you back, or tell someone to call you back, he might decide you're right about seeing the space. A voice mail gives you a better shot at yes versus no, that's all. The space is going to do most of the job selling him."

Burnett literally bounced in his seat. "And once he sees the space he'll be sold."

CJ envied the kid his youthful enthusiasm even as it annoyed her. "Once he sees the space all you'll know for sure is if there's no chance at all. He'll tell you he doesn't want it if that's the case. Otherwise, the real selling starts."

Burnett's enthusiasm wasn't the least bit quenched. "I know, it's just that it's a good fit for him."

"Yes, it is, but I've seen plenty of perfect fits fall through." She finished the last of her salad and let the rest of her day flit through her mind. Sales meeting, two conference calls, an interim presentation over drinks—more or less a typical afternoon and evening. She wanted an early night because tomorrow was another long Friday at the shelter. Emily hadn't called to tell her not to come back, so she was going. "If you want to practice what you'll say, we can do that on the way back to the office."

"Thanks, but I think I got the gist. You've been great, CJ, thank you. You don't have to give me all your trade secrets, you know."

"They're not secrets, just common sense and experience. It'll be a pleasure to watch you close the deal." I'm not doing it for you, kid, she might have told him. She was addicted to closing a deal, and if not one of her own, then one of his would be a temporary fix. It would be a mistake for him to think she did anything out of the goodness of her heart. Kisses from angels and people who thought she was good enough to date their friends— they changed nothing. Her inner scoffing laugh sounded just like Aunt Bitty. "I think you went about getting this lead in a very clever way, and if you keep that up, sooner or later you're going to hit a deal too big to handle, and that's when I'll expect some payback."

Burnett readily agreed. As they braved the heat, CJ again thought the kid pinged her gaydar, but she had no real use for the information if it was true. If he knew she was gay, he didn't let on. She never socialized with coworkers, so it just wasn't relevant for the day-to-day conduct of her life.

Between conference calls later that afternoon she thought briefly of calling Abby to see if she was free. Calling just two weeks after their last get-together would send the wrong message, she reminded herself, even if the night would no doubt be distracting.

Besides, what did she need distraction from? Her goals were what they had been for years now, her days spent always moving toward those goals. A throaty laugh and dancing eyes and a single kiss, well, they would fade from her memory all on their own. A night with Abby wasn't necessary for that.

She kept telling herself those facts as she dialed the number, then hoped to get Abby's voice mail, in which case she'd hang up. But Abby, sounding tired and out of sorts, answered.

"Hi, it's me. Busy tonight?"

"No—do you want to come over? I just got home from my rotation and it was incredibly shitty."

"I'll bring some dessert. I've got a presentation but could be there by eight."

"I'll get a few winks, then. Dessert sounds good. You know... what I like." Abby's voice had taken on a decided purring edge.

"I do, I think. But if I get it wrong you seem to find it easy to correct me." Jerry appeared in her doorway, forcing CJ to change her tone. "So I'll see you later, then."

"Boss there? I could say anything I liked, couldn't I? Would that make me a bad girl you'd have to punish?"

"We can discuss that."

"See you at eight." Abby hung up, leaving CJ to fight a blush.

"Are you working with Burnett on his big restaurant deal for the Prospector?"

"Sure. He got a solid lead and I'm reviewing his work."

Jerry frowned as he bounced forward on his toes, making the keys and change in his pocket jangle. "I'd be more comfortable if an experienced broker was the lead."

Oh no, CJ thought. She hadn't given up being lead so Jerry could steal it. She would spike that idea right now. "Believe me, first sign I see of him faltering I'll grab up the slack."

Maybe it was the too innocent smile that convinced Jerry her intentions were sinister, but he went away looking both pleased and put out.

During the next conference call and the proposal presentation over drinks later in the evening, she found herself anticipating the night with Abby, which wasn't like her. Passion usually asserted itself when she was actually with Abby. The smell of her shampoo or that sexy perfume she sometimes wore, the shape of her body—it took only a moment in her presence for the attraction to blossom. It wasn't like her to be thinking about sex during a business meeting.

Driving to Abby's, CJ had to admit it felt different tonight. She didn't want just sex, though that was definitely on her mind. She wanted something more, maybe just the comfort of familiarity. Maybe not to be alone with her thoughts or the memory of a kiss that didn't mean anything. Whatever it was, the very existence of something other than physical desire with Abby was new and therefore unsettling. It wasn't a particularly welcome sensation, either, but it was also an itch needing to be scratched.

Her troubled thoughts got a lot simpler when Abby answered her apartment door wearing a short lavender robe that clung to her body. Her short hair, still damp from a shower, curled around her shoulders.

Abby took the box containing a small walnut and caramel tart and led the way to the kitchen. "I think we should save that for energy later." She set the box on the counter and turned around to find CJ right behind her.

"Damn, CJ, how did you know I really wanted to see you tonight?" She undid the tie on her robe and CJ helped her slip it off her shoulders.

"Must be telepathy, because I have been thinking about you all afternoon." She tugged the robe out of Abby's grasp and the silk puddled around Abby's feet. "I love your naked body."

Their kiss was as heated and filled with desire as any they'd ever shared. It was the way a kiss was supposed to be, not full of silent, innocent moonlight, but overflowing with their rapid breathing, little gasps, even the sound of skin brushing against skin.

Abby tasted like sex, like a woman, and there wasn't any need for CJ to be thinking about anyone else, about what a different woman might be like. Even as she aggressively explored Abby's body, though, she realized her thoughts were wandering. She wanted to devour Abby whole and yet it was another voice she heard in her mind, urging more.

Abby tipped CJ's head back for a long kiss. "I love the way you turn me on." Sliding off the counter, she pulled CJ down the short hallway to the bedroom.

CJ didn't have to think of anyone else for her pulse to hammer in her throat. They were quickly spread out on the bed, naked, straining. "Let's take all night."

For an answer, Abby raked her nails across CJ's shoulders, her words lost but the groans and pleas were perfectly clear. It wasn't hard to ignore the other voice she could hear, rising in her fantasy of platinum hair spread across the sheets and long legs wrapped around her hips.

They both fell asleep some time later, bodies still entwined. Stirring in the night, CJ pulled the warm body closer after she found and draped them both with the sheet. Whatever their separate needs had been, they'd both found mutual satisfaction. She drifted to sleep again, feeling oddly pleased that Abby hadn't called out her name as she usually did.

Only in the morning, making a bad breakfast of half a walnut-caramel tart, did she wonder why. It wasn't a question she could ask. CJ left Abby sleeping, and headed for home. In the shower she felt the scratches Abby had left. Toweling off she discovered the sore muscles and ache in her back from the prolonged love making. Hot and hard, they'd both gotten what they wanted. CJ regarded the circles under her eyes and tried to tell herself that she was making more of her own uncertainties than they merited.

They'd both wanted to get laid, and that's what they'd done. Except she'd been thinking of someone else, and that was most certainly not part of what Abby understood to be the truth of their relationship. She'd never used Abby as a stand-in for someone else and she supposed she ought to feel bad about it. She would, except that Abby had been different, too. No fuss about CJ's lack of commitment, no cries that included CJ's name. Just sex, on both sides, for the first time—wasn't that what she had said she wanted?

The collar of CJ's white blouse draped to one side as she helped Karita move the bed frame farther down the wall. For several moments Karita struggled with conflicting feelings. The long curve of CJ's neck, taut with muscle, was undeniably attractive. Her shoulders tightened as she strained against the heavy frame and Karita was finding it hard to look away.

Even more riveting was the scratch that stretched from the base of CJ's neck to some out-of-sight point on CJ's shoulder. At least Karita assumed that's where the scratch would end. The skin wasn't broken but it had probably occurred in the last twenty-four hours.

The blouse gapped and shifted as CJ gave one more heave to the heavy frame and Karita's mesmerized gaze found matching scratches, no doubt all made by the same set of nails at the same moment in time. She caught herself before she imagined what position she would need to be in to scratch CJ in just that way. Well, she nearly caught herself. Just like she had nearly caught herself from reliving that kiss every time she didn't look at CJ's mouth. She wasn't looking at it now, either.

Girlfriend, Karita thought, CJ's got a girlfriend, remember? You kissed someone who has a girlfriend—not your shining moment, remember?

Was there another set, farther down CJ's back? None of your business, she told herself sternly, and stop ogling. Since when did some nice muscles draw her mindless attention? This preoccupation was only going to lead to more trouble. "Here is good enough. We can get two port-a-cribs in this way."

"Those are kept in the last room on the right?"

90

"Yes."

"I'll be back with the first one in a jiffy."

Karita watched CJ speed away, telling herself to do other things with her eyes. She draped the first set of sheets on the narrow bed. Busy hands would keep her eyes from misbehaving.

The arrival of the first crib was an acceptable reason to look up. "The crib sheets are in—"

"The closet. I remember. I'll get two sets and the second crib."

A light, bright blue blanket finished her bed-making tasks and Karita took a moment to tack down the loose corner of the *Finding Nemo* poster. She could hear CJ on her way with the second crib. "Did you remember—"

"Mattress protectors, they're right here. Show me how to set these up?"

"You must have done some babysitting along the way. Most non-moms don't know about the protectors."

"Lots of little cousins when I was growing up."

"No siblings?" The online profile of CJ on her firm's Web site didn't make any mention of family. Karita fought down a blush and was glad CJ couldn't read her guilty mind. It was just a kiss, just a kiss, just a kiss. "The outer shell is the base once we get the legs all popped out. You just snap up the rails, push down on the center...like that."

"Very clever. Then the shell goes on the bottom..." CJ quickly assembled the baby's linens, looking so absorbed in the task that she must have forgotten the question.

Karita repeated, "So, no siblings?"

"Nope. How about you?"

"Just me. My folks died in a car accident when I was two."

"I'm sorry. That's rough." CJ started on the second crib.

The perfunctory sympathy stung a little bit. "I was raised by my grandmother, who was an unusual woman, but very loving. If I'd ended up in foster care—now that would have been rough." Karita reached for one of the folding crib rails at the same time

91

as CJ and their hands brushed. The sizzle that ran up her arm was very unsettling. She left the rails to CJ while she finished up with the base.

"That's for sure. What's next?"

Karita wondered if CJ had spent time in foster care. She consistently skittered away from details of her childhood. She'd been battered, that was almost a certainty, but she didn't give off that wounded-child-within aura that Karita found so heartbreaking in many of their clients. "Sheets or dishes, your choice."

The doorbell was faintly audible from downstairs.

"I hope Emily can get that." She hurried toward the stairs so she could tell if Emily was going to answer the door.

CJ wasn't far behind. "It's extra busy tonight, isn't it?"

"We've only got the Tarzan room left at this point. Hopefully another of the shelters still has space. The Rockies are in a championship race, apparently."

"Yeah, they eliminate two other teams from playoff spots if they win tonight, and there's not quite four weeks left of the season. Labor Day weekend is often the big weeding out point for the playoffs."

"So a big deal."

"Depends what you've bet on."

"Exactly. Men who can't afford to bet and do anyway, hanging out with buddies, a bunch of beer—and we're full." Karita paused to listen. "Emily's got it. I'll go see how many and make up the last room."

Emily was taking a report copy from a Latina police officer that Karita vaguely recognized. The new arrival had obviously been to an ER and was stitched up, and she carried an infant— two or three months old, Karita thought—just as gorgeously cocoa brown as she was.

"May I hold the baby for a bit? You look about done in." Karita waited for a nod before reaching for the child. "Who's this, then, sleeping so well?"

92

"Janeeka. Her daddy doesn't want to be her daddy."

"Then she will need a lot of mommy, and tonight, maybe someone else to get her settled to sleep." Karita nudged the tiny fist with her little finger and the hand opened to grasp it. The reflex usually worked and the substantial squeeze she received was just what her aching heart needed. She smiled at the mother, ignoring the bandage that probably hid six or seven stitches across her forehead. "She's beautiful."

She turned toward the dining room and it was a moment before she realized that Emily and the cop were still chatting. A glance over her shoulder revealed a rare shy smile on Emily's face and the cop was absolutely rapt. Emily was flirting. Well, if you were Emily, that was flirting. Ninety-nine out of one hundred lesbians would miss it, but it did look as if the tall deputy with dark lustrous eyes was having no trouble picking up the signs.

Emily broke off the conversation and sped toward the dining room, all business. Karita made a mental note to tease Emily later. That's what friends did, wasn't it? Friends and possibly soon-to-be ex-lovers? Was she already an ex-lover? After all, they always ended their intimate encounters with a promise that it would be the last. She knew they were both sincere but the need that had first brought them together still existed. Why would it be the last? Well, the attractive cop was one possible reason, she guessed.

She saw to it that the mother was comfortably seated before giving the baby back. She'd find CJ and they'd make up the last room. She was already out of the room before she realized how much she was looking forward to more work by CJ's side and try as she might, she couldn't scold herself out of the feeling. It was another reason why she might just be Emily's ex, for real, at this point. Well that would be silly, wouldn't it? She pressed her lips together as she went up the stairs. Why would she give up something she enjoyed on the hope of nothing in its place? She reminded herself again that she wasn't going to get involved with CJ. She was a Mandy clone, another road to a broken heart. She wasn't going to be someone's pretty bauble. A kiss was just a kiss, and CJ had made it quite clear she wasn't interested in anything more.

Life was supposed to be simple. So why were her feelings for CJ so complicated? Why did she make up her mind one minute and have to decide all over again the next? Where was a magic mirror on the wall or a fairy godmother when a girl needed one?

The bedroom window framed the rising moon. In late summer it shimmered with pure white and cast enough light to read by. By the time she left for the night, the moon would be in the west, and she would follow its beguiling path all the way home. Karita sighed and closed the drapes. There were no answers for her there either.

Chapter 7

CJ put the kettle on to boil, assuming Karita would soon want the cup of tea she'd mentioned needing over an hour ago. She could use something heavy with caffeine herself. The active night with Abby hadn't left her with a lot of energy. She was seriously starting to flag, and it wasn't even eleven. The undeniable jolts of adrenaline that flooded her whenever she saw Karita were starting to leave her jittery instead of jazzed.

Someone entered through the back door with a jingle of keys and scuff of boots. Startled, CJ turned from the stove.

"Hi. Who are you?" The newcomer, in crisp blue jeans and a rugby shirt, had jock dyke written all over her, but her gaze wasn't confrontational as she studied CJ.

"CJ—community service refugee I believe is the correct term for me." She was willing to bet that the woman's flexing of her impressive biceps was completely unconscious.

"Oh, right. I'm Lucy."

"Oh." Quickly, before the silence became awkward, CJ said, "Karita told me tonight about your mother's passing. I'm sorry."

"Thank you." Lucy shook back her shaggy blond hair as she

headed for the lockers. "It was time and it was how she wanted to go—no long illness in the hospital. And I got there before her final stroke, so…" She busied herself with the locker key.

CJ wouldn't mistake the nonchalant tone for lack of feeling. She'd already heard from Karita how Lucy had cared for her partially paralyzed mother for the last few years. How complicated Lucy's feelings must be.

Her thoughts were interrupted by Karita's reappearance. She embraced Lucy heartily and they chatted until Karita broke off at the sound of the kettle whistling.

"Did you put that on for me?"

"For myself, too." CJ glanced at her watch. "It's past my bed time."

Lucy fetched mugs from the cupboard. "Are you the early to bed, early to rise type?"

"Usually. I was up a bit later than usual last night, though."

Karita gave her a funny look and might have even blushed slightly before she turned abruptly to the tea selection. "CJ's one of those rare women who actually has a girlfriend, unlike the rest of us poor sods."

How had Karita figured out she had been with Abby last night? CJ knew she hadn't mentioned it, which made Karita quite the observant detective. She wasn't exactly proud of the spur of the moment phone call, and she was thinking when she got home she might well have a message from Abby breaking things off. The more she thought about their urgency and high heat the more it seemed like they both had been getting something out of their systems, for good.

Regardless, if Karita had the impression that she and Abby were hot and heavy there wouldn't be any repeats of the kiss. The sleepless nights and nameless yearning would end. She would rededicate herself to the list and crossing off names, without women in her life complicating things. She needed things to be simple for a while.

Stirring her tea and making small talk, she reminded herself that she was close to freedom, close to having no ties to her past. She couldn't mess it up now.

"Are you okay?"

Karita's voice broke into her thoughts and she realized she'd not been listening. "Oh—sorry. I'm fine. Just tired, and thinking about business."

"Commercial real estate," Karita said to Lucy's inquiring look. "She's also a girl with a career that pays well, like you."

CJ said to Lucy, "What do you do with the rest of your life?"

"Don't get weird on me when I tell you, okay?"

"Okay," CJ promised.

"I see dead people."

For just a moment she thought about the girl in the Gathering who had claimed to converse with apparitions, but there was nothing fey about solid, confident Lucy. She hazarded, "Mortician?"

"Oo, you're good, though I prefer funeral director. I come here because I need to be around living people."

Karita, her voice going soft, added, "And after you did an open casket for a woman who'd been beaten to death you thought you'd see if you could avoid having to do that ever again."

"Yeah, well, that too. Damn, there's the dryer. I can handle it. You two take a load off while I take a load out." Lucy headed toward the laundry room.

Karita sipped her tea before volunteering, "She's a good woman."

"Incredibly buff, too."

"She works out religiously and I'm told plays an awesome outfield—whatever that means. She's not had much of a private life the last few years, though."

A silence fell, heavy because of the light and frothy conversation that neither of them seemed able to find whenever they were alone. The ticking of the kettle cooling faded and even the creaking of the settling house ceased. It's so quiet near her, CJ thought, except for the pounding of my heart, damn it.

"Are there more records to sort? I don't mind doing it," CJ said.

Karita set her mug down on the far side of the table. "There are always more records. Let me get you this week's stack."

"I can do computer entry, if you need it."

Karita emerged from Emily's office with a pile of papers. "Sorry, I can't give you the passwords. But if you sort them, that'll give one of the regulars a chance to do some of it for Em. That'll be a big help to her."

"Why did she start this place?"

Karita shrugged. "She got involved in Stand Tall, but I don't know how." At CJ's puzzled glance, she explained, "Stand Tall is an umbrella group that keeps everybody involved in crisis care for battered women talking to each other. There are larger shelters that do longer, transitional stays, and halfway houses, group homes, but there are also a lot of one-night only emergency houses, like this one. And just because a woman is beaten up in Jefferson County versus Denver doesn't mean she should get different response, treatment and resources. Stand Tall solves a lot of jurisdictional issues, and it allows us, for example, to bill the correct governmental agency for the pittance they'll give us for a night's shelter for the clients who fall below poverty level."

"I noticed on the intake forms that you get a lot of low-income women—that's because higher income women have other choices, isn't it?" CJ was grateful for any topic that drove away the memories of that kiss.

"Yep, because domestic violence knows no demographic income brackets. The only difference is the safety net a woman might have available to her. Thankfully, the digital era also allows for the law enforcement agencies to talk to each other like never before. A batterer who beats a girlfriend in Wheat Ridge isn't going to be unknown when he beats up his wife or kids in Aurora."

"The information era has made it harder for lots of bad

guys." CJ hoped her tone was level.

Karita didn't look up from pouring more hot water into her mug. "You know what I wish every woman knew? That for seven bucks she can find out if the guy she's dating has a record in Colorado. Most women say they didn't know he was violent until they were already terrified of what he might do."

"That only works if the S.O.B. gives her his real name." CJ bent over the papers, rapidly pulling out the Jane Does before alphabetizing the rest.

"The majority do. They're good boys, with mothers who swear their darling son wouldn't ever hurt anyone and besides, she's a tramp who asked for it. You only give a false name if you think what you're doing might be wrong. Most repeat batterers think it's okay."

"Not quite true," Emily said from the doorway. She wore her signature sweatsuit—in navy blue today, but CJ noticed the addition of small gold earrings. "Far too many know it's wrong because they beg forgiveness the next day, and bring gifts and promise it'll never happen again. Could you take our new arrival up to her room?"

Karita set down her mug. "Does the baby need formula?"

"I'll make it in a minute," Emily answered, "and send it on up."

She slumped heavily into a chair at the table after Karita left. "I forgot to tell you not to come back after I heard Lucy would be with us again."

Glad the subject was off false names, CJ tried for some charm. "Very true, so here I am. I'd be grateful if you'd sign some paperwork for me. It's in my locker."

"Okay, fair enough. How are you feeling tonight?"

CJ lifted one eyebrow as an answer.

"Oh yeah, I forgot. No psych one-oh-one for you."

Women like Emily had come in and out of CJ's life as a child. She wasn't going to start trusting one of them now, but the urge to hide behind a superior you-can't-break-me smirk wasn't going to be her reaction either. "I admire what you do here. How many women do you get to break the cycle?"

"Enough to keep me here, hoping. A lot of women," she added, heaving herself to her feet, "do manage to get their batterer into counseling, with our help. That's a big deal, because the cycle of violence really breaks when the batterers stop before passing it onto their kids."

CJ kept sorting, wondering what kinds of cycles were still circulating through the Gathering. She hadn't thought about the children still in the life, with more born every year. She could hear the echo of some cop from long ago, calling CJ and her cousins nothing more than vermin, an infestation.

When Emily finished making the baby's bottle, CJ offered to take it up. "I'm not sure what to do with the Jane Does, so if you could take a look, that would help."

"Oh, they get a number added. I'll let you know where to start when you get back."

The house was falling quiet, and the change, from a few hours earlier, was palpable. There was no one crying, not even a baby.

She tapped quietly on the door of the last room on the upper floor and was let in by the mother. The light was very low, soft and golden.

Karita was in an old rocking chair, cooing softly to the infant. Her almost white hair surrounded both of them and it reflected the golden light, like a halo. The image seared in CJ's mind and she couldn't shake it—Madonna and child, right there, where she could touch them.

"Just in time," Karita said.

Trying to be quiet, CJ crossed the room to hand over the bottle. The baby looked to be on the verge of fussing.

Karita took the bottle, but never lost eye contact with the child. "You're warm and dry, and here's some food. Just that powdered stuff, not so good, but Mom will have the good stuff for you later, when you wake up again." Her tone was pleasantly sing-song and in just moments, the child was gulping lustily, tiny eyelids drooping.

CJ was about to leave when she realized the mother was struggling with the nightshirt CJ recognized from laundry she'd done earlier.

"Let me help you—do you want me to unhook your bra?"

After a short silence when the woman's pride clearly warred with her common sense, she said, "Yes. Thank you. I can't twist that far right now."

CJ quickly did the necessary steps, and helped maneuver the pajama top into place. "There you go. I think there are nursing lap pads and plain cloth diapers for clean up in the top drawer. We really appreciate it if you put anything that gets soiled outside the door. Someone will gather it all in the morning."

She let herself out of the room again, after one last, greedy look at the platinum head, so fair and light, bent over the wrapped bundle of baby. Again she thought of Madonna and child, but this time she couldn't push away Aunt Bitty's voice of reality. That light was for innocents, not the likes of her. She would never earn that kind of grace.

To hell with you, Aunt Bitty. I make my own choices, and I'll check myself into hell itself before I do anything to darken Karita's life. Not because you beat into me that I was worthless, but because it's the right thing to do, for both of us.

Maybe she didn't believe that happiness was in the cards for her, but that didn't mean she should court being unhappy. She tried at least to control that much of her life.

An hour later she'd completely sorted the intake forms and folded the rest of the laundry. Lucy had settled at Emily's desk to do data entry while Karita and Emily talked in low tones in the utility room. Their conversation occasionally included words like *insulation* and *plumber*, with the occasional reference to a picnic earlier in the summer that made them both laugh.

Far as CJ could see, from her tired place at the table, there was nothing more she could do that night. She put her head down on her arms. If she stayed that way for long, she'd fall asleep.

Her prediction was nearly true—a hand on her shoulder jolted her out of a doze.

"You should go home," Karita said. "I'll be leaving myself in a few."

Dully, CJ said, "Will you get to your car okay? I'm right outside again. Sorry, that makes me selfish, doesn't it?"

"I'm glad you don't have to walk. I'll be fine—Emily will take me to my car. She's about to call it a night too. Pauline is doing the morning shift and will be here in just a few."

Gulps of cold water shocked her awake, especially after she dabbed some on her temples and eyes. She'd make it home, but thank goodness it wasn't far. Karita looked like she could stay awake another twelve hours. CJ wasn't sure she'd ever been that young, but Karita was only, what? Six or seven years younger? She would always seem youthful, while she herself by comparison, would always feel old.

She was in her car before she remembered the paperwork she had meant to get Emily to sign. It really needed to be mailed back to the court—it was late as it was. She checked the surrounding area again and nothing was moving, so she made her way to the back porch, hoping a quiet knock would be heard.

A furtive whisper stopped her in her tracks, then the words took on meaning.

"We really shouldn't."

"Can we not debate that again? Let's talk about it tomorrow morning."

Another noise, close, then Karita said, "This time can we get to a warm bed first?"

Emily laughed. "Yes, baby. The bed will be warm—after a few minutes."

The sound Karita made burned into CJ's ears. She tiptoed away, thinking she'd get her papers signed tomorrow, even if it was an extra trip. Her mind worked overtime picturing Emily slowly undressing Karita, realizing that Emily knew just what would melt Karita completely. That Emily, with her big heart and honesty, was someone Karita could trust that way.

So much for the Madonna image. Karita was a red-blooded woman and real, every bit of her. Aunt Bitty pointed out Karita was dating that young woman CJ had seen in the deli, was getting sex with Emily and had been kissing CJ—all at the same time. She wasn't a Madonna, she was a tramp.

"No," CJ said to her reflection in the rear viewmirror. "She's not a virgin, she's a giving, loving woman." You could have had some part of that, she told herself. There was something so true and open about Karita that her love didn't get cheaper the more she gave it away. On the contrary, it made it more of a treasure.

She is not for you. CJ repeated it like a mantra on the short drive home. The moon was gloriously full and bright and normally would have lifted her spirits, but the silver light was cold and no closer than she would ever get to the same light that seemed to glow from Karita. CJ didn't doubt for a moment that she could steal a lot from Karita, including her ability to trust, her innocence, maybe even her heart. CJ's lineage was full of accomplished con artists and she'd been weaned on the skills. Hadn't her father always said he'd never seen a natural like CJ, that conning women was the one thing CJ was good for?

She gripped the wheel until her knuckles were white. She was good for other things. She would not give in to her ancestry or upbringing. She didn't con people anymore. She was out of the life. She would work one more night at the shelter and that would be it.

She is not for you. CJ pulled into her parking space and repeated it slowly. "She is not for you."

Neither, apparently, was Abby, and CJ certainly didn't blame her. The message began, "I'm a coward doing this by voice mail, but then again it's always been me leaving you messages, hasn't it? The other night was great, but I don't think we should do that again. This other resident finally asked me out and I don't think I should date her and still be sleeping with you so—I have to give it a try, you know? You and I aren't…we're not going anywhere even though it's a lot of fun. I want to go somewhere with somebody. Anyway. I have to leave for work. You don't have to call me back if you don't want to, but I hope we can still be frie—"

CJ pressed delete.

She got out the list, studied the names, and tried to add the amounts in her head again. The concentration wasn't there—her mind was a whirl. Abby's needy passion vied with that sound Karita had made when Emily touched her just the right way.

Nothing's changed, she told herself. Her latest lover had decided to move on. She would find another if she wanted. So the tall, platinum blonde was under her skin, big deal. She'd survive the crush, and she'd not miss the woman when it passed.

A relaxing shower fooled her into thinking she'd fall asleep soon, but the hope was short-lived. The alarm display gave off a low hum and in the distance a car started. The refrigerator clicked on and off. The background when she'd been a child, trying to sleep, had always held the clamor of an argument, the sound of something or someone breaking. In detention, the creak of shoes on cement as guards paced had kept her awake, punctuated by the slam of doors and the distinct click of automatic locks.

The world had never been a quiet place until Karita kissed her.

It didn't mean anything.

She had never been much good at lying to herself and sleep eluded her.

It hadn't been a bad night. It had actually been uneventful in spite of filling every room at the shelter. Karita spooned behind Emily, softly kissing her neck. She felt filled to the brim with tenderness for this woman, which wasn't unusual, but still— something was different.

"Baby," Emily murmured. "You have the most amazing hands."

"Oh yeah?" Karita smiled into Emily's shoulder blades and twisted the hand nestled between Emily's thighs. Emily pushed back slightly. "That hand in particular?"

"Yes, that hand." Emily stretched, almost purring. "Could you do that maybe for a couple of hours?"

Her fingers tickled lightly at the damp tendrils between Emily's legs. "Okay, but honestly, if I keep this up you're going to fall asleep."

Emily rolled onto her stomach. Her muffled voice rose out of the pillow. "It could happen, but I promise I'd wake up ready to get serious about doing delicious things to you."

Karita swiftly covered Emily's body with her own, pleased that the sudden full body contact drew a moan from Emily. "I have a different idea."

"Yeah?"

"I think you need something right now." Karita pushed her hand firmly between Emily's thighs again, this time taking a direct route to sweet, wet heat. It was fun, and hot, and sexy, like it was every time they were together, but Karita continued to be aware that something was different.

Emily's responsiveness was the same, the eager and lusty way she pushed Karita onto her back so she could wrap Karita's legs around her shoulders—that wasn't changed. It must be me, Karita thought. That kiss…and she made herself not think about that anymore, because she was with Emily. Emily's touch aroused her just as much, and her mouth, oh her wonderful mouth, it was just as thorough. Karita gave herself to the pleasure of it. It was supposed to feel good and it did.

They cuddled again, and Karita let out a long, pleased laugh. "That was marvelous. Oh—I remember now what I wanted to ask you about. About that cop earlier? She was *muy bella*."

"She's very cute, no doubt about it."

"Are you going to ask her out?"

Emily wouldn't meet Karita's gaze. "Right—on one of my many free nights."

"Next time she's in before ten p.m. just ask her to join you for coffee if she's got the break time. I can do an intake, you know that. Just say you never got dinner, which is nearly always true, and does she have time for a cup of coffee while you have a bite to eat—at Eddie's, just around the corner and down the block. I bet she says yes."

"The fact that she's knocked on the shelter door a bunch of times in the last month is the only thing we have in common."

"That you know about. That's why people date."

Emily snuggled her closer. "She's totally hard-bodied. I doubt she'd be interested in me."

Karita lightly squeezed one generously formed breast. "You have a few good features." Even as she trailed a fingertip over Emily's nipple, Karita knew she'd likely not do so again after tonight. When she'd kissed Emily on the porch she hadn't known that the memory of kissing CJ would intrude, but now she did. "Em…you're attracted and she seems interested as well. But here we are in bed again."

Some of the drowsiness in Emily's eyes fled. "You didn't want—"

"I did. I kissed you because I did…want. But I think my reasons may be the same as yours tonight. And they're not the reasons we've always had in the past. Nurturing and random sublimation are okay by me, but…"

"Okay," Emily said slowly. "I'm here with you right now because I'm thinking about Anita—"

"Pretty name."

"Thinking about Anita," Emily continued, "and I'm too lazy or scared to ask Anita on a date so eventually I can ask her into bed instead of you. So who are you too lazy or scared to ask out, and curled up here with me instead?"

"Someone I shouldn't be thinking about. But it's not right to use you so I can not think about her."

"CJ. I've seen the way she looks at you."

"She looks at me?" Karita inwardly cringed at how juvenile

106

she sounded.

Emily propped herself up on one elbow. "Not the usual way, not with her tongue hanging out. But she is always looking for you, or at you, when she thinks no one is focused on her." Emily kissed her softly. "I can't blame her. Just looking at you makes me feel better, no matter what."

"I'm not right for her."

Emily frowned. "I'm far more concerned about her not being right for you. She's a ticking time bomb of issues, and you'd spend all your time dealing with her shit, and all the while she'd be refusing professional help and there you'd be. You know what it's called."

"Co-dependent." Karita stifled a yawn. "Yes, I know. And at the same time, I'm barely afloat financially and she's a highly successful real estate broker with testimonials about her ability to make deals that everyone loves."

"Google her much?"

Karita blushed to the roots of her hair. "Okay, maybe. Obviously, success and cash mean a lot to her—just like Mandy. We know how that went."

"Mandy was stunted. From what you told me she was all or nothing. If you didn't give her all, she gave you nothing. CJ is a different deal. She's shrink-wrapped her pain and thinks that makes her life tidy." Emily kissed her with more heat. "And if I have to make love to you every day to save you from some karmically bankrupt yuppie's clutches, it's a sacrifice I'm willing to make."

Karita giggled into Emily's kisses. "No, you're going to be courting the lovely Anita. Or letting her court you."

Emily closed her eyes and pulled Karita close. "So, we're not going to do this again, are we?"

"No," Karita said. They'd said it before, but this time it felt final. The wave of tenderness she felt for Emily rose in her again, with a sense of loss. She trusted, however, that they'd both grown and changed, and they would always mean something special to each other. They might not have this type of intimacy again, but the loving friendship was for always. She'd never regret having spent these nights together.

Elske er elske, Gran would have said. Love is love. In spite of Mandy, she still believed that feeling and giving love made more love. It was enough magic to believe in, at least for tonight. Such a thought would have usually let her drop off to sleep, but it took a few more minutes because of the tiny voice asking, "But what about tomorrow?"

Chapter 8

"You told them I was your date?" CJ set down her briefcase and pressed the boot button on her computer.

"No!" Burnett spluttered into his soda. "No, I told Cray we were work colleagues and you'd like the show too, even if you were a woman."

"But why are you taking your new would-be client to a gay revue?" To CJ, the venue was far, far too personal.

"I'm not taking him. He just mentioned he wouldn't be able to meet for a quick proposal review because he had tickets to the Babylon. I said I hadn't seen the new show but had heard good things. I was about to wish him a pleasant night when he said he had two extra tickets friends couldn't use."

"Does he know you're gay?" CJ wasn't sure she even knew, but she decided if he was he might as well just tell her.

"I'm guessing yes, or he wouldn't have brought up the Babylon. I'd say he doesn't really ping the gaydar, but if you saw him in a gay club he wouldn't look out of place either."

Just like you, CJ could have said. This conversation was not how she had planned to start her day. "So you told him you were asking a woman to go with you?"

"Well, I emphasized the work colleague thing," Burnett said. "Of course, I thanked him for the offer, too."

"Okay, since I'm a work colleague, it's quite possible he'll think you're bringing business to a social engagement, which it sounds like wasn't his intention." CJ knew she'd probably enjoy the show. The write-ups had raved about the campy humor and music. But the show was Thursday night and she'd not get home until midnight. She had a tenant build-out construction budget review at seven Friday morning and her last stint at the shelter that evening. There was no way she could handle that. She felt far older than thirty-five to say it, but she was too old for that kind of schedule.

Burnett's smile was completely without guile. "But if you dyke it up he'll know you're family. Unless you want him to presume you're a fag hag."

For a very short moment, CJ wasn't sure what to say. Then the light in his oh-so-puppy-dog eyes flickered ever so slightly. Did he honestly think he could play her? She gave him a prim look. "Dyke it up?"

"C'mon, break out that leather jacket and the Gold Wing gloves."

"Don't get cheeky."

Burnett, to CJ's shock, laughed. "You should see your face."

"Hey, listen." She gave him a level look. "For this deal you need to think of me as your boss, and you don't talk to bosses that way, got it?" Damn it, the corner of her mouth started to quiver. "Never, *ever* mention a Honda to a Harley gal."

Burnett hooted with glee and CJ couldn't help but laugh, too. Evidently, Burnett had missed the part where she made it plain she could squash him like a little bug if she wanted. He had succeeded in playing on her sympathies—not at all the puppy dog she'd taken him for.

"So," she said with a sigh. "When and where will I meet up with you for this cheerful outing?"

True to her word, Pam had called for lunch again, and seemed in such good spirits that Karita immediately agreed. This time she arrived at the deli first and opted for falafel drizzled with a pungent tahini dressing. Halfway to one of the few empty tables she realized that CJ was leaning against the wall, obviously waiting for her order.

An odd sensation suffused her chest—was that her heart leaping? Was she blushing now? After being somewhat successful at not dwelling overmuch on the kiss, the memory of it was suddenly vivid, especially that feeling that with CJ there would be a fire like she had yet to experience. No, no, no, she told herself. She stabbed herself mentally with memories of Mandy to try to control the smile she knew gave away far too much.

CJ watched her approach with a welcoming look that lacked the carefully masked tension of her demeanor at the shelter. "Hi, stranger."

"Hey there." As if she didn't already know the answer from Google, Karita asked, "You work close by?"

"A couple of blocks. I'm hooked on the egg salad so once a week, here I am. How about you?"

"The law office is about five blocks that way." She gestured with her bag. "I'm meeting someone."

"Another lunch date?" To Karita's puzzled look, she continued, "I saw you last week. She's very cute."

"Oh, you mean Pam. It's not a..." Maybe it was better that CJ think Pam was responsible for the blush she was dead certain now stained her cheeks. A completely cowardly choice, she acknowledged, and not one an elf would pick. But she wasn't an elf, right now she felt like one hundred percent woman, and the most female parts of her body were trying to get the upper hand with her common sense. She knew she sounded unconvincing when she said, "It's not really a date."

"If you say so."

"She's just a friend." Dang it, it was too hard not to be honest.

111

CJ opened her mouth to say something, then closed it.

"What?" Karita gave her a teasing look. "You got a problem with me?"

"No problem, ma'am. I was… Is Emily just a friend?"

Karita knew she went from flushed to beet red. "How did—"

"I'm teasing," CJ said quickly.

"No you're not. And I just confirmed it. You should be an interrogator."

"I'm sorry, really. I did mean just to tease. I went back last Friday to get Emily to sign something and overheard you on the back porch. Before that…" She shrugged. "You seemed like close friends, that's all."

"We are." Karita had no idea exactly what she had wanted from this conversation, but revelations about her sex life were definitely not it. "We are. And I love Emily a lot. It's just not… We just…sometimes…"

"I'm not judging you, really. I'm hardly a prude." CJ looked at her feet for a moment, then said, "Personally, I think relationships suffer from high expectations. If the people in the relationship get what they want out of it, everyone else should just wish they were so lucky. I've known a lot of really moral people who were miserable in their marriages and spent their lives pointing out how everyone else was sinning. I think it's envy, plain and simple. People who don't know how to be happy can't stand that other people have figured it out."

"That's the root of judgment in the world isn't it? Taking your own emotional issues and blaming other people for them? It's what a batterer does, albeit to an extreme degree." Karita hoped she was no longer red as a raspberry. What must CJ think of her? "Batterers are the ultimate bullies, hurting someone else to make themselves feel better. Oh!"

"What?"

Karita blinked in surprise at CJ. "I just had a thought I hadn't had before. The friend I'm meeting—it's a work thing. Something I should tell her, that's all," she finished hurriedly after they heard CJ's name called at the counter. "See you tomorrow night, right?"

"I'll be there. Gotta do my time." CJ pointed. "Your date's here."

"She's not—" CJ was already out of earshot.

Dizzied by the loop-de-loop of emotions during the last few minutes, Karita gave Pam a cheery wave and nabbed the last vacant table for them. Acutely aware of the moment CJ disappeared into the warm afternoon, Karita took a deep breath, willing the fluttery feeling in her chest to subside. It was all animal attraction, and nothing more. She unwrapped her falafel and couldn't help but take a big bite. Food would settle her stomach and that would be the end of her ridiculous thoughts; a swirl of potent pheromones wasn't going to make her consider that maybe she didn't have the first clue about love.

Pam joined her after ordering. "You look like you're starving."

"It's tahini sauce, it's like an appetite aphrodisiac for me. One whiff and I gotta have it. You are looking much better this week." It was true. Pam's hair was pulled back in a colorful clip, and her eyes had some of their usual sparkle.

"Thanks. I feel better, that's for sure. Talking to you last week really helped."

"I had an additional thought for you—just popped into my head when I got here."

"Yeah? Go for it."

"How good a lawyer is Susan House?"

"Good enough." Pam shrugged. "Marty is the brains of the outfit, though."

"I wouldn't know how to judge, but the thought I had was she spends so much time telling all the associates how worthless they are, that maybe she does it because she needs to feel better about her own skills. It's not a terribly brilliant thought," Karita added hurriedly. "It's just that when people are insecure about themselves they mistakenly think they raise themselves by standing on other people. Maybe you threatened her more than just a secret gay love affair. Maybe you threatened her as a lawyer."

"Oh, well—I hadn't thought of that." Pam's name was called and she left the table with a frown of concentration that was quite cute.

Karita ate more slowly, not wanting to finish before Pam even joined her. As soon as Pam was seated again, she apologized. "I should have waited for you."

"I understand. Unlike me, you only have an hour."

"More like forty-five minutes."

"Then you can watch me eat and I'll walk you back to the office." Pam dug into her bowl of chili. "Anyway, thanks for the idea about Susan. Even if it's not true, it's comforting to think it might be."

"Glad to be of help. How are your plans coming along? Still moving?"

"Maybe not. I have two interviews tomorrow for associate jobs."

"That's great!"

"Well, I have to thank the wicked witch—she did send me a good letter of recommendation which means I can list her as a reference. I'm sure she'll be gritting her teeth to do it if someone calls her. So for now, my folks said they'll cover my rent for a bit on the hope I land something right away. They've been spectacular about it all."

Karita grinned. "Maybe, just maybe, they love you?"

"Maybe they do. My mom sent me an article on artificial insemination, which I take to mean she still expects grandbabies."

"Do you want to be a parent?" Karita hadn't yet given it a lot of consideration. She loved children, though. In a few more years, maybe when she was thirty, she could give it some real thought.

"Given my student loans I can't say it's high in my priorities. But eventually, I think I'd like a family." Pam stared at her sandwich, then shot her a fleeting glance.

There was a little silence, during which Karita was abruptly reminded of her coffee date with Brent. She had the feeling that she'd missed the moment when she ought to have used the "good to be friends" speech on Pam. "I was an only child, and raised by my grandmother. She kept a roof over our heads by providing day care for neighbors, so there were always kids underfoot. Maybe that's why I'm waiting a while. At the end of the day I have only myself to feed and clothe and I'm pretty easy to please."

"Your grandmother sounds like an amazing woman." Pam stirred her still steaming chili.

"Oh, she was. We lived in the house she'd bought with my grandfather when they first married, and while they lived there the neighborhood changed—lots of Vietnamese immigrants. By the time I went to kindergarten I was the only white-skinned blonde in the school. Even though nobody singled me out or bullied me, I apparently came home weeping day after day because I was so different. Why didn't I have a mom and a dad? Why was my hair so thin? Why were my eyes so boring? She came up with a solution."

"Which was?" Pam's eyes had definitely regained their sparkle.

Karita felt an "uh-oh" in the pit of her stomach. "She told me I really was different. It was to be our secret, because nobody else would understand. I was an elf, you see, and if I practiced, I would be able to do magic."

"Oh, how cute!"

Karita chewed the last bite of her falafel, dabbed her mouth and managed a chargined smile. "She predicted I already had a little magic, and if I repeated a charm she taught me, we'd see for sure. It was a charm to be happy and if it worked I probably wouldn't cry the next day at school. And it worked. Worked—like a charm."

"That's a wonderful story."

"It is." Karita agreed, wholeheartedly. The only problem

had been that unlike Santa Claus and the Easter Bunny, she'd never stopped believing in Karita the Elf. It had been private joke between her and Gran, learning new charms—Norwegian sounded so elvish—and thinking through situations based on how an elf would respond. She had read everything she could get her hands on about elves, trying to identify her origins. She had nurtured the belief in spite of all evidence to the contrary, because it did make her feel special. It was woven into who she was, the possibilities at least. "I often ask myself, when things are tough, what an elf would do."

"Well, maybe you're not an elf, but you worked some kind of magic on me last week. I was so depressed and then I felt so much better."

"Talking about something helps."

"Yeah, especially with a friend."

Karita was about to seize the opening, when Pam went on, "I hope you don't think this is sudden or anything, but would like to go out? Dinner or a movie or something?"

Too late…and maybe that was a good thing. It annoyed her that CJ popped into her mind. She could also hear the echo of her own words to Emily, that dating was how people discovered if they had things in common. "I, uh…"

"Oh. I'm sorry. I thought—oh, are you seeing someone? I didn't know."

"No, I'm not seeing anyone." She was free as a bird, and besides, Pam was interesting, and attractive and energetic and very nice to talk to. Why shouldn't they date a bit and see where it led? Why should she say no because of some kiss? "I was just surprised, I mean, I'm not a lawyer. I don't even have an undergraduate degree."

"What does that matter? Lawyers can be shits. What did you do instead of college?"

"I did finish a basic two-year degree, but I hated being in a classroom. So I joined the Peace Corps, and then I took care of my grandmother in her final illness. I inherited a little house from her up in Kittredge and moved here not quite two years ago. That's pretty much the whole life story." She scanned Pam's face carefully, hoping her bare bones recital didn't make Pam think *flake*.

"The Peace Corps—that sounds fascinating." Pam finished a large bite from her sandwich, then said, "Did you go to Africa or South America?"

"Because of the neighborhood where I grew up I speak basic conversational Vietnamese. Yeah, I know, what a gift I got out of initially feeling so out of place. So they sent me to teach English to kids in Vietnam. It was *really* interesting, and so worthwhile. I loved nearly every minute."

Pam's smile deepened. "Sounds like you got a lifetime of experience. College isn't for everybody. Besides, there's always next year if you want to do formal studies. Tell you what. Let's have dinner Saturday night and talk about you and your life and what you want. Because we already know I want to go on being a lawyer."

Karita found herself smiling. Lots of conflicting feelings were churning in her stomach, but Pam was undeniably engaging. "Okay, dinner. It's a date."

Cray Westmore and his partner, Alvin Canard, seemed charming enough. Both wore crisp and stylish trousers with open-collared shirts and blazers. But where Cray was in sedate gray and white, Alvin sported black and lilac. Even from thirty paces away, CJ could tell they were a couple.

CJ wasn't exactly used to "dyking it up." She had brushed out her tight, trim hair style but hated that result, so gelled it back into place with a little more angle to it than usual, but the mop of curls in the back was the same as every day. She would have to hope that the black jeans, red cowboy boots and cobalt blue polo shirt said, "Not dressing for the guys."

They made small talk as they went into the faux red-velvet crusted theater lobby. A small sign proclaimed, "If you're thinking you're in a whorehouse, good." CJ maneuvered herself into a corner where she could watch the doors. She didn't like crowds much, but the faces turned toward her were all unfamiliar.

CJ tipped her head meaningfully at the wine bar and Burnett quickly asked what everyone would like to drink and sped off to secure their requests.

"I don't want to talk about business tonight," CJ said into the little silence that fell. She gave Cray what she hoped was a sincere look. "But can I ask how long you've been designing restaurants? That's an interesting specialty."

"Actually, that's my fault," Alvin said. "I'm an interior designer—yes, I know." He shrugged expansively. "Faggot in fabrics, what a surprise. But I love restaurant design. I can't boil water, but I like making a space that evokes food."

Cray picked up the story seamlessly. "Once I saw Alvin working on a space and realized how much he loved it, I thought I'd had enough of designing apartments. I still do that—gotta pay the bills—but if I do the architectural design on a restaurant I have a good chance of watching Alvin at work. We make a fabulous team."

"Cray knows what I mean by the most random words, and he understands that to me, little differences matter."

"He says things like, 'if you give the ceiling a little more oompa I can lose the burgundy and go winesap.'"

"They say women see umpteen more shades of color than men, but Cray never makes me feel like my caring about the difference between beige and ecru is silly."

CJ watched the two of them interact and knew they had to have been together at least a decade. How different their exchanges were from the stops and starts she had with Karita, or even had had with Abby when the subject wasn't sex. As the lobby of the theater continued to fill, she shifted closer to the couple. When there was a little lull, she offered, "I like taking clients to Elway's because from the door to the table to the menu, it is exactly what it appears to be."

118

"Oh," Alvin shrugged. "They could do so much better. But the design is consistent. All you have to do is drive by to crave a good, manly piece of meat."

"Don't go there, dear, you'll make CJ blush. So are you Burnett's boss?" Cray gave her an easy smile. "Do I need to talk him up, tell you how great he's been to work with so far?"

"I'm not his boss," CJ admitted. "More of a mentor."

"I've heard your name around."

"All good, I hope."

"Mostly." Cray still seemed at ease, but he was obviously choosing his words with care. "Maybe a few people think they got talked into more than they needed, but nobody seems to feel they got...what's the word I'm looking for?"

"Screwed?" CJ had no trouble figuring out where he was going. They weren't talking business, of course they weren't. "It's bad business to screw people. Real estate is all about word of mouth and repeat clients. So, as with anybody who works on a percentage—" She paused to nod at Alvin who tipped his head to acknowledge that he also earned his living based in part on sales. "I might point out the more expensive items on the menu, but nothing outside the client's capabilities to sustain."

"Burnett has been very easy to work with. So far whenever he gets in touch he has a reason, and if it's one thing I appreciate in the age of text, voice mail and e-mail, it's communication with a clear purpose."

CJ filed that away and smiled brightly at Burnett, who was managing to effortlessly carry four glasses of wine through the increasingly crowded lobby. Somewhere in his past he'd been a waiter. She didn't remember that on his résumé. "You know what I've been wondering? What kind of parent names their son Burnett?"

Burnett handed around the glasses. "Zinfandel, merlot, shiraz and cabernet. Better known as 'that red wine from the box.' I was told it was cheap and easy, just like the show."

Cray and Alvin both laughed. They all clinked glasses and

amiably agreed that the wine wasn't that bad.

With a nod at Burnett, Cray asked, "So what's the answer to CJ's question?"

"Ah, my parents. There's not enough wine in the box for that story. The last time I talked to them I told them that naming me Burnett had in fact made me gay. It was as sound a theory as theirs was about Satan."

"How long ago did you have that conversation?" CJ sipped sparingly from her glass. She didn't feel much like wine tonight and no way was she going to court another traffic situation with an officer of the law. There were now too many people in the lobby for her to keep track of, making her tense. Any old "friend" could be within feet of her before she saw them.

"Going on four years. My grandmother was very cool about it, though. How did your parents feel about your being gay, CJ?"

She shrugged. "My mother died when I was five." Before anybody could express sympathies, she went on with a smile, "and I didn't know I was gay at the time. My father has never given me any grief about being gay." It was absolutely true. Cassiopeia Juniper Rochambeau hadn't known she was gay. She'd even been in a girls' detention center for four years and hadn't had a clue. At a community college in upstate New York, CJ Roshe had finally figured out she really, *really* liked girls.

To her chagrin she missed something Alvin said, but laughed along with Cray and Burnett. The house lights flickered and they abandoned their glasses in favor of claiming their seats. Being gentlemen, they let her into the aisle first, which was fine as it put Burnett next to Cray and left CJ without the need to make small talk.

The next forty-five minutes were fun, as the revue presented everything from Queen to ABBA with sparkling costumes and broad comedy full of sexual entendres and quick jibes on current headlines. No doubt about it—gay men were gifted with acerbic wit and many of them looked better in high heels than CJ did.

There wasn't a gay icon left out, but everything was presented with such camp that it was freshly fun and infectious. The two drag queens playing the women of ABBA, in tall latex boots and long platinum blond wigs, had nothing on Karita, however, at least in CJ's admittedly biased and decidedly foolish opinion. "Waterloo" was a bit too on the mark.

She excused herself to the ladies room at intermission and had little success at banishing the persistent memory of Karita leaning casually, elegantly, against the deli wall. Of the silken hair running over her fingers. Of a living, breathing Madonna, sacred and yet touchable. Of Karita's warm hands cupping her face and the world fading away to nothing.

After the intermission they resettled. A sweet love song from the headliner brought them back into the mood of the performance, but left CJ feeling restless. Sentiments like forever and soul mates—that was for people like Cray and Alvin. They were nice, oh that word again, nice. They had nothing dark to pretend didn't exist.

Burnett leaned over to ask, "Are you doing okay?"

"Sure. Am I not looking like I'm enjoying it?"

"You suddenly looked tired, right then, that's all."

"Probably because I am. I'm fine." Puppy dog eyes, right, CJ thought. The kid could break hearts with those eyes. She wondered why he didn't have a boyfriend. He was nice, too.

The show's big finale had all the performers onstage in new costumes with a full-scale tribute to Sylvester. CJ joined in the overhead claps and "oo-oo" exhorted by the dancers and the evening ended on a high note. She was tired, but she was also glad she'd come. Instead of thinking about Karita nonstop, she had only thought about her from time-to-time.

Burnett, well-coached, offered to treat everyone to dessert and coffee at the Rocky Mountain Diner, just a few blocks north. It was a weeknight, and CJ had predicted the client would decline, but Cray and Alvin immediately accepted. She plastered a bright smile on her face, hoping she no longer looked tired, and they strolled out to the street.

"I love September," CJ said. "The nights get cool." The temperature was probably around seventy, no colder, but a far cry from the heat only two weeks ago. The afternoon thunderstorms had already abated and the spare-the-air warnings had stopped for the season. Alvin protested that it was too close to the freak blizzards of October and Cray pointed out that there was nothing freakish about weather that happened every year.

"It's freakish if you're from Virginia, which I am," Alvin said.

"But then you'd have to say the total lack of humidity here is freakish, and it's my favorite feature of Denver." CJ nodded thanks to Burnett for getting the diner door. They were quickly seated, and they all turned down the late night repast of the buffalo meatloaf that was offered by the perky waitress. Instead, coffee, three desserts and four forks were requested, and the conversation turned to the show and other similar entertainments.

When the desserts were delivered Alvin turned to her with an assessing look. "Do you have a girlfriend, CJ? We have this friend, a corporate lawyer, and she's a wonderful woman."

"Thanks, but no thanks." CJ could tell that Alvin's heart was in the right place, but she was not getting talked into a blind date which she would then have to answer questions about. "Set Burnett up with someone. A lawyer, or a doctor, but not one of those types like on TV. A podiatrist, with regular working hours and a fondness for hiking and fishing."

"So Burnett is into outdoorsy guys who like feet?" Cray looked speculatively at Alvin. They both said simultaneously, "Eric," and burst out laughing.

Burnett gave a philosophical shrug. "Sounds ideal, but since I moved here I haven't invested any time into my love life. I am my grandmother's most constant support and that scares off some guys." The two men nodded, leaving CJ to presume one or both of them had aging relatives in their lives as well. The talk turned briefly to politics, then to food and wine.

A diverting hour later, Cray turned to Burnett and said,

"Drop by around eleven tomorrow and my assistant will fit you in, okay? Bring a package and we'll do a quick look at the site."

Burnett merely smiled his response, but CJ could almost hear his mental happy dance.

There was a delay about getting the check, and Burnett urged the two men to take their leave. "It's my treat—it can hardly make us even for the tickets. You've got a drive all the way up to Conifer, right? So you should go, and I'll make sure CJ gets to her car safely."

There were assurances all around that it had been a lovely evening. Once Cray and Alvin were out of sight, CJ slumped into her seat. "Really nice guys, but I'm beat."

"How'd I do?"

"You were terrific." She patted his arm. "Congratulations! You've got a live proposal tomorrow."

"If I think about it much I'll get nervous. I'm going to go ask about the check." Burnett slid out of the booth and headed for the reception desk.

Relaxed from the good company, CJ closed her eyes. She was tired, but the evening had been undeniably fun. The memory of Karita's touch returned. The world grew still again, marvelously quiet, made up of only the warmth and purity of Karita. It wasn't safe to think about her like this, she told herself, but it felt so good.

The quiet was shattered by a woman asking, "Cassie? Is that you?"

She sat upright, realized she'd not studied the layout for the nearest exit—she'd gotten lazy. She hoped it was offense and not fear that showed in her eyes as she said, "Huh?"

The other woman, at first glance, might have been a blood sister, but all the Rochambeaus were dumped out of one mold. The same glossy black hair, deceptively generous mouth and dark eyes, fringed with heavy lashes, stared back from CJ's mirror every morning.

"You're Cassie June, right? Don't you remember? My daddy

and your daddy worked that utility stock deal."

Oceans roared in CJ's ears. She could hardly sort out the words through the panic that drove her heart rate into the stratosphere. *Don't look for cops.* Uncle Vaughn's half-brother's eldest—cousin Daria. They were the same age. She hadn't seen Daria since before that last con, the sting that had landed her in Fayette. *Keep eye contact.*

All she could think to say, aware that her palms were sweating, was, "I have no idea what you're talking about." *Plan your escape.*

Daria gave her a knowing look. "Neither of us has changed that much in twenty years."

Not nearly enough, CJ wanted to say. She at least had her father's nose and cheekbones, and her avoidance of the sun had left her skin tone several shades lighter. Most people, she hoped, wouldn't see her with Daria and jump to the conclusion that they were related. *Plausible lies, keep it simple.*

"Look, you've got me mixed up with someone else." How would an innocent person act in this situation? Get rude, make a scene—that would just get her remembered and give Daria reason to follow her or try to find her again.

It was a conscious effort to maintain eye contact and think, over and over that she wasn't Cassie June anymore, and therefore this woman really was asking about someone who didn't exist. "Unless you went to WSU? Though I'd remember if you'd been Gamma Pi."

Daria's certainty wavered, but she didn't give up. "Washington or Wisconsin State?"

"Washington." A trickle of sweat seeped from her armpit down her rib cage. Her scalp was damp and hot. Every protective instinct in her body was screaming at her to stand up, say "Excuse me" and walk out of the diner and out of Denver forever. Someone from the Gathering had found her. She'd been braced for this moment for years. Now it was here.

Deny, deny, deny, she thought, then run. That's the only way. If I bolt now she'll know she made me. If she can't get money out of me directly, she'll see if there's a reward, or she'll just turn me in for spite.

Daria leaned conspiratorially over the table. "Look, I won't blow it for you. He looks like he's got something going for him. But if you need a player...I'll be here tomorrow night around ten."

"I really have *no* idea what you're talking about." CJ gave Daria's outfit a scornful look, hoping the cruelest insult one woman could give another would finish the conversation. She didn't want Daria to hear her name or talk to Burnett. "And since I don't know you, I don't see the point here."

She grabbed her purse with annoyance while praying that sweat didn't drip down her face before she was out of sight. What had happened to the nerves of the coolest con her father had ever worked with, according to him?

Burnett was on his way back to the table.

"Ready, sweetie?" She rose to head him off, and linked her arm with his.

His puzzled look didn't help, but she couldn't blame him. "Sure, CJ."

Out of the corner of her eye she saw Daria mouth "CJ" and then smile, very slowly.

Her shoulder blades shuddered as she turned her back on Daria—she couldn't help it. Any moment she expected a slap, a push, a blow to the head. But turning her back on Daria was the most vulnerable thing she could do. She hoped it was what someone with nothing to fear would do.

"Are you okay?" Burnett asked, the moment they were outside the diner door. "You're shaking."

"That woman was a bit crazy is all. She kept saying she knew me. I figured it might scare her off if she thought I had a big, strong boyfriend."

"Do I need to work out?"

She managed a shaky laugh. "Oh, I think she was harmless, just weird." She realized she was walking quickly and slowed her pace. "I parked in the big garage. Where are you?"

"Same as you—made sense."

CJ listened for footsteps behind them, but heard nothing. Her shoulder blades twitched several times, as if they sensed watching eyes.

Burnett walked her to her car, and saw her off with a cheery wave and, "I'll have that package for Cray on your desk to take one last look at in the morning."

She waved back.

She didn't know if she'd be there in the morning. The quiet she'd felt, daydreaming about an unattainable woman, about exploring that amazing kiss and the feelings that had welled up inside her, was gone beyond reclaiming. Her life, her work, her meager dreams of a future where nobody cared about what had happened to Cassiopeia Juniper Rochambeau—all gone in the time it had taken for Daria to mouth "CJ" and smile with predatory certainty.

Chapter 9

"Thank God it's Friday." Brent breezed his way into the office and Karita was relieved to see he wasn't nearly as stiff with her as he had been for the last few weeks. Perhaps he'd met a princess—she certainly hoped so.

"I hear that." She clicked back from mute to pick up the conversation with the IT support line. "The Intranet is up, but the Internet is down. Yes? I did that. Our system cold boots at four a.m. and the Internet died around seven, apparently. No Google, no Yahoo, no Wikipedia. No LexisNexis, which is more the problem at the moment."

She listened to the service rep's speculations about the possible source of the problems, but focused on the bottom line. "Three is too late—we both know that means five. Can you tell me one o'clock so I can tell my boss eleven and someone really is here by three?"

Marty paused in the act of leaving an envelope on her desk.

"One o'clock it is. I'm going to hold you to that." Karita disconnected and gave Marty a guileless look. "Someone will be here by eleven."

"Have you always fudged times like that?"

"Only when it shelters your blood pressure from life's harsh realities." He snorted, and she distracted him by saying. "I have good news, though. You told me to remind you when the quarantine was up on that adorable Pomeranian, and it ends today at noon. Like I said, there's no credentials so you can't register her, and she's got a luxating patella, so you can't show her. But she's a total doll, quite smart, and far as I know only barks on command."

Marty's excited nodding turned into a wide, beaming grin. "That's great news. I'll bring my wife up to get her out tonight then."

"I'll let Nann know to expect you." She turned her head sharply at the sound of a raised voice, and unfortunately knew immediately who it was.

"Are you fucking stupid? What shit hole of a law school did you go to? Get that crap out of my sight and bring me something that shows you have a brain!"

Marty sighed, but said nothing. They both ignored the next, similar outburst, until Karita could stand it no longer.

"Marty, everyone who works with her needs your help. Good people have been chewed up and spit out. What happens if she tries that tone with a client—or a judge?"

He leaned over the desk and dropped his voice. "I can't fire my brother's widow. I know some people want me to, but I can't do it."

"I'm not saying you should fire her, much as I think she deserves it." Though she wanted to see Susan nailed to something, she abruptly realized what an elf with no magic would do—she took a page from Emily's book. "Help her. You're the only one who can make her get some counseling. There are times I want to see her treated the way she's treated other people, but that just perpetuates it."

He sighed more heavily, then winced at the sound of another outburst. He didn't look at Karita again as he straightened his shoulders and headed for the rear of the office suite.

The argument abated and the hushed tones of serious business resumed. Karita stretched out her neck, grateful that all the tenderness from the altercation at the shelter last week had subsided. She was just relaxing after fielding a flurry of incoming calls when the local messenger service delivered an envelope marked for one of Marty's biggest cases. Her standing instructions were to deliver anything related to it directly to him without any delay.

She hesitated outside his office for a moment, recognizing both voices even through the thick door, and not sure if Marty telling his brother's widow she needed anger management counseling was the one exception to her instructions. Face it, she told herself, this is a damned-if-you-do and damned-if-you-don't situation. Their voices grew quiet for a moment and she decided to go ahead and knock.

Marty did sound annoyed when he called out, so she opened the door slowly, pushing the envelope through first. Then she put her head in and said, "It's Wilson v. Coors."

"Thanks. Bring it on in."

She let his door swing shut behind her and crossed the lush gray carpet to set the envelope on his desk. She did not look at Susan but she could feel the rage around her in the air. As mean as Susan had been to Pam, she couldn't help a pang of sympathy. Susan must be miserable, all the time.

She turned to leave, then jumped slightly when Susan spoke.

"I really don't like it when people talk about me behind my back." Her eyes were dilated with anger. All at once Karita saw the tightly stretched skin trying to hold a world of pain inside, and failing. One light tap with a feather and Susan would shatter.

"Sue." There was a definite edge of warning in Marty's voice. "Don't take anything out on Karita. She's the only person who isn't telling me to get rid of you."

"How can you say that right in front of her?"

Karita froze in place, not sure if she should continue to head for the door or stay.

"Because I trust Karita's discretion and her motives, but you're right—"

"Well, I don't trust her motives, not at all." Susan glared at Karita. "Don't give me that innocent look. I saw you talking to her yesterday. Just because you don't understand how I could do that, in a weak moment when I was lonely and vulnerable, well that is no reason to persecute me. I can just guess the stupid lies you told Marty about me. You should keep your fucking mouth shut."

"I don't know what you're talking about," Karita protested. "I didn't say a word about any of that."

"And now you're lying to cover up your homophobic vendetta—"

"What are you two talking—"

"I'm gay, Susan. And I didn't say a word about Pam to Marty. Not one word."

A long silence fell and Karita realized after a moment that her mouth was open. Aghast, she fumbled for words.

"I'm so sorry, Susan, I didn't mean to do that!"

Susan's face was deathly pale with only two bright, feverish spots of color in her cheeks. Maybe, Karita thought, she realized what her own anger had set in motion.

"Sue, did you sleep with an employee? Just tell me the truth."

She nodded.

The anger now radiated from Marty's side of the desk. Karita gave him a pleading look, but he wasn't focused on her.

"That is completely unacceptable. Completely and utterly unacceptable professionally and morally. You are a partner in this firm and you exposed all of us to liability and then am I to understand that you fired the employee? Have you any idea?"

"Marty, I didn't know what I was doing. I miss Abe so much!" Tears began to flow.

"I miss him too, Sue. I have missed him every day these past two years. That's the only reason you're still here. Look at me."

Susan gulped and then gave Marty her attention, her chin still quivering. Part of Karita wanted to believe it was an act. She'd seen crocodile tears often enough. Her instincts, though, said that Susan had no real idea how she felt about anything. She'd blotted it all out. Some people used alcohol or drugs, exercise or sex, but Susan had chosen anger.

"This is what you're going to do. You're going to counseling. You should have gone when Abe died. And you're going to get therapy about your sexuality, while you're at it."

Shocked, Karita said, "Marty, you can't get cured of being gay by therapy."

He gave her a look that made her want to step back. Okay, not her place, but before she could voice an apology he said, "I *know* that."

He looked at Susan again. "Whatever it is, if you're gay, bisexual, if you were just curious, whatever it is, Abe loved you and I love you and I want you happy with yourself. If you decide you don't want to be a lawyer anymore, fine, whatever. But you're not going to take it out on everyone around you while you wallow in your misery and drag this firm down with your appalling lack of judgment. Am I clear?"

Susan nodded as she again burst into tears.

Karita fetched a tissue from the box on the credenza behind Marty. She passed it to Susan, then said quietly, "I think I should go."

"Karita," Marty said equally quietly, though his intonation was heavy, "I hope my trust in your discretion isn't misplaced."

"No, Marty, it isn't. This won't leave the room." Honesty was the best policy. "I'm friendly with Pam, but I will not discuss this with her."

She closed the office door firmly behind her and only then felt the hammering of her heart. She'd just come out to her boss and outed someone else at the same time. She had thought doing something like that would lead to disaster. Instead, it didn't seem possible that things so messed up could be resolved so easily and quickly. Some other shoe had to fall, didn't it?

Her nerves were twitching up and down the lengths of both arms and legs. She made her shaky way back to the lobby. Okay, so Friday was off to one heck of a start. At least it would end with the most fulfilling time of her week, at the shelter working side-by-side with Emily. Rocking babies, soothing frightened women, making sure their clients felt that there was someone who cared, who valued them.

Her mind ping-ponged between the fulfillment of her work at the shelter and the knowledge that she had just jeopardized her job. Marty had seemed okay with the idea of Susan being gay, but that could be all for show. Even though she liked him, it didn't mean he couldn't be a closet homophobe. She knew it was possible to love someone who was totally devoid of empathy—thanks so much for that lesson, Mandy.

The office felt cold, so she recalled warm things. The curl of a baby's fingers around her thumb, the heat of Emily spooned to her back, the rush of sensation when she'd kissed CJ—that hadn't been just heat. That had been magic.

What was the point of dwelling on it? She scolded herself for recalling the kiss again when pursuing anything else would just get her hurt.

She reclaimed her seat at her desk and deliberately did not think about who else would be at the shelter working tonight. She fielded several calls, signed for another package and wondered if she'd have to find someplace else to work. Just because getting fired for being gay was wrong didn't mean it wouldn't happen. Marty deserved a chance, she told herself, before she borrowed trouble. She'd not given him that chance when he'd hired her because she had been so worn down by Mandy's hatefulness and lack of empathy. She would wait, not think about kisses and women who were frogs, and see.

She didn't have to wait long. When she got back from a

short coffee break she found a sticky note on her headset. Tears immediately sprang to her eyes.

Marty had written, I have a niece I think you'd like.

One thing CJ knew for certain—she couldn't carry almost forty thousand dollars in cash around with her. The bundles of fifties weighed less than four pounds, but it would be her karma that she'd get mugged, or someone would steal it from the car. She had no choice but to leave it at home, in the safe, unless she truly intended to leave town and not return.

She rolled over in bed, still awake at five a.m., and went over her choices again. The smart thing to do was to run. She felt as if Daria, now that she had the scent of frightened quarry, would pop out from behind every tree or from around every corner, one hand out and the other on a phone with the Kentucky State Police tipline on the speed dial.

She needed to leave CJ Roshe behind. She'd been a fool to use her real initials when some of the people she was running from had functional brains. In the days before integrated law enforcement and other government databases, it hadn't been that hard to walk out of the Kentucky Division of Juvenile Justice facility and register for community college in far away New York under a different name.

Only a little patience and finesse had been required to get an ID card, and at the time, New York didn't even require a photo. A little money here, a well-told lie there had netted her a Certificate of Live Birth stating she'd been born at home—the truth. Only an inspired detective could figure out CJ Roshe didn't exist. She wasn't sure anyone could figure out that Cassiopeia Juniper Rochambeau had become CJ Roshe. Nobody but people from the Gathering could connect those dots. There was one code in the Gathering: Anything that could be turned to profit—was. If knowing that Cassie June hadn't stuck around for the transfer from Fayette's juvenile facility to the adult population could be turned into money, that was just smart thinking.

CJ Roshe was one long con, a history built on a lie, a house of cards. She had anticipated, every day, being found out and had told herself she was prepared for that eventuality.

"You believed your own con," she said aloud. "You went native."

She wanted to be CJ Roshe. She had gotten hooked on the success of making deals, of running legit cons on the world. She'd become used to the money rolling in, enough to let her tick the names off that list and keep a clean, secure roof over her head. Damn it, she even liked that Burnett admired her, and why should she care what he thought? Raisa and Devon and Cray and Alvin wanted to set her up with friends because they were completely bamboozled into thinking she might be nice. There was nothing nice about her—it was all an act to keep Cassie June Rochambeau from being found by the State of Kentucky.

She'd known she could never tell Abby who she really was and that had always been a convenient out, an escape hatch for her feelings. She could no more tell Karita than she could Abby. Karita would be…horrified. Anyone who knew the whole story would be. Until that kiss she'd thought she could survive anything. She'd done unforgivable things and lived to try to overcome them. She didn't think she would ever recover if she caused Karita's bright eyes to lose their light.

So she ought to run. Nothing here should make her stay. Nothing but the realization that maybe this wasn't a life she'd created to hide behind. Maybe this was the life she actually wanted.

Her alarm went off and she silenced it quickly. She was so tired. Scared. Ashamed. Guilty. She had a busy day on her calendar—her hollow laugh echoed from the walls as she sat up in bed. CJ Roshe couldn't run away today, she had community service to complete. Given the things she'd done it would be too ironic to end up back in jail courtesy of a stop sign.

"The numbers are on page two." Burnett flipped the portfolio open for her. "You look awful."

"Gee, thanks." CJ kept her attention on the contract numbers as her fingers flew over her calculator. "These all look good to me. Break a leg."

"Thanks. I'm going to make it short and sweet, and when I get back, lunch is on me. After the wine and dessert last night I can afford the sandwich place across the street, if we share."

"Get out of here." CJ couldn't help her fondness for the kid, but she knew her tone was flat because he gave her an odd look. "I'm coming down with something, maybe. I'm not used to bread pudding at midnight."

Burnett picked up the proposal as she pushed it across her desk. "I'm serious about lunch."

"As long as it includes coffee, lots and lots of coffee."

She didn't have the energy to give him another thought. She listlessly assembled her own package for a potential new client, another big University of Colorado alumnus referred by Nate Summerfield. With any luck at all this could mean a solid connection to the type of men who had skyboxes at Broncos games and very large offices and warehouse operations they might need to upgrade or relocate.

She paused with her eyes closed. From the moment she'd sidestepped the guards during the transfer between facilities she had been single-minded in two things. First, that no one from her past ever find her. Second, that the names on the list she'd made in Fayette would all, without exception, be crossed off. Accomplishing the latter demanded the former. She should be halfway to Canada by now, not thinking about deals she could get in three years, five years.

Her luck in Denver had run out. Part of her wanted to rail about how unfair it was to be haunted by a past that belonged to a teenager, living at risk over the three months she hadn't spent in an adult facility, all because she'd turned eighteen before her juvenile sentence had been completed. She hadn't heard from anyone in the Gathering since she'd been sentenced to Fayette but with deadly certainty she had known that there'd be a Rochambeau in the adult facility. They would have been on the lookout for her, and they'd reclaim her to the life.

There would have probably been letters waiting from her father, who had still been sitting in Big Sandy doing his time. Mail from unfit parents to inmates in Fayette's juvie facility was withheld, but as an adult he'd have been able to get in touch with her. Mail or word-of-mouth, it didn't matter; Cassie June would never escape. No social worker had wanted to hear about her fears that after four years of focus on schoolwork, on staying out of trouble, she'd be back in the life the moment she crossed the adult prison threshold.

It wasn't fair, but she couldn't even think those words without the memory of Aunt Bitty's response when she'd told her something was unfair. The bloody nose had underscored the message: *Life isn't fair*. Fairness was what their marks expected and that's why marks lost their money. If she expected to be treated fairly that made her a victim just waiting to be discovered.

Was that the only choice? Thief or mark? It was the only choice in the Gathering, but she'd been out of that circle for twenty years. She was a fool, because apparently she had decided those rules no longer applied. Daria could make them apply, all over again.

Coffee, she could use some coffee. She didn't budge from the chair.

No matter how much she rubbed her eyes, the data danced on the pages, but she doggedly worked on the proposal until it was at least a decent draft. She'd hoped to put it in today's mail but maybe she'd best wait until Monday. If she was here Monday.

She was so tired she put her head down on her desk. The next thing she knew Burnett was shaking her awake.

"You really are sick, aren't you?"

"No." Jitters from the sudden awakening put a quaver in her voice. In the next moment lethargy threatened to turn her bones to liquid. "I just need lunch."

"Okay, let's go, get up, come on, get a move on."

"There's that tone again, the one you shouldn't use with your boss." She couldn't remember if she'd eaten breakfast. "Show some respect."

"Sorry, ma'am." He visibly gulped at the look she gave him as she slipped on her suit jacket.

"How did your meeting go?" she asked as they made their way to the elevator bank. "Any questions you couldn't handle? Did you see the site?"

"Yes, and Cray didn't rule it out, but he was concerned about the tenant allowance for structural."

Tre exited the elevator as they got on, saying over his shoulder, "I got a line on a new retailer from the paper you gave me. Thanks again."

"Good luck with it," CJ answered automatically.

As they discussed Burnett's next steps, they passed Gracie's, where she'd first seen Karita. A glance inside didn't reveal the object of her thoughts. Ahead, though, someone turned a corner sharply. Was that Daria? Could an accomplice be behind her?

She kept walking though her skin was crawling. It had been this bad those first few days out of Fayette, trying to get herself out of Kentucky.

Burnett didn't turn in at CJ's favorite deli, but instead guided her to a bare bones sandwich shop that had, he promised, fabulous brownies.

"I'm buying," Burnett said when CJ got out her wallet at the sandwich counter.

"Nah, I'm not like Jerry. I won't stick a rookie with the bill."

"He didn't…" Burnett gave her a searching look. "I thought it was weird he took care of the Elway's tab without coming back to the table. But he didn't pay it, did he?"

Damn, she thought, she was too tired to remember her lies. "It's not important. By all means, your treat for lunch."

"Jeez, for about a year—that's a lot of brownies I owe you." Burnett handed over bills to the cashier. "When I started working in the office, a couple of people said you worked strictly alone and that you were…"

"A bitch?"

"No, just kind of private and standoffish. That you were great at what you did, didn't like people making mistakes, but who does?"

"I'm not a nice person, Burnett."

"If you say so." He all but rolled his eyes as he picked up the laden tray. With an expert twirl he carried it one-handed over his shoulder the short distance to a tiny table. "Your repast awaits, madam."

"Where did you learn to do that?" The change in subject was welcome. "Last night you remembered everyone's choice of wine and carried the glasses like a pro."

"Who hasn't waited tables to get by? Or did you manage to escape that fate?"

CJ gave him a wan smile. "A million years ago in college in New York—waiting tables paid the bills. I never was much good at it. A coffee shop with a priority to push the pie didn't require previous experience."

He unwrapped his sandwich after taking a large bite of his brownie. "I was proficient at slinging drinks. It was a dance dive."

"Ah, you were a barmaid."

"Please." Burnett sniffed. "I was a cabana boy."

CJ laughed, but broke off as Burnett abruptly turned a vibrant, mortified red.

"What's wrong?"

"I didn't mean to tell you that."

"Why ever not? Honest work is…" Burnett looked like he wanted to drop through the floor. "Oh. Unless… Does cabana boy mean what I think it does?"

After a stuttered beginning, Burnett managed to say, "It means a lot of nights I went home with bruises on my knees, yeah. I was sixteen and a runaway. It wasn't the kind of place that

138

filled out employment forms and I lived on the…tips."

CJ gave him a long, level look. "You're twenty-seven and you look very alive to me."

His gaze stayed fixed on his untouched sandwich. "I'm alive, but I'm not proud of some of the things I did to stay alive."

She spoke without choosing her words, just told him what she knew. She was too tired to think better of it. "You don't have to be proud of it. We don't always know at the time what the real price of a decision is, and when we're young… When we're young and there's no one to guide us, sometimes the most we can hope for is to survive long enough to know that maybe we shouldn't have done that. You can't have regrets if you're dead."

He took a deep breath, but wouldn't look at her.

She could say the words, and believe they truly applied to Burnett, but she'd never think them true for herself. "Did you ever hurt anybody?"

"No, no, never. If anybody got hurt it was me."

"So the only person you have to ask for forgiveness is yourself." And therein lies the difference, CJ thought. Forgiveness for her was not such a simple matter. Someone had gotten hurt.

"That's easy to say, but not so easy to know." He finally looked at her. "How come you don't take your own advice?"

Nonplussed, CJ thought that she'd completely misjudged the kid. He was, well, no kid. She tried to sound mysterious and unconcerned when she answered, "Oh, different crimes, different times."

He was having none of it, apparently. After finally taking a bite of his own sandwich, he asked, "Did you ever hurt anyone?"

She decided to shut him down with a dead serious stare and the unvarnished truth. "Yes. Yes I did."

"I don't believe you."

"Nobody would." She continued to stare at him.

He took another bite and made a show of dabbing mustard from the corner of his mouth. "That look is freakin' scary."

"It's meant to be."

The puppy dog eyes flashed with amusement. "Try your brownie. If you like it I'll bring you one a week for…" His brow furrowed. "Did you tip twenty percent?"

Impossibly, she laughed. So much for her don't-mess-with-me stare. Clearly, if it came to full on confrontation with Daria, she'd have none of her old skills. "Yes."

"Okay, so one a week for two years, one month and two weeks."

The laughter helped even as all her inner voices chided her for being weak. The strong and smart thing to do was to pick up her purse and walk out the door. Even smarter, she added, with an edge of hysteria, would be to take the brownie with her as well.

She laughed again, adrift from any sense of the reality. Acting as if her house of cards were still standing, as if it were a real house and not a tissue of lies built on lies, wasn't how to complete a con. She'd been a natural, her father had said so, and here she sat, looking at Burnett and thinking if she could have had a younger brother, she'd have picked someone like him. From the other side of the potent hit of the brownie and a triple shot espresso, she found herself grateful for community service and at least one more chance to spend time with a woman who ought to be nothing to her.

When she left the sandwich shop the afternoon seemed surreal. Was that Daria around the next corner? Her father in the shadows of the parking garage? A duly authorized representative of the great State of Kentucky walking toward her?

It struck her then that in one of life's ironies the only place she was going to feel safe was the shelter. It was the last place in Denver someone like Daria or her cohorts would look for her.

Chapter 10

Having no meetings after work allowed CJ to arrive at the shelter earlier than she had the previous two Fridays. The swelter of summer had already passed and the temperatures hadn't crossed the 80-degree mark. If there was one thing she didn't like about the weather in Denver, it was how rapidly the seasons changed. Autumn in Kentucky was slower, easier.

Emily let her in, saying, "I remembered to mail those forms you dropped off Saturday. They went out Monday."

The door clicked shut behind her and CJ felt tension drain out of her body. "Thanks a lot. I appreciate it. What can I get started on?"

"Laundry, what else? A new volunteer caught up a lot last night."

CJ lost no time in moving wet towels into the dryer and getting a full load of sheets underway. She felt at loose ends as she went back to the kitchen and couldn't help but glance at the papers Emily had spread out over the table.

"Ah, working on a grant application?"

"Yeah. It takes forever. I've finally got copies of all the

documents everybody asks for, tax returns, incorporation papers, list of staff, all that stuff. So now I'm working on the cover letter."

"Marguerite Brownell? She's a big symphony supporter, isn't she?"

"Yes. Old money, cattle and mining, mostly. She gave cash to a children's burn ward—an administrator who works there told me. Just gave it out of the blue after reading an article in the paper. So I'm asking for money to train volunteers on working with traumatized toddlers." Emily sounded as if she was certain she'd never see a dime for her effort, but she was going to give it a try anyway.

"You're making a direct appeal—it's not a foundation or something like that?" CJ quickly glanced at the papers and hid her frown. She didn't know much about Marguerite Brownell, just the name. "Look, this is my last night and you can just be mad at me, what else is new. Why are you asking for so little?"

"Increasing my chances of getting something."

"Three thousand dollars isn't going to hit her radar."

"That's what she gave the burn ward, for a special kind of bathing table. She'd apparently read about the need for one and decided to help out."

"So unsolicited she offered up three thousand dollars. How much will she give if you actually ask?"

Emily gave her an irritated look. "Have you done grant applications?"

"Nope. I just get hardened Scrooge types to part with millions, and sometimes millions plus ten percent because the view is prettier. Do you have five minutes, and can I use your computer?"

"Five minutes. Then you leave me alone?"

"I'll leave you alone if you want."

Emily heaved a sigh as she led CJ to her office. She tapped in her logon and offered her chair. CJ quickly opened the browser and directed it to Intellidome. The welcome screen popped up and she typed in her user ID and password.

Emily gave the screen a skeptical look. "What am I looking at?"

"This is a service my company pays for—costs an arm and a leg, but if you want to know what someone's worth, what they owe, what they spend their money on, what corporate boards they serve on, what their tax returns look like, this is the place." CJ typed in a search for Marguerite Brownell.

"Isn't this an invasion of her privacy?"

"Public information, just assembled for easy searching. Some people guard their privacy zealously, but some people don't. If we had the time we could go to the newspaper archives and discover details of her social life. We could go to the library and search through annual foundation reports to find her name." CJ pointed to one of the links. "Because she's filed for divorce and apparently her attorney forgot to ask for the right arrangements, her tax returns at that time ended up in the public filings of the proceedings. Happens a lot." She kept the irony out of her voice. "Anything that happens in a courtroom is public unless a judge says otherwise." Except proceedings involving minors, she could have added, where the default was the other way around.

"So what does all this information do for me?"

"Well, I'm looking at her adjusted gross income from three years ago. You are asking her to part with one-sixth of one percent of her annual income. I think you should ask for one percent, and offer her something worth her while."

"I need money for staffing. I figured she'd be vulnerable on issues about children."

"She has no kids—and so might be." CJ started to point out another element of the Intellidome data, but the light in the room danced with silver. She knew Karita was there, she knew it in every synapse of her body.

"What are you guys doing?" Karita leaned in the office door. How could anyone make a faded blue top and soft, worn jeans look like haute couture? She wasn't even trying.

"Spy mission," CJ said. She followed the link to social affiliations.

Emily added distantly, "For the grant application."

"It's not a grant application." CJ scanned the list of clubs and societies that Brownell publicly supported. "It's a direct appeal. You're walking up to her on the street and asking her for twenty thousand dollars. That takes…different rules. She's not going to give it to you based on copies of your bylaws."

"So she's a member of the Greater Metro Area SPCA—"

"She is?" Karita now crowded behind CJ as well. "I wonder if she'd support Nann's rescue."

"I saw her first," Emily said.

CJ turned to look at Emily and saw that the two of them had twined their arms around each other's waists. It seemed completely unconscious. Ignoring it, CJ said, "She likes to support the arts, animals and children. I'm looking at what she doesn't support. Not a sports team on the list. No booster clubs, no athletic events. She might give to walk-a-thon type things, but not at a level that she's getting picked up as a regular sponsor."

Emily was clearly getting overwhelmed. "I just want three thousand dollars to do some training."

One of Karita's eyebrows was reaching toward her hairline. "No sports? Like…maybe…she doesn't like pro sports? Oh. I see where you're going."

"I don't." Emily glanced at her watch. "And your five minutes are just about up."

CJ loved pressure. She always had thrived on the idea of doing the impossible in the shortest time. "Dear Ms. Brownell. On Saturday night, the University of Colorado and its biggest rival will face off at the annual Homecoming game. That night, at least seven children and their terrified mothers will be brought to the Beginnings Women's Shelter possibly because the game didn't turn out the way daddy wanted."

Karita whistled.

After a stunned silence, Emily said, "God, that's

manipulative."

"Pro-sports advertising isn't? The link between pro-sports events and the incidence of domestic violence is real, right?"

Emily nodded, but her tone was laden with exasperation. "It's indisputable, just like the link between drinking and domestic violence. Neither *causes* somebody to beat someone else, but they set the stage for the lowering of restraint, or act as an outright trigger for existing batterers. Battering is like a toxic by-product."

Karita leaned over CJ's shoulder and the scent of her shampoo—hints of vanilla and rosewood—washed over CJ's senses. Peering at the screen she said, "I feel like a fool. I could have looked most of this up at work. We've got Lexis. I don't know this service."

"It's not as deep on court filings and probably longer on the social stuff. A lot of it's free via Google or Yahoo searches, but Intellidome organizes the data. I'd have to follow twenty-thirty links to get this list of social groups. Oh, she *has* done a walk-a-thon—Susan G. Komen Foundation. Breast cancer. And it looks like she brought in a thousand bucks a kilometer. So where she gives, she's very likely to bring in others."

Emily ran her hands through her short curls. "This is more than I can sort through."

CJ knew she couldn't forget about Daria. She shouldn't be putting down more roots, more ties, when it was perfectly clear she'd already put down far more than was good for her. Karita's hair chose that moment to slide from her back and over CJ's shoulder, whispering past CJ's ear and leaving a trail of silken warmth along CJ's neck. She heard herself say, "Let me do this for you. I'll bring back a letter and packet next week."

"Oh, that's wonderful," Karita said. She straightened up, and CJ felt cold where Karita's hair had temporarily rested along her shoulder and arm.

"Your community service is up," Emily said. "Why would you do this?"

CJ took a moment to log out of the online service before answering. She didn't look at Karita but the glow of her pleasure, that CJ was doing something that made Karita happy, left CJ feeling sun-dazzled. Instead she focused on Emily and what she would want to hear. "I come from a long line of people who talked other people into parting with their money. My ancestors got here a few centuries ago via a prison boat into Georgia. My generation, at least—I'm trying to use that lineage and stay out of jail."

Even as she said it, she knew it wasn't just what Emily needed to hear, it was the truth. Maybe she was a thief, and a consummate liar, adept at knowing what people needed to believe before they'd agree to her plans, but she wasn't going to do anything that sent her back to any kind of prison. She might have just discovered, however, something she could do with all her worst qualities that somehow, in the end, turned out okay for everybody involved. Frankly, she was suspicious that such a thing was even possible. It was too easy, the rewards too high.

The doorbell rang and Emily, first one to the monitor said, "Wow—two women and it looks like five kids. It's early, too. We'll need DVDs in the common room."

Karita quickly slipped out of the tiny office. "The Looking Glass room is the biggest if they want to share the space."

"Wait until I find out."

CJ thought about getting out her BlackBerry and writing up the ideas she had for the Brownell appeal, but instead she headed for the linen closet. Sheets and towels were always needed.

She heard Karita say something lightly teasing to Emily about "Anita" and recalled the casual contact between the two. Anyone wanting to get involved with Karita would have to take Emily into account. In the language of the Gathering, if Karita was the perfect mark, Emily was the spoiler. They might not be headed down the aisle but they were clearly bonded. Not that she was thinking in those terms—Christ, didn't she have enough to worry about? Daria had turned up like a death card in a bad life reading.

So she was going to just go through the rest of her life hoping Daria didn't come looking for her? If she was going to be that stupid, why didn't she just ask Karita for a date right now and buy the entire handbasket? Sure, she wanted to be the woman who put shadows into the clearest, most glimmering blue eyes on the planet. She wanted to be responsible for tarnishing the most precious thing she'd ever seen. That's what a thief would do, wasn't it?

Heaven help her—her shoulder was still warm from where Karita's hair had draped over it. If she wanted to live she had to run, but running would be the end of any life worth having.

"I think your idea sounds great." Karita smiled at CJ across the bed they were making. That CJ might be around the shelter after tonight was a very pleasing idea. She wanted to help in useful ways that only she could—she was no Mandy, no karmically bankrupt yuppie, to quote Emily. "And thank you for offering to help out Emily with it."

"It's an extension of my existing skill set," CJ said. She seemed almost shy.

"Were you serious about your ancestors? They came here incarcerated?"

"Serious. That's what I was always told, anyway. A very long line of...unconventional thinkers."

"My people were apparently chasing fish, but we don't go back that far. Gran was twelve when they left the old country. She'd teach me little magic phrases and it wasn't until I was grown that—could you hand me that pillowcase?" She tucked the pillow under her chin and began working the case up. "It wasn't until I was grown that I realized they were in Norwegian."

"What else would they have been?" CJ turned to pick up a blanket and Karita hoped that she was done blushing by the time CJ looked at her again.

"Oh, we had a running joke about it being elvish." She didn't analyze closely why she wanted to tell CJ about that.

"That suits." CJ still wasn't looking at her. "You could pass for an elf with a little ear surgery maybe."

Karita realized she'd been holding her breath. CJ didn't think it was stupid, maybe. "Well, I'm not sure it's ears so much as a state of mind."

"Certainly not fake ears. DNA is DNA. Some of us were born elves, and some of us were…not. Blood will out." CJ looked at her then, her dark gaze so conflicted that Karita started to ask what was wrong, but CJ added, "I forget who said that."

"Isn't that what the Internet was invented for? To look up obscure facts to avoid tossing and turning at night?"

"I'm certain that's what they had in mind, sure." CJ gave her a droll look.

"You're right, you know. After the big game, there will be at least one child here specifically because dad didn't like the outcome."

Lucy appeared in the doorway looking freshly scrubbed from the shower at her gym. "Do you guys have any spare shampoos?"

Karita fished one out of the grocery bag on the bed. "Need anything else?"

"This will do it." Lucy caught the tossed minicontainer. "CJ, are you doing anything tomorrow night? I've got a spare ticket for the Roadrunners soccer game. They're NCAA Division Two champs."

CJ blushed and Karita found herself holding her breath again. "I, um—maybe Karita—"

"She doesn't like sports," Lucy said quickly. "Besides, she's got a hot date with some lawyer babe."

"Is that so?" CJ quirked an I-thought-you-said-it-wasn't-a-date eyebrow at her and Karita squirmed. "I don't know much about soccer."

Lucy hooked a thumb in the waistband of her jeans. "Nubile young women in shorts. What's more to know?"

Karita envied Lucy her easy, gamin grin. She seemed completely casual around CJ while Karita struggled to avoid sounding like a twit.

"Would that make us dirty old women?"

"Yes, it would."

"In that case, sounds fun." CJ plumped up the pillow in her hands. "Do you want to meet there?"

"How about a bite to eat first? Wynkoop Brewing Company has great beer."

"Sure. That's in LoDo, right?"

Lucy's laugh was easy. "Yeah. I haven't babe-watched in LoDo in at least two years. Game's at seven. Do you want to meet at Wynkoop at five?"

"Sounds terrific."

"Cool." Lucy breezed away, leaving Karita to combat unwelcome jealousy.

"Nubile young women, eh? Is that your type of thing?"

"I don't know." CJ's voice was oddly strained. "It'll be a first. Sounds like Lucy could really use a night out."

"She hasn't had many for quite a while, that's for sure." Abruptly puzzled, Karita tipped her head at CJ. "What about your girlfriend? The one I saw you with at the coffee bar?"

"We broke up. It wasn't all that serious and she met someone who could be and that was that."

"Oh. You didn't say."

"No, I didn't. So Pam's really a date?"

"Yeah. She asked and I thought, well, why not?"

"What about…" CJ gave a meaningful look at the floorboards between them and Emily's office.

"We're not—we didn't exactly break up because we weren't exactly dating. It was more of a, well, a thing…"

"Friends with benefits thing?"

Karita frowned. "I'd like to think more than that. Em is really special to me. But the time in our lives when we occasionally needed more is over."

"Oh."

They gazed at each other across the bed. I don't even know why I'm going out with Pam, Karita thought. How had life gotten so complicated? It was as if their lives kept trying to overlap but then their paths got tangled and redirected. Fate was having a laugh.

Emily called out from downstairs and CJ started, then quickly said, "I'll go."

After showing the two women with the five kids the room they would all share, Karita couldn't find CJ and presumed she was for some reason in the dining room where Emily was doing the intake on a new arrival. A few minutes later a small, pale woman with a dark-haired little girl, maybe five or six, emerged with CJ gently shepherding them toward the common room where *The Muppet Show* was playing. The little girl was immediately drawn to the television but not before Karita noticed how stiffly she moved. Her mother, no more than thirty, moved delicately, like a woman of eighty. Nothing marked their faces but Karita was willing to bet both had been kicked while already on the ground. Even though she'd learned that getting angry on the behalf of their clients wasn't a useful response, she felt it, and she knew that Emily did too. Anger was one of the forces that kept them here, and they put it to productive use, trying to beat the long odds.

CJ slowly walked the mother along the first floor to the rear bedroom, pausing at the linen closet for sheets and towels. "It's the Rose room," CJ was saying. "I think your daughter will like the colors."

After a glance at her watch, Karita headed for the kitchen to help with producing the night's running fare of popcorn, milk and juice. Emily had already set the microwave to work on the first bag so Karita took on watering down the apple juice by a third, as recommended by their volunteer pediatric supervisor. Emily had lined up reusable plastic tumblers of all colors on the tray by the time Karita began pouring.

"We make a good team, you know?" Emily went to start a second bag of popcorn while Karita continued filling the small cups.

"I know. I hope that it's always true."

Lowering her voice, Emily said, "Anita turned me down a bit ago."

"Oh, I'm so sorry."

"But she said yes to next Tuesday."

Karita squealed with delight. "Told you so! That's wonderful. And you are so cute when you blush."

Emily gave her a weak-assed attempt at a scowl. "Am not."

"Are too."

"Is what?" Lucy, arriving from the laundry room, pinched a couple of popped kernels from the large bowl.

"Cute when she blushes."

Lucy arched an eyebrow. "If you like that sort of thing." She ducked Emily's playful slap.

Pauline appeared from the back porch, all in a rush. "I'm sorry guys. I got held up at work. I'll get out of my scrubs before the clients see me. Hey, leave me some popcorn. I missed dinner again." She disappeared into the tiny bathroom just past the row of lockers.

Emily picked up the bowl. "We've got seven kids so far. Lucy, could you make another bag in about five minutes?"

Karita followed Emily into the common room, explained to the mothers what was in the juice cups and the room's tension eased as everyone shared food. The house was always better with the giggles of children.

She realized the little dark-haired girl's mother wasn't back and she didn't want to say yes to any food without checking about allergies with her mother. "I'll just go ask your mom, okay? Be right back."

As she approached the Rose room she could hear the quiet sound of weeping and the unmistakable murmur of CJ's husky voice. She paused, just out of sight, not wanting to startle or intrude.

CJ was saying, "She's really going to hurt in the morning. They heal faster but it still hurts."

Through her tears, the mother said, "He's never hit her before. It was just me. I don't know what to do."

I should intervene, Karita thought, remembering that CJ had fainted after her first intense encounter with a client. She leaned quietly into the doorway in time to see CJ sit down on the bed next to the client.

CJ touched the other woman on the hand, briefly, and said, "My father didn't hit me until I was about your daughter's age. I was pretty used to it because my aunt was quick with a slap if she caught you looking. I remember it though, because it was different. I didn't know he'd stop. When he started on my mother I never stayed around to see how and when he stopped. I didn't know how long I'd have to take it and that was really scary."

"Why did he do it?"

"I don't care." CJ's tone was flat and Karita found herself swallowing back tears. "He never hit me again, though."

"Oh. That was good, then."

The chilling, emotionless edge to CJ's voice sharpened. "Well, it depends on your thinking. The next time he went off on my mom he killed her."

Karita's heart twisted so hard in her chest she nearly gasped. Dear Lord, she thought, it explains so much.

"I don't have many memories of her now. He started hitting her and I ran for it, like always. I wonder if I'd stayed if he might have spared her some because he had me to hit too, but I'll never know. She was dead the next morning and after that he didn't hit me. He and my aunt would slug it out sometimes, but he left me alone."

The tissue the woman was twisting around and around in her hands came apart. Her eyes were wide with shock. "Weren't there cops? Did he go to jail?"

"Not for that. We, our clan, moved a lot and after we were

gone if an unidentified body floated up out of a lake or river, well, nobody cared. She wasn't the only one who got lost along the way. He beat my mother the way your man is beating you. Punches and kicks to the body. I don't know why she died. Maybe a rib broke and tore open a lung. Or kicks to the kidneys, or maybe he finally choked her to death because sometimes he just felt like throttling her."

The woman put a visibly shaking hand to her throat.

"What happens to your daughter after he kills you? That's what you have to keep asking yourself. What happens to her? My father let me live. Will hers?"

Karita realized she'd let it go on too long. The client was overloaded. CJ was probably doing some good but Emily was the professional. The creak of the floorboard betrayed her presence and CJ glanced up.

Karita tried her best to look as if she'd just arrived but she knew her shock probably showed in her face. "Is it okay if your daughter has some watered down apple juice and microwave popcorn? The other kids are all having some."

"Is there milk? She didn't get any at dinner. She needs it for her b-bones." The woman's composure dissolved completely and she buried her face into CJ's arm.

For a shocked moment, CJ didn't move, then she put an arm around the thin shoulders.

"I'll get Emily," Karita said quietly. The grateful look CJ gave her sent Karita speeding away.

With a few short words she filled Emily in, but didn't relate the gist of CJ's story. She joined the crowd in the common room, smiled at the right times, laughed with a couple of the kids, but all the while she kept thinking about what she'd overheard. From the nearly two years of working with Emily she knew that she had to separate her pity for CJ the child from her empathy for CJ the woman. CJ was no longer a child. Even if Karita ached to put her arms around the little girl inside, it wasn't a little girl she would be holding. Given her other feelings, given that kiss, it would be disastrous for her to confuse her impulses.

Emily had been right—CJ was a ticking time-bomb of issues. Beyond a doubt, warm and safe arms, a loving touch, would help. For a few minutes, it would help. And then the issues would still be there. Wanting more than a hug would still be very, very real.

CJ peeked into the common room from the doorway before heading to the kitchen. Karita wanted to follow her but knew herself too well. She would want to comfort the child, pour all the magic she had into the wounds, but that could lead them to a crossroads where they made choices without being certain of their reasons.

Right now it wasn't CJ who needed space, it was her.

Revelation was not good for the soul. Or the stomach, CJ added to herself. Another sleepless night loomed, and this time it wasn't Daria that kept her awake, it was her own inexplicable urge to put into words things she had never said aloud.

If it hadn't been the last of her obligatory hours, she was quite certain Emily would have told her not to come back. After she'd finished a long talk with the woman CJ had been comforting, she'd found CJ in the kitchen and said, "You did good, but you're not a licensed therapist, CJ. I'm responsible for treatment, and I'm liable for everything that happens here. I think you did the right thing to show your empathy, but it's not something any client can hear."

"I understand," CJ had said. She did, too. "I'm sorry."

Emily had seemed to accept CJ's apology. Nevertheless, she'd said, "I know it's early, but why don't you call it a night? Given the hours I'm sure you'll put into the Brownell thing, we're more than even."

"Are you sure? You've got a full house."

Emily had looked at her, and those steady brown eyes had seemed to miss nothing. "We'll manage."

We means her and Karita. She's putting distance between Karita and me, CJ thought, then she chided herself for her unkind interpretation when Emily added, "CJ, I do a group, you know. You're welcome to come to it."

CJ had declined. She knew Emily meant well. She was looking forward to advising Emily about fundraising, to seeing if that could be helpful. But she didn't want to be a client to Emily. Or Karita. Or Lucy or Pauline, even.

Only bars were open this close to midnight in this part of town, and there was no way she was going near a bar at that hour. She didn't need a drink. If anything, she needed something grounding, like a cup of coffee and the time to stir, sip and think. She made a quick U-turn and was relieved to see that the only other car on the road continued in the direction she had been heading. Daria hadn't found her yet. With a quick left, she headed for Pete's Kitchen. Coffee and some fresh baking powder biscuits with butter sounded perfect.

She got a parking place out front because a patrol car was just pulling away. The diner seemed quiet, though, and it was likely the cops had just been in for their own late night snack. It was the kind of place that served breakfast all day, and when the bars closed Pete's got busy dishing out pre-hangover plates of waffles and omelets.

The waitress, who sported a pink hairnet over her gray hair, gave her a casual wave toward the back, and CJ picked a small booth where she could see the door. She supposed she shouldn't be here, because all-night diners were the kind of place that attracted Daria and her ilk. At the counter, proving her point, was a small, overly casual twenty-something white man who was taking great pains to look like a teenager. She guessed he was either turning tricks or picking pockets, or both.

"What can I get you, hon?" The waitress was still behind the counter, wiping down mustard bottles with quick efficiency.

"Coffee and biscuits, if you've got some up."

"Won't have fresh ones for probably thirty minutes, but I could have you a plate of French toast in five, get him to leave off all the sugar, if that's more what you want."

"That sounds perfect. Just two slices of bread—a snack, not a meal."

"I hear you, hon." The waitress hollered the order over her shoulder, squirted the last of one bottle of mustard into another, then wiped her capable hands. Moments later she was at CJ's table to pour a cup of steaming black brew into an unpretentious white mug, leaving CJ to add fake sugar and the contents of a tiny cup of mystery creamer.

It wasn't the organic fair trade brew that Gracie's turned out, not by a long shot. Regardless, the first sip was heavenly. The second, in defiance of nutritional reality, seemed to calm her racing nerves. She idly watched the man at the counter making eye contact with two guys who noisily entered, but they ignored him and found their way to a booth beyond a vivacious group of women who were discussing a concert they'd just enjoyed.

"It's not the end of the world," she found herself muttering under the cover of the other conversations and the clatter of cutlery. "You've always known he killed her, you've just never told anyone before." The truth of her mother's death was long since grieved over. The wound had sealed over with scar tissue, but certainly a battered women's shelter was likely to bruise it. Emily had probably been expecting just such a disclosure all along, and it did annoy CJ to be in any way predictable to other people.

She expected to always be predictable to herself, however. She hadn't realized she was going to tell the woman about her mother until the words were said. Now she was sitting in an all-night diner because she'd completely surprised herself. Life had been too surprising of late. "That," she muttered at the coffee mug, "is an understatement."

Daria, Burnett, volunteering to do some fundraising for Emily—all surprises. They paled next to the biggest one: Karita's kiss. The surprising intensity of Karita's mouth on hers, so quiet—the astonishment, the wave of peace, the sense of a beginning. None of it was anything she could have again, so why was she staying when every instinct said she should leave? The wonderful, welcome feelings warred with her fear in a repeating loop until the waitress distracted her.

"Here you go, hon. Syrup?"

"No, thanks. This looks great. Just what I wanted." The two piping hot slices of French toast already had a puddle of melted butter in their centers. CJ added salt and pepper before slicing them into bites.

It was comfort food like she'd been making for herself since she had been tall enough to reach cooktop controls. She was pretty sure it was Aunt Bitty who'd shown her how to whisk eggs and dip in bread, but there wasn't anything she'd ever thank Aunt Bitty for. Or her father for that matter—life is a right, and she shouldn't be thanking anyone for letting her stay alive. She shook off an errant flash of memory, of finding her mother's body in the morning and thinking, at first, that Mommy had slept on the floor before, but never so late.

The restlessness of her thoughts and the revelations of these sleepless nights reminded her of the first nights she'd spent in Fayette. Some things hadn't been different at all from her life before that point. Neither the detention center nor the Gathering had privacy, both had honed the skill of observing the world through peripheral vision, and everybody thought what was yours was theirs, if they could take it.

The key difference was that there had been no Rochambeaus or other clans in the juvenile facility. Nobody knew who she was. Nobody knew why she was there. It had taken her less than twenty-four hours to realize she did not have to go back to the Gathering. She felt no blood loyalty or familial duty. In many ways, Fayette, at the age of fourteen, had been her birthplace.

The parade of social workers had one goal in common, which was making sure she could get a job when she got out. She'd learned how to wire a lamp, change out a pipe, even adjust an engine's timing. The reward for learning those things, and completing classroom work, had been library privileges, which included access to music as well as books. She'd discovered jazz and mysteries, in that order. The Gathering was home schooling in subjects not on any child's curriculum, and her hunger for textbooks—even woefully out-of-date ones—had pleased her keepers. All in all, the day one of the guards had called her "CJ" had been a very good one. She'd been CJ ever since.

"Should I warm that up for you, hon?"

"Sure." CJ gestured at her cup. "The toast is great, thanks."

"Enrique knows his griddle. Come back at six and it'll be my hollandaise on the eggs Benedict."

As the waitress went back to her chores at the counter, CJ again gave the man-passing-for-teen her brief attention. He was having a long, money-poor night, from the look of things, though he had an easy going smile for any and all who came through the door. She supposed he'd already cased her, and concluded that she was a lonely business type who'd been dumped by her date or she wouldn't be eating at Pete's by herself at this hour.

Lonely? Maybe, just a little, but in Fayette she had learned the difference between loneliness and solitude. Solitude allowed her to look back at Aunt Bitty and see the cruel, damaged harpy that she was. Finally, she had seen the Gathering not as a proud remnant of an alternative way of life, but a self-perpetuating social canker that fed on violence, thieving and exploitation of *everything*. Her father, without a doubt, was a murderer, at least twice over.

Clarity about her past hadn't changed the present, however. She'd known she had to tell the social workers things they liked to hear. She'd made bad decisions, and wanted to make good choices from now on, yes she did. She'd found Jesus—some of them loved that one, praise the Lord. They didn't need to hear her say her father was a murderer—they already knew that. That's why he was in Big Sandy, for the con gone wrong and the dead man. What did it gain her to tell them he'd also murdered her mother? What on earth had it gained her tonight to tell a perfect stranger?

That's why she was drinking coffee after midnight, enjoying

her solitude in a crowded diner. She didn't understand why she'd broken silence. Karita had undoubtedly heard her little story, and now Karita thought she knew what made CJ Roshe tick. Like the jailhouse shrinks, she had no idea what CJ remembered and why she kept her list of names.

Searching all her memories, the bad ones, the not-so-bad ones, going back as early as she could, CJ couldn't find a single one where she'd done something without knowing why. She gave store clerks a five-dollar bill, then said it was a ten and cried loud and long until they gave her the difference. If she didn't Aunt Bitty would hit her and she already knew what Aunt Bitty had done to Uncle Vaughn. For a long time, that was her reason for everything she did. By the time she was nine she could run any number of quick confidence tricks. No matter how hard she tried, the only compliment Aunt Bitty had ever given her was, "Your eyes could have a whore paying for sex."

Fear of Aunt Bitty and the ever-present knowledge that at any moment her father could decide that she, too, didn't deserve to go on living, had made her eager to please, but it wasn't the only reason she had excelled as a con. She had been her father's willing apprentice. In the solitude of Fayette, she'd figured out why. She'd conned people and lied and taken their money because she enjoyed it. Thieving was in her blood, in her genes. She was good at it and the thrill was undeniable.

She sipped her coffee. That was also something social workers hadn't needed to hear.

It was the same feeling with selling real estate now, a feeling of pleasure and success, staying just this side of the ethical line, not because she was doing the moral thing, not because she'd reformed or found the Lord, but because talking people out of money through legal means kept her out of jail. So why, tonight, had she broken silence? Why was she spending time and energy helping Burnett? Why wasn't she running for her life from Daria and the inevitable swarm of cousins? Self-preservation was her bottom line, but she had put herself at risk and she couldn't name anything good that would come of it, no sure thing. All she had was tissue paper dreams.

She'd chatted up Karita because she couldn't take her eyes off her. She'd flirted with her at Gracie's, talked to her at the shelter, even offered to help with a piece of her life, and she didn't even intend to get Karita into bed. What kind of con was that?

CJ Roshe was Cassiopeia Juniper Rochambeau in hiding. She couldn't be someone's girlfriend, or mentor, or even buddy. Yet she was still in Denver when she ought to run because she wanted CJ Roshe to be real. That meant this time the con she was running was on herself, trying to make lies into truth.

After a glance at the man still lingering over his coffee at the counter, CJ put some bills together and carried the check over to where the waitress was wiping plates. "Keep it," she said, when the woman mentioned change.

A trip to the bathroom was definitely in order, and she was ready for some sleep, in spite of the caffeine. She would go home, get out the list, remind herself who she was and why she did things, and go to bed. For now, ignoring Daria and even ignoring Karita, was what she needed to do.

As she emerged from the bathroom she saw that the chatty group of women had clustered near the cash register and everyone seemed to be offering a ten or twenty and asking for change so they could split up the check. From where she stood she counted three wide open backpacks and two more purses offering up cell phones and billfolds. What she noticed the man at the counter had as well. His brow was furrowed as he stood up as if to pay his check as well. He stretched casually, making no sudden moves. By the time he was in position, CJ was behind the group, her arms spread and making a big show of pushing the huddle out of her way.

"Sorry, it's a bottleneck, sorry, excuse me..." She pushed purses and backpacks around to the front of their owners. One backpack she had no choice but to bump off the woman's shoulder so she was forced to catch it before it hit the ground. "Sorry, clumsy of me—oh!" She added loudly, "This guy wants by us."

The women naturally gave ground, reassembling themselves into less space. Nearly all of them glanced at the thoroughly annoyed man. CJ didn't make eye contact—no point to him knowing her actions hadn't been accidental.

With all those eyes on him, it made sense for him to pass over a dollar for his coffee and hurry out the door.

"He was cute," one of the women said.

"They're all cute to you," a friend promptly announced and the hubbub resumed.

After another minute's wait, CJ hurried out to her car and got safely inside. She laughed into her reflection in the mirror. Cassie June would have probably had three of the wallets and walked away whistling. Four years in detention had taught her the importance of choosing the right side. But it didn't change who she was. She hadn't wanted to spare the women the loss of their ID and credit cards to some lowlife predator, she'd just wanted the thrill of outsmarting the guy and him none the wiser. A short, quick con, and she'd won, and that's what mattered to her.

That was her life, and Karita would never understand it. She'd be repelled if she knew that every day, every hour, CJ had to choose to "do the right thing." It was as unnatural a frame of mind to Karita as generosity and inherent goodness was unnatural to CJ. They really had nothing in common, and no magical kiss, no amount of lusting and flirting, would change that.

It was the truth, and it annoyed CJ that she was still repeating it an hour later, staring at the bedroom ceiling.

Chapter 11

Sucking on her bruised thumb, Karita thought it was time for a heartfelt but distinctly un-elflike curse. "Goddamn!"

She stuck her thumb into her iced tea and glared at the narrow weatherstripping and even teensier copper nails. No doubt she was going about the project entirely the wrong way, but she was horrid at do-it-yourself projects and being willing to learn and try didn't seem to make a difference. Gran had never lacked the helpful ingenuity of her neighbors when it came to fixing something with little to no expense—it had always been easy to trade a few hours of home repair for a few hours of babysitting.

Marty was probably right. The last time she'd mentioned the many fixes the little house needed, he'd suggested she take out a mortgage on the land and pay for licensed contractors. Living without a house payment was pretty dandy, though, and it seemed like a smart idea to at least do what she could on her own before committing herself to monthly payments.

Maybe weatherstripping all the west facing windows, from whence came the icy winter winds, wasn't one of the things she could do.

The throbbing of her thumb abated, but it was oddly reminiscent of the throbbing somewhere behind her heart when she thought about last night. She could still hear CJ's flat, emotionless tone as she said "He killed her."

Her own turmoil had only worsened when she'd discovered that Emily had sent CJ home, and that CJ had left without saying good-bye. She didn't know when she would see CJ again. She kept chiding herself for being hurt—what did she expect? They'd kissed, and okay, for her, it had been an amazing kiss, but a kiss did not make a relationship, or create obligations or change the fact that they both had dates later tonight, with other people.

She didn't have a clue why she'd thought it wise to go out with Pam and she surely didn't know why CJ had said yes to Lucy. It was idiotic that for want of a little courage she'd said nothing that meant *anything* to CJ. So it had been a great kiss, a fantastic kiss, and she had felt a yearning heat she couldn't even name. Movies always had a kiss solving everything, easy as melting butter in a hot pan. Well, it didn't work that way for her, obviously. That kiss had made it harder to think through her feelings, and more difficult to talk to CJ.

She and Mandy had talked nonstop. Everything had been interesting. Damn it, she'd loved Mandy and thought she'd been loved back. So much laughter and passion gone up in smoke the first time life got a little bit tough to juggle. Better to have found that out early on, Karita tried to tell herself. What if you'd been the one sick and needing a hand to hold instead of your grandmother? She wouldn't have been there for you. Sooner or later she was going to call you a flake, and say you were stupid.

Deeply annoyed that she was having the very same argument with herself, she gave whacking nails with the tack hammer another try. Then she said several more bad words, but did successfully control the urge to hurl the hammer out the nearest window. Her mood alone said she shouldn't be around harmful objects. A shower and a night out with a friend—it wasn't too late to be just friends with Pam—was what she needed.

If she hurried her shower a little she'd have just enough time to stop at the rescue and do a couple of quick chores for Nann. Puppies and kittens always made her feel better.

Ninety minutes later Karita mopped her brow wearily as she leaned against the desk in Nann's office. She was so glad Pam was the cell phone type.

"Pam, I am so sorry. I stopped off for just a minute at the animal rescue where I volunteer and got caught up in the deluge. There's a growing wildfire south of Mount Fallon, and it's driving lots of critters up the canyon."

Pam's voice was slightly tinny, but otherwise clear. "I'm running a little late myself. Do you want to cancel?"

"I'd hate to, but that's purely selfish. I mean I'm starving. But we're overrun."

"Well, why don't I grab a pizza or something and join you? Maybe I can help out."

Karita picked at some of the multiple types of animal hair that clung to her best pair of slacks. Dog or cat? She peered closely. Marmot. "That's way more than the call of duty. You don't—"

"No problem. My folks raised sheepdogs and I love animals. This is great actually. I'll skip going home to change and be there all the earlier. Give me an address."

Karita explained how to find the converted store, and added, "Can I be a total scrounge and ask you to bring two pizzas? I don't think Nann has eaten all day. Oh, and she's a vegetarian, too."

"If I get half of one with pepperoni will that spoil the other half for you?"

Karita laughed. "No, I don't mind pepperoni cooties."

Karita went to tell Nann the happy news and then spent the next half-hour doling out water and chopped fresh grass to feed the rest of the marmots that occupied two sets of the outdoor cages. Some of the critters were half singed, all were scared and out of their element. Once the fire was contained they'd release them all back into the area. She peeked at the mountain lion, whose cage faced away from the others. The burned cat was heavily sedated until risk of infection passed, and it wasn't tending to drink much water. Nann was worried it would need a saline drip, and she wasn't equipped to administer one. They'd have to call the Department of Wildlife for one of their experts. To her relief, the water bowl showed some consumption. She noted the level on the clipboard hanging outside the cage.

When she went back inside the clamor was overwhelming. The vast majority of the new arrivals were dogs, most of whom had tags, but their owners were in the evacuation zone. The barking was non-stop and the mouths to feed almost triple the usual.

A weary-looking, forty-something volunteer firefighter arrived with a young Labrador and an older Husky. Right behind him, a welcome sight indeed, was Pam, with two wonderfully aromatic pizza boxes. Karita hoped her eyes said, "Thank you," before she gave her attention to the dogs.

The firefighter surrendered the makeshift leads with a sigh of relief. "How many more can you guys take? We're still sending folks here when they come up to the line with critters they've found."

"I'll have to check with Nann." She clucked soothingly to the dogs. "Be right back."

She glanced back at the doorway and was pleased to see Pam offering some pizza and the volunteer looking like he'd been brought back from the brink of exhaustion at the prospect. Once on the other side of the separating door, she called, "Hey, Nann, two more large breeds. Do we have a cutoff yet?"

Nann looked up from applying salve to a poor puppy's blistered paws. "Well, they said they weren't going to increase the evac zone, so we're okay through the night for whatever they find. We need a vet here, though, so I called my brother. If they get to full containment we can start making calls in the morning. Oh, and the answer is still no, sorry, we can't handle a buffalo."

"There's a stray buffalo?"

"Evidently one got out of the Genesee herd." She wiped her already sooty face, adding a gleam of ointment to her cheek.

"Pizza's here, by the way."

"Oh, I think that's the best thing I've heard all day."

"It gets better. Pam's folks raised sheepdogs, so she's ready to roll up her sleeves after she's fed."

Nann popped the squirming puppy back into the cage with two others its size. As she joined Karita on the way to the lobby, she said, "What does it mean when the prospect of pizza and a willing body leaves me thinking about nothing but a nap?"

"That you work too hard." Karita introduced the two women and promptly helped herself to a large slice of deep dish cheese and olive. "Does the newbie have to do the litter changes for the cats?"

"Hey," Pam protested. "I brought the food."

"I already did it," Nann said. Her bright red hair had half-escaped from the ponytail tie. Somehow, combined with soot across her pale cheek, she still managed to look elegant. "At least I think I did."

"I'm just teasing," Karita said. "I usually do it when I'm here, so I will, if you didn't."

"Nice place you got here. I gather you're not usually this busy." Pam mopped a dollop of tomato sauce off her chin.

"You gather rightly." Nann collapsed into one of the hard chairs, chewing and talking at the same time. "I'm a sucker for hard-luck stories. I had a veterinary practice, just starting out, when someone brought me an eagle with a broken leg. Before I knew it I was far more interested in our local animal ecology than I was in general vet duties."

"So you went a different route than you had planned?" Pam chose the chair opposite Nann. "I'm between jobs in lawyering and thinking of a possible right turn in my life as well. Estate and probate work is really lucrative but having had time to reflect, I'm more interested in family law, adoption, marriage equality, things like that."

Karita segued from the cheese and olive to the mushroom and zucchini. It didn't last long either. She debated the wisdom of a third slice as she listened to Pam and Nann talk about animals, children, families and hiking. Pam certainly was laughing a lot. Nann's freckles were practically glowing. At first Karita thought Nann's bright color was merely the effect of finally getting some food into her stomach. On second thought, though, it was quite possible the glow was the dinner companion.

She decided on a third slice—mushroom and zucchini again—and watched the other two women chat. She was used to seeing women roll over and ask for pets around Nann. The impish leprechaun look was very engaging. The leprechaun, however, usually needed to get clonked on the head before she'd see a naked woman doing a shimmy-shimmy dance just for her. One adorable butch in the neighborhood had brought Nann freshly baked cookies, twice, and the poor woman had only registered to Nann as "the corgi." Right now, however, Nann's hands were going every which way while she talked and Pam looked positively dazzled.

It happens that easily, Karita thought. Eyes sparkle, words flow, and the attraction is there. So why is it so hard to find that with CJ? Why couldn't they get into an easy place and just get to know each other?

Pam burst out laughing again, and it seemed like an auspicious time to whisper Gran's hopeful charm. If that didn't work, then later she'd clout Nann with a bucket and be more direct. Something like, "Single. Lawyer. Fetch!"

A beep from her calendar program broke CJ's concentration, and she stretched in her desk chair before shutting off the appointment alarm. Coming into the office had been a good idea. The quiet of a Saturday allowed her to stay focused, and she always accomplished more at the office than if she took work home. Her lack of concentration yesterday had thrown her off schedule in some of her planned prospecting for new clients, and today she'd more than made up for it.

Focusing on work had settled her nerves. She felt on track again, pursuing her career in order to sever all ties with her past. She hadn't thought of cleansing the past as a way to make CJ Roshe real, but maybe that was the goal, after all. There were things she wanted that she'd been telling herself she couldn't have. Evenings out with friends, for example. Dating someone more frequently than once every seven weeks. Following a first kiss with a second and if it turned into more, having some kind of life she could offer. But CJ didn't get to be real if Cassie June was still bound to her crimes. Twenty-two thousand square feet of class A office space would get the next name off the list, and deposit a substantial chunk toward the one after that.

For variety, she'd also worked Intellidome hard in Emily's cause, and had what she hoped was a viable fundraising appeal that started with Marguerite Brownell and ended up roping in even more monied sources. She was pleased with the overall proposal and looking forward to showing it to Emily. She'd try to do that on Tuesday evening. Not that her choice of that day had anything to do with when Karita volunteered again, she half-heartedly told herself.

Oh, give it a rest, she thought wearily. Late night coffee, repeating the names remaining on her list until she finally slept, a lazy morning, a brisk walk and some hard work had convinced her she could live without distractions. One moment she would congratulate herself for exercising her skill set on the right side of the law. Then she thought about Karita and turned into a lovesick fool, a do-gooder who helped out worthy causes, a sap who gave away her expertise for free.

Trying to sort it out gave her a pain right behind her eyes. Aunt Bitty sniped at her lack of brain power, but CJ muttered back, "It's not my brain that's the problem."

Well, hell, she thought. After a perfectly good afternoon's work, she was back where she'd started, at the very same fork in the road. Thankfully, it was time for her date with Lucy. Doubtless, it would be distracting, a date with a woman she wasn't interested in sexually. She wasn't sure she'd ever had one of those before.

It just proved there was a first time for everything. That it was also the first time she'd spend an evening wondering how another woman's date was going hadn't escaped her notice either, but she wasn't going to dwell on that, thank you.

She turned off her computer, snatched up her keys and headed out into the long golden shadows of late afternoon. On such a lovely day it was easy to pretend Daria had been a bad dream.

Lower Downtown was still sleepy even though the sun was nearly touching the Front Range. LoDo's urban hip retailers and glitzy eateries had already lit their neon signs, but they couldn't compete with the late summer sun. CJ knew from dates with Abby that an hour after sunset Denver's gay district would be sparkling with life.

CJ swung around Sixteenth one more time, hoping to luck out on a parking space. The wonderful thing about the Rockies was that no matter what, she always knew which way was west. The only place she'd ever been lost in Denver was the concrete canyons of the highrise business district.

A van finally pulled out of a metered spot and she snapped it up. When the engine fell quiet she took a moment to study the banks of mountains. The closest was a mere seven thousand feet, but behind those foothills were nines, tens and elevens. Coworkers boasted of hiking the twelves and fourteeners beyond those. On a clear winter morning the rows of ascending peaks were breathtaking. An afternoon like this one, hazy from remnants of summer heat, let the light play tricks, and the sheer size of the Rockies made them seem like an extension of the city. She could put out her fingertips and almost touch the indigo concaves and purple shadows.

Of all the seasons, autumn in the Rockies was her favorite. Two weeks ago Denver had sweltered in the high nineties. Next weekend, according to the forecasts, was the first warning of possible snow showers in the foothills. The orange and red of ash and maple would splash into the long stretches of evergreen conifers. Later tonight, the evening air would feel as if it had been scrubbed clean by the snow-covered peaks before falling to the city streets. I don't want to leave this, she thought. *This is my home.*

The hills of Kentucky rolled. In September they were gold and dusted with gray and blue. She couldn't remember ever really looking at the landscape or feeling as if it was a part of her life. She'd spent most of her time watching the world out of the corners of her eyes, but she still remembered fragments of childhood. The quiet puff when a pussy cattail popped, the ratchet rhythm of crickets, the tickle of a squirrel taking seeds out of her hand—mostly she recalled lazy summer afternoons when it was too hot to move and almost too humid to breathe, and even Aunt Bitty rested.

Too bad those memories were so short. Each one segued into the sound of an argument.

A cluster of young women—probably from Metro College—strolled past her. Even in college, a long way from Fayette and the Gathering, she'd not traveled in a pack. That had been her life as a child. As a teen in detention and community college student, even the time spent waitressing, she'd stayed a loner, preferring to strike up one-on-one relationships with teachers and advisors. When she'd managed to transfer into a New York state college, she'd been a little less wary of people, though she always kept one eye on the nearest exit. The first person who had ever touched her with nothing but good feelings in mind had been a teaching assistant from the previous semester.

Her hands had been a revelation. CJ smiled to herself, because it was a very sweet memory. She liked women, and that was something she didn't have to hide for fear someone would take it away. Maybe, she mused, you had to have a bigger secret than being gay to make being out of the closet a non-event.

Lucy was waiting outside the brew pub, and waved a greeting

from the half block away. She was a very nice looking woman, probably considerate and strong in bed, and, after the constraints of her life caring for an ailing mother, ready for more than a little serious romping between the sheets. CJ already knew she wasn't going there. She wasn't even sure why she had said yes to Lucy's invitation, and wasn't willing to consider she had been proving to herself that she wasn't going to let one kiss from one woman change everything.

No, that kiss hadn't meant a thing. She wasn't staying in Denver when she ought to be gone. She wasn't telling some of her deepest secrets to total strangers, either. She wasn't ruling out, in advance, a potential new relationship that could be as undemanding, yet sensual, as the one she'd had with Abby.

"Are you ready for some brew?" Lucy was dashing in jeans and a Roadrunner booster jersey, and her short brown hair gleamed with gel. CJ was glad she'd chosen a dark blue long-sleeve rugby shirt and jeans. A suit would have been out of place.

"Absolutely. It was a long week."

"Yeah," Lucy said. A shadow flickered over her face. "I really needed to get out and it's more fun when you're not alone."

She held the door for CJ, who charmed the hostess into a cozy table near the window. "We can start the ogling early," she told Lucy as they sat down. She pointed out a leather-clad very high femme—probably a bartender on her way to work at one of LoDo's clubs.

Lucy peered after the woman, then gave CJ a smile. "I feel like a kid in a candy store. At first I thought my brothers were planning the funeral too soon, but now I'm glad it's behind me. My mother would want me to move on. She said she was stealing my youth."

"Sounds like she cared about you."

Lucy nodded, her eyes glistening. "She did. I was talking to Em last night and she's right. I mean, I deal with grieving people all the time. People feel guilty that their loved one died because it makes their life easier, and I'm only human, too."

"There are people who feel glad someone died because it gets that person out of their life." CJ added quickly, "You must see that at the shelter sometimes."

"Yeah." Lucy gave her a searching look. "Good riddance sometimes comes to mind—can't say it breaks my heart when some guy who gets his jollies off kids ends up dead in prison. Okay, that's a pretty grim topic right off the bat, isn't it? Let's order some food."

A brief discussion led to a happy agreement to share the grilled pizza of the day and sample the Railyard Ale and the Two Guns Pilsener.

When the waitress delivered two tall glasses of amber and tawny ale, Lucy's eyes lit up. "To a night out," she toasted.

They clinked the glasses, sipped, swapped glasses and sipped again. CJ felt a sense of relief as they smiled at each other. Her instincts said that right now Lucy was looking for friends, not lovers.

"Em never said how you got sent our way. How'd you cross paths with Denver's finest?"

"It's a very short story involving a little too much wine at a business lunch, and a stop sign. I wasn't over the legal limit but community service saved me seven hundred dollars or so. And I have to say…it's been interesting."

"It can be heartbreaking sometimes. The holidays especially. Christmas night. New Year's Day—the night after all the bowl games. It also gets all my urges to have kids out of my system." Lucy tried the pilsener again.

"Not in your plans?" CJ thought Lucy was probably closer to forty than she was. "Not mine, either. I mean, not from my womb, at least." She gestured vaguely at that part of her body.

"I work a lot of nights and I like it. Plus, well, I know lots of people in my line of work with great families, but I don't want to raise a child around death the way I was raised. I've got a couple of nephews and that's working for me. Plus, well, I always feel like I'm going to break babies. I'm not a natural like Karita."

"Amen to that."

"I've never actually seen anything like it." Lucy leaned back in her chair. "A baby screaming to high heaven and one touch—kid starts to quiet. She gives off such a soothing aura."

Tell me about it, CJ wanted to say as she swallowed more of the earthy, ripe ale. But she didn't want Karita touching her the way she would a child, though, quite the opposite. That was part of the problem, she realized. She didn't want to be anything but a woman to Karita. No pity, no healing, no friends with benefits comfort. That's why she wasn't really jealous of Emily, she realized. Emily didn't have what CJ wanted from Karita. She hoped her tone seemed normal as she said, "She's a special person."

Lucy nodded after she sipped again. "I think what amazes me most about her is, given her looks, she could model or hang on some tennis star's arm and live the good life. Instead she's helping battered women and defenseless animals."

The waitress delivered their pizza, carved it up and plated two slices, sparing CJ any need to respond. CJ deeply inhaled the mixed aromas of olives, sun-dried tomatoes, goat cheese and linguisa. "Jeez, that's like a drug."

"Perfectly legal, too."

Lucy didn't talk about Karita again until they were picking out seats on the bleachers at the soccer game. CJ managed to mention Karita to see if Lucy would talk about her more—how fixated was that, she asked herself—and Lucy didn't disappoint her.

"I was so wrapped up with my mom I knew I didn't have the energy to really date anybody seriously, so I never asked her out. Plus, being Karita, she'd get sucked up in the health care with my mom too, that's who she is. And we'd be about that, not actually building our own life. Besides, she's really a very happy woman with the life she has, and I think I'd make her unhappy. I'd be wanting a plan for next year, one for five years from now. That's who I am. And that's not her. She needs someone maybe a little more grounded than her, but who can still fly. I'm pretty earthbound."

"So am I," CJ said. She and Lucy had a lot in common, and if Lucy, who knew Karita better, thought she'd squash some of the joie de vivre out of Karita, then CJ would certainly do the same. She's not for you, remember? You have other plans. Sure, she mocked herself. Other plans that include thinking of this town as your home, thinking you even *deserve* a place to call home.

The two teams took the field, eliciting spectator cheers. Most of the crowd was female, which CJ certainly didn't mind. The players looked young and fragile, that is, until the game started. Then their intensity and skill flashed like knives and the match was on.

Lucy knew the sport and was happy to explain rules and the general defensive and offensive gambits. CJ was content to enjoy the spectacle. She caught on enough to know that whenever a player with the ball got close to the other team's goal it was time to stand up.

She jumped to her feet with Lucy at just such a moment. "Is she getting in the lane?"

"Yeah, but she's no Kylee Hanavan. The squad is still good, though. I don't know if we'll get another championship, but— run it down the lane, pass it—score!"

The crowd went crazy. The Roadrunner women on the field ran around in circles, then dogpiled on each other. Women, rolling around on the ground, especially young and nubile ones, well, CJ thought, that was worth the price of admission.

Karita stifled a yawn. She'd just checked the ears of her fortieth or fiftieth dog and felt stupid with exhaustion. It had been her fault that half the marmots had gotten out. Pam had been a good sport, and had helped her catch the terrified creatures that hadn't escaped from the compound via some hidden marmot-sized tunnel. She was pretty sure she'd hear their whistles and chirps in her sleep.

Nann sank down on the waiting room sofa. Karita was pretty sure she was asleep before her head touched the back cushion.

From the window facing the parking lot, Pam said, "Nann?"

"Uhm." Nann was trying to open her eyes but was having no success.

"Nann, there's a llama in the parking lot."

"Just one?"

"That I can see, yeah."

"Damn. Ought to be two." Nann burrowed her head farther into the back of the sofa. "They're happier in pairs and packs. Herd animals."

"Nann?" Karita joined Pam at the window. "Pam's not making it up."

Karita led the way outside to join the tired-looking woman who had the llama on a lead. She hoped it was full-grown because it was an inch or two taller than she was.

The llama reared back its white head to give her and Pam a haughty look, then it promptly spat.

"I found it in my backyard, down the highway." The woman's gray hair was disheveled, and her khaki trousers were spattered with mud, but she looked pleased with herself. "My partner said I was nuts to try, but I got my dog's leash around it and it calmed right down, except for the spitting."

Pam took the leash, saying, "I wish I'd paid more attention to the llamas when I was in Peru."

Nann arrived, looking half-awake. "You were in Peru? So was I." To the Good Samaritan she said, "You did great, Wanda. Catching llamas is hard work, especially when they're isolated. Keep that Dalmatian of yours away from them—she could get kicked."

"Sadie didn't want to play with something that big."

"Smart dog. Well, if you see any others, call and we'll help get them under control. There aren't any llama farms near here, so I'll have to assume there's a distraught owner further down the canyon."

175

With a tired nod, the woman said she'd keep an eye out. "The elk are on the move, by the way. I had two bulls and two herds of a dozen cows go through my yard. It's always like that when there's a fire. At least they're not bugling."

"You can say that again." Karita kept a wary eye out for more spitting. "First time I heard an elk bugle was the middle of the night and I swear I thought it was the banshees."

"Llamas don't have a rutting season," Nann said. She thumped the animal on the neck and Karita noticed that it was not spitting at Nann. Typical.

She gave the llama a wide berth. To Wanda she said, "Do you need a lift home?"

"I would appreciate that, actually. It's about a mile."

Karita went inside for her keys while Nann and Pam walked along the gravel path that led to the back of the facility.

Nann was excitedly answering Pam's questions. "You can hire a llama wrangler trail guide and a couple of llamas as pack animals for some of the more strenuous hikes. It's really fun. They're very adaptable."

"Where were you in Peru?" Pam had one hand casually on the llama's flank, and looked totally at ease. "Before I went to law school I spent three months in Peru with Greenpeace."

Karita lost sight of them and didn't think they even noticed she had left.

By the time she got back from driving Wanda home—Wanda and her partner had lived in Kittredge for thirty years and Karita was welcome to borrow any tools she might need—Nann had the llama calmed and Pam finally looked as tired as Karita felt. To her immense relief, Howie had arrived, which meant Nann could finally go home.

Karita gave Nann's brother a broad smile. "She got you here again, did she?"

"I'm the only vet who works cheap enough for her."

Howie's wife appeared from the back. "And she gets two for the price of one. All y'all should go home. I just heard on the CB they've got the fire contained."

Nann gave a weak hurrah, and promptly gathered up her jacket and keys. "Thank you both so much. I wouldn't have survived without you." She glanced briefly at Karita, then her gaze lingered on Pam. "I really appreciate it."

"It was my pleasure." Pam's smile belied her exhausted tone. "It's too late this season, but maybe next spring we'll give a llama trek a try."

Gran, Karita thought to herself, maybe it's not magic, maybe it's just wishful thinking and lots of luck, but whatever it is, it's a good thing. She couldn't help but notice how easy it was to spot the promising chemistry between Pam and Nann, and between Emily and Anita. Was she able to draw any such easy conclusions about her and CJ? Life's little ironies weren't all that funny.

She walked out with Pam to their cars. It didn't seem possible that it was only just past nine.

Pam was yawning again, and Karita asked, "Do you want some dessert or another bite to eat?"

"I don't know why I'm so tired."

"You just spent the last three hours getting up and down off the ground, and hauling fifty pound bags of feed. We're both going to be sore tomorrow."

"We could get a drink at the Little Bear, up in Evergreen."

"My place is just a half-mile that way." Karita pointed southeast. "I make very good coffee and I'm pretty sure I have a couple of chocolate chip cookies left. I think that will get you safely home far better than a drink."

Pam nodded agreement. "You're right. One sip of alcohol and I'll be asleep."

As she led the way toward home, Karita hoped that Pam hadn't misunderstood the invitation. She had gone with her first impulse, which was to offer whatever Pam needed so she didn't fall asleep on her forty or so minute drive home. Even though Pam and Nann had hit it off, technically, Pam was still Karita's date.

As she pulled into the driveway she realized Pam was going to be her first visitor in quite a while, and she hadn't mowed the grass recently and the garage door opener still didn't work. She was relieved, however, to see that she had done the dishes that morning. But the weatherstripping project was spread out all over the living room.

"I inherited this place from my grandmother. It's cute, but it needs work."

"Great location, though." Pam looked a little bit nervous, as if she, too, had realized that they were two single women on a strange but official date, and now alone in a place where a bedroom was available.

They continued chatting while Karita made coffee, and Pam asked about her parents. Cookies restored their energy, as did the coffee, and it was well after ten before Pam said, "I should be going or I'll get sleepy all over again. Thank you, this was perfect."

"It's the least I could do."

"This was probably the most unusual date I've ever had, but it was fun." Pam paused at the door. "Can I be honest and say that I had hoped maybe the night would end differently?"

Karita tried a joke. "You mean ending without llama spit on you?"

"No, I meant like this." On tiptoe, she kissed Karita lightly, once, then kissed her again more firmly. "Something along those lines."

"Oh, like that." Pam was no frog, and Karita had to admit her lips were tingling. The memory of CJ's lips—there was no resemblance between the sweet little buzz she felt right now and what she had felt with CJ. A few weeks ago she might have mistaken the buzz for more than it was.

"Is it the llama spit that was distracting?" Pam smiled, though her eyes were serious. She searched Karita's expression and evidently found some reassurance there, because she went on, "I'd been thinking all week that it would be a kind of tidal wave sort of thing to kiss you."

"Even without llama spit I'm not sure about the tidal wave. I like you, and maybe we just had to find out since we're both single." Karita paused. "Now we know."

"Heck, I did wonder what it would be like to kiss someone eight inches taller than I am. I'll cross that off my To Do list." Pam stepped out onto the front porch and Karita followed her to her car. "Do you think Nann will need help tomorrow afternoon?"

Karita did a little dance behind Pam's back, then composed herself before Pam could see her. "I definitely think she'll need help. And she really likes the carrot-ginger soup from the little store up the street."

Pam settled into the driver's seat and gave a little wave. Karita waved back, all the while thinking that, for a date, it had turned out quite well. Karita couldn't help but wonder how Lucy and CJ were faring. Probably sans llama spit, for one thing.

Gran had never taught her any charms to do harm. Elves didn't bring bad feelings into the world, she'd said. Nevertheless, Karita took a deep breath of the cool night air, cleared her mind and wished Lucy a date just as successful in every way as the one she'd just had with Pam.

Pam beeped her horn and Karita waved one last time before going inside, all by herself.

"That was great fun," CJ said as they reached the spots where they'd parked side-by-side. "Thank you so much for inviting me."

Lucy leaned back on the trunk of her car. "No, thank you. I really wanted to get out and it was fun to show off my useless knowledge of the sport. Someday, I will be on Jeopardy and the categories will be soccer, soccer gear, women who play soccer, beer and Brandi Chastain. What is a black sports bra, Alex?"

CJ laughed. "That'll make sense to me at some point, right?" The last few hours had been very pleasant—she'd thought of Daria only in passing and even less frequently of her mother and that very old pain.

"So, CJ." Lucy abruptly looked serious. "This is that awkward point in our date when, since I did the asking, I have to wonder if I can kiss you."

Taken aback, and undeniably charmed by Lucy's forthright approach, CJ could only say, "It's not about whether you can, but whether you want to, isn't it?"

"Your opinion counts, of course. I'm just thinking it might be worth the possible slapping."

"I'm not the slapping type." Oh, CJ thought, that wasn't exactly a no, was it?

"Good. Here goes."

Still grinning, Lucy pulled CJ close. Their lips brushed and CJ smiled into the kiss. Lucy's firm, athletic body was warm, and the arms that slipped around her waist were strong, protective even. A woman could do so much worse, she thought, but what she already knew was confirmed: definitely the wrong arms, the wrong body. She opened her eyes to find that Lucy's were open as well.

Lucy laughed against her lips. "Okay, how about we stop now?"

"You bet."

Lucy put her hands in her pockets, but she didn't seem the least bit embarrassed. "So now we know. We get to be friends."

CJ's smile faded and she said sincerely, crazily, like a woman who didn't have reasons to bolt for the nearest state line, "I'd like that."

As always, however, she didn't get to stay crazy. Alone in her sparse apartment it was easier to recall the avaricious glint in Daria's eyes. There was no way she could keep a friend, not when she had other priorities. Not when at any moment her common sense might win and she'd gather up the money and the list and head for some place new.

Showered and ready for bed, CJ ran her finger over the last three names as if they were written in Braille instead of the scrawling hand of a fourteen-year-old. She had no business thinking she could have a home and anything else that went with it. She forced herself to read the oldest newspaper clippings. "Minister, father of three, shot dead" was the headline she never wanted to see again, but it was in her life, forever.

Chapter 12

Karita could live with the fact that Susan House wasn't speaking to her. Yesterday and today there had been a distinct chill in the air, but at least there had been no outbursts at any of the staff. Maybe counseling would eventually help, but for the moment, Karita comforted herself with the knowledge that Pam had officially moved on, and that was all that mattered.

Marty, on the other hand, was the same as always. She was starting to close up her desk and make her log for a hectic Tuesday when he stopped at her desk with a photo of his wife holding the adorable little Pomeranian. "All settled in her new home."

"Did you give her a name, yet?"

"Well, my daughter likes PomPom and I like Stays-Off-Furniture."

Grinning, Karita shook her head. "That's a losing battle. Poms are so social. They love eye contact and that means up in your lap. What does Minna say?"

"PomPom."

"So, I'm thinking PomPom is the winner."

Marty took back the photo. "You'd be right."

"Look at it this way. It's smaller than a llama and it doesn't spit." Her phone chirped before she could explain and Marty headed for his office. She tapped the line and greeted the caller.

"May I speak to Karita Hanssen, please?"

"I'm Karita. How may I help you?" Even before she finished speaking, Karita knew who it was. The husky voice was unmistakable.

"It's CJ. I'm working on this project for Emily and I have a question I thought you could answer."

Karita was so glad Marty had left—her ears felt like hot irons against the side of her head. "I'll do my best."

"I've been reading some of the findings of the research into domestic violence and different social events. Like you all said, there's a link between incidences of battering and sporting events. Football, auto racing, hockey, basketball, the works. Given that, would she be opposed to trying to get money out of people who might be big supporters of those sports?"

"I don't know," Karita said slowly. "I'm not aware that any of the sports have even acknowledged the research as valid. They make the same kind of argument that alcohol manufacturers do—drinking doesn't cause drunk driving. People getting behind the wheel while drunk causes drunk driving."

"I didn't mean the teams or the owners, but the big spender fans. Some of whom might rub shoulders with a persuasive woman like Marguerite Brownell."

It sounded ambitious, and far beyond anything Emily had envisioned. "Are you talking about raising guilt money out of them?"

CJ's voice warmed with humor. "I wouldn't call it that. I was just thinking that if we can get Brownell, or someone like her, to put on a bell, she could lead a herd to support the After the Big Game program for children and their mothers."

"That has a nice ring to it." Karita was impressed. "It can't hurt to ask. I have a feeling you could persuade her to agree to anything."

CJ was silent for a moment. Her voice wasn't as warm when she said, "I wouldn't want to persuade her to do anything against her principles."

"Of course not. I didn't mean that you would. I was just… teasing."

"It's okay. Thanks for listening. I was going to try this out on Emily tonight."

"Make it before seven thirty—she's got a sort of coffee date thing."

"Will do. Thanks again."

Karita mulled over their exchange, but could glean nothing useful from it. Her day had brightened immeasurably however, knowing that she'd see CJ again tonight.

CJ put down the handset, asking herself what she had hoped to gain by calling Karita at work. So she'd heard Karita's voice and knew she was alive. What had she expected? Karita to announce she was either dating or not dating that cute young lawyer?

There was a commotion at the door to her office, and she heard a stifled giggle, then whispering. Annoyed, she called out, "What's up?"

Burnett peeked around the jamb, glanced behind him, then gave CJ a huge smile. With a theatrical leap he filled the doorway, arms and legs spread. "Tah-duh!"

"What? You got a commitment from Cray?"

"No, silly woman! Even better!" He danced forward and she realized that half the office was behind him. Tre carried a paper plate with a coffee shop muffin in the middle, and a lit candle stuck in the middle of that. Jerry brought up the rear with a mixed expression of indulgence and…envy?

"It's not my birthday," CJ said.

"No, it's not." Juliya opened the Metro section of *The Denver Post* to the inside back page.

Burnett burst into, "Foooooooor, she's a jolly good fellow…" and the rest of the crowd joined in.

"Is this my missing newspaper?" CJ looked down at the bottom inside corner where Juliya was pointing. The headline read "Three-Year Sales Champ Named Denver's Woman Realtor of the Year."

Next to the headline was the photograph of her from the company's Web site.

The feeling that suffused her—hot and embarrassed and pleased, all mixed together—took her breath away. She wanted to laugh because the next thing she thought was that nothing so nice had happened to her ever before, with the exception of Karita kissing her.

For a shining moment she sat there, "gobsmacked," to quote Tre. Her colleagues finished singing and burst into applause.

"It's about time," Juliya announced. "Sales champ is an understatement because you don't get credit for all the tips you pass on. When I hit that slump last year the lead on that medical group saved my life."

"Blow out the candle," Tre encouraged her. "I think you deserve it because the Vietnamese Chamber of Commerce is signing tomorrow— "

"And Cray says he's going to do a blueprint—"

"That stack of business cards you got at the Mile High Round Table was a gold mine—"

"The South Metro Economic Development meetings turned out to be a great payoff—"

CJ blew out the candle and was glad of the chance to hide her face. Everyone was saying such nice things, but they didn't know that she only passed on tips and leads she didn't think she could use and it seemed a shame that someone else couldn't get the payoff. She wasn't the nice person they seemed to think—she had them all conned, didn't she?

It hurt to think of them all that way, as merely her cons and not part of a team. Wasn't it realistic, though?

There was no way the muffin would feed everybody, but she chopped it into wedges and invited others to share. She did it to save the calories, not because she was unselfish, she told herself brutally.

"Here's the best part," Juliya said, after licking her fingers. She pulled the first section of the paper from underneath the Metro pages. "Right up here—there you are!"

A teasertag line directed readers to learn about the woman named Realtor of the Year. It must be a slow news day.

Sunlight from the window behind her turned cold. Her vision swam.

Juliya's exultant voice came from far away. "Your picture came out so well, even the small version. Front page of the *Post*! You'll have to get extra copies for your family!"

She couldn't leave without seeing Karita one last time. She wanted to leave her ideas for Emily's fund-raising, too. If she'd actually done something good for someone, they could damn well get a chance to use it. She didn't want to go but now she was paying the price of success. Do a great job and your picture ends up on the front page of the paper. Who knew?

Every corner in the financial district had a newspaper stand, or at least felt like it did. A glance in the window at Gracie's had her likeness casually spread on every table. Little versions of her face stared back at her wherever she looked, like something out of a Hitchcock film. Daria would find her now. Any of them could find her now.

She didn't remember driving home, but as she got out of the car she automatically checked the entrance, alleys and nearby parked cars in her apartment complex. She peeled off the business clothes that represented CJ Roshe and pulled on jeans, sneakers and a long-sleeved shirt. A plain backpack got stuffed with the bundles of fifties—the gun she relocked in the safe. Someone would find it, but there was no helping that. She actually hoped it was the authorities because the gun would finally be disposed of safely. She reassured herself that her fingerprints from the only minute she had ever held it were no longer on it, and hadn't been since she'd reclaimed it from the irrigation pipe where her father had stashed it.

Her yet unneeded winter parka she stuffed into the pack on top of the money, then put it in her largest suitcase. A couple of pairs of shoes, slacks and a few shirts and undergarments went into the case as well. She got the file folder with her list from her office and pushed it down amongst the clothes, decided she would take her laptop after all and then zipped the suitcase closed. She'd dump her cell phone and BlackBerry after seeing Emily. Her car she'd leave at the Salt Lake City airport though she intended to take the train toward the north from there. Half the people from the Gathering knew how to track a car's vehicle ID number—they knew how to eradicate it from the vehicle, too—but few would have the moxie to trace her passport through Canadian customs.

Canada would be okay. They even allowed gay marriage, not that it would ever do her any good. She could learn to end her sentences in a question. Curling might be as much fun as soccer. She wouldn't miss work, wouldn't wonder if Burnett had made his first big deal, not even if Emily raised a pile of cash. There was only one thing she would really miss, damn it. It was painfully clear that only one thing counted.

Why did she have to find out that something could matter to her as much as this, only to have to run such a short time later? Don't say it isn't fair, she told herself. Karma dances to its own tune. You were kissed by an angel and changed forever. It was greedy to have dreamed of more.

Rationality wasn't her strong point, right then. She knew, without a doubt, that Daria would show up at her place of business tomorrow. She'd hint, make it clear she could humiliate CJ, drop a clue or two about her past. When no one else was paying attention, Daria would talk about the Kentucky tipline that paid for information about fugitives, but all would be well if CJ paid. And paid.

That wasn't the scary part, though. It was the way they would try to get her back. Remind her of all the great cons she'd done, what a natural she obviously was. Her own DNA would betray her. All those ancestors with careers as thieves would try to drag her back into the life. She'd only gotten out of it before because prison gave her a chance to make a break for it. She wasn't going back to prison again. Television could romanticize life behind bars, but she hadn't forgotten. She didn't want to find out if the memories of detention could negate the call of the thief inside her.

Daria scared her, but it was her own nature that had always terrified her.

Canada it was. She didn't know was how easy or hard it would be to get ID in Canada. Last time she'd had to do it the world had been pre-jihad, pre-speed-of-light information. Nevertheless, she'd go so far north it wouldn't be worth it to any of them to come looking for her.

She rolled the suitcase out of her apartment and didn't look back. She thought she might be hungry, and it was a habit to crave coffee. The sun was setting in crimson due to wildfires in the foothills, but she didn't look overlong at the beautiful mountains. There were mountains in Canada.

Like the drive home, the cross-town journey to the shelter was a blur. She took the open spot right in front of the house and saw no one in the vicinity. With only the folio containing her materials for Emily in hand she walked briskly to the front porch and rang the bell. Less than an hour and she would be on her way.

A minute later the door opened and Karita was there, smiling at her in shy greeting as she held the door widely so CJ could enter. "Congratulations, Realtor of the Year."

"Woman Realtor of the Year. The man gets announced tomorrow. You saw the paper."

"Yeah, on a newsstand when I was leaving work. You just missed Emily. She left with Anita about five minutes ago. I doubt she'll be more than a half hour, though. She knows you're expected and Tuesdays the clients tend to arrive later in the evening."

"No problem," CJ said. The sight of Karita weakened her resolve. Her head was losing to her heart, and didn't want to hear that losing now would be losing the whole game. She ached to be closer, to hide inside the reality of the silver light. It was a weak moment, wanting Karita to somehow cradle her in safety, to rescue her from the piranhas. But the piranhas would then gnaw on Karita instead, and CJ was not going to make her own life easier by putting her past into someone else's present, not if she could help it.

Karita was chattering about the ways Tuesday nights differed from Friday nights. "We usually only accept women escaping a situation that happened in the last twelve hours, but tonight we have two clients who are in the system and need a stay-over in transition from a halfway house to a group home. They tend to be women without kids since those with kids get into a slightly higher priority in the system."

"So tonight's not a night when you need extra staff on hand." CJ tried to commit the long, lean body to memory. Karita was all lines in her legs and arms, but then her neck and hands curved. The smooth silk of her hair framed the cheekbones, the lips, the shoulders—it was so easy to see her as that Madonna but nothing about the way CJ felt was ethereal.

"Not usually, though Ulli is here most Tuesdays. She lives in the neighborhood and gives a few hours to check the kitchen supplies and make up a shopping list."

CJ was introduced to the gray-haired, grandmotherly Ulli, who clucked and tsk'd her way through an inventory of the cupboards.

As if to make a liar of her, a police department social worker with a client in tow arrived and Karita took both of them into the dining room for the paperwork. The kitchen seemed chilly and dark without her. After just a few minutes the social worker left and CJ chatted absently with Ulli, all the while going back and forth between the memory of what would likely be the only kiss she'd ever share with Karita, and the knowledge that once she got a full tank of gas her next stop would be somewhere in Utah.

Maybe she should just leave the folio for Emily and go. Let Emily sort through the ideas. Emily didn't have the time to do any of them, nor the contacts, but maybe someone else would come along and implement it for her.

It took a moment for her to realize that the thumping she heard wasn't random. She'd been in the shelter long enough to do the logical thing—she looked at the monitors. She blinked at the one for the front porch—she only had a brief glimpse of a blue jacket that might have been a police officer's before the jacket's wearer reared back and smashed a baseball bat into the cubbyhole where the security camera was fastened. The monitor went blank and the next thump was clearly on the front door.

Her heart pounding, fingers refusing to obey her, CJ still managed to get the phone on Emily's desk to her ear and the buttons pressed for 9-1-1. Ulli had been kneeling on a counter, but was already next to CJ at the desk, who passed the handset over. "When the operator answers, just tell her what's happening. A really angry man with a baseball bat is pounding on the shelter door and has already taken out the security camera. Just tell them—"

Ulli began repeating CJ's words as CJ dashed for the dining room. Karita already had the door open and was encouraging the terrified client, who flinched violently at every blow to the door, to go upstairs.

"What's the procedure?" CJ put one arm around the client and half dragged her toward the stairs.

Karita's voice was shaky with adrenaline. "Tell them to lock themselves in their rooms, together if they want. And to stay there until a police officer tells them to come out."

CJ did as Karita instructed. One of the clients immediately took charge of the newcomer and locked the door with them both in her assigned room. The other client wouldn't answer her door at first, and CJ gave up trying to get an answer. She'd no sooner turned away when the door was opened a crack.

"You tell that bastard to leave me alone."

"We don't know who it is, but please stay put and keep your door locked."

"It's my bastard husband, that's who it is."

CJ could only see a pale eye and a hint of blond hair. "How do you know?"

"I told the son-of-a-bitch not to come looking for me here when I called him."

Skeptically, CJ asked, "What phone did you use?"

"I got one of those disposable cell phones."

"You were supposed to give that up while you stayed here!"

"I'm not letting Miss La-Dee-Dah downstairs burn my minutes."

CJ pointed a shaking finger. "He's here to get you. You've put everyone in danger."

The woman shut the door in CJ's face and turned the lock. Damn it, CJ thought, I don't care what Emily says, some people don't deserve help. She was only a few feet away by the time she heard the woman yelling into her phone. The thumping on the door stopped, so maybe their screaming match would distract the husband until help arrived.

The crashing of breaking glass told her she'd been too optimistic. She could hear his uninhibited ranting, which included ironically calling out, "Open up! This is the police!" Maybe he was a cop gone berserk.

Glad of her sure-footed sneakers, she skittered around the corner at the bottom of the stairs, frantically looking for Karita.

"You stay on the line with the police," Karita was saying to Ulli. "Get in Em's office and lock that door."

"We should all get in there." CJ cleared the kitchen door. "He's not in yet, but any second."

Karita screamed a warning, and CJ ducked as the husband yelled, "Wrong, bitch! I'm already here."

Duck, scramble, get under—it all came back to her. It was a kitchen, staying low was crucial. Nothing hot on the stove. Knives, Aunt Bitty enjoyed throwing knives. CJ was crawling under the farmhouse table in an instant, kicking the chairs out from under it into her assailant's path. She didn't know how long she would have to last, but she hoped to get to the other side of the room before he did, and then on the other side of the office door with Ulli and Karita. With the three of them to brace it, they might hold him off until help arrived.

"Where's my wife?" The table jumped in place from the impact of the baseball bat.

Out the other side, CJ lunged for the office door. Ulli was in the far corner, clutching the phone. CJ started to pull the door shut before she realized Karita was not in the room with them.

She threw the door open again and felt the blood drain from her face. Karita was standing within reach of the baseball bat. Hands at her sides, she made steady eye contact with the crazed man. He panted, momentarily stymied as she stood her ground.

"I will tell you where she is, but you have to put the bat down first."

"I can find her myself."

A security guard, CJ thought. The blue jacket, the dark polyester pants, vaguely like a police officer's, but not. Maybe a gun, maybe not.

Her voice steady and calm, Karita said, "I know which room she's in. The police are on their way. You only have a minute to choose. Put the bat down. It's your one chance to be unarmed when the police get here."

A siren rose in the distance, supporting Karita's suggestion.

"He's high on something." The words were out of CJ's mouth before she was aware of her impression or that she was going to speak.

Her pounding heart muffled his words, but CJ was pretty sure he sneered, "I'll take you with me," as he leveled a Babe Ruth swing at Karita's head.

192

Karita's disbelief was nearly fatal, but she threw herself out of the way in time. The bat embedded in the Sheetrock behind where Karita's head had been moments before. CJ shoved the table as hard as she could, catching him in the hip while he tried to free the bat from the wall.

He shoved the table back at her so quickly the edge caught her in her belly. Doubled over, she slammed her knee into a chair. Her knee buckled and she hit the linoleum hard, taking the weight on her elbow and wrist. Lots of things went pop but all she could think about was Karita's proximity to Aunt Bitty—no, not Aunt Bitty, that asshole with the bat.

Karita didn't think he'd kill her.

CJ knew he would.

Karita was backpedaling across the kitchen, putting herself between the maniac and the office where Ulli was yelling desperately into the phone. How long had it been, CJ wondered. It felt like forever—three, maybe four minutes. The siren seemed no closer.

She struggled back to her feet, picked up the nearest thing to hand—the dish drainer, and threw it at him. She completely missed and thought how embarrassed Lucy would have been by that throw but he focused on her, like a crazed, huffing bull.

"Karita, get in the office and lock the door. I can take care of myself!"

"No!"

"I can't protect both of us—you make sure Ulli is safe."

Karita ducked inside the door, but didn't shut it. "Don't be stupid, CJ. Run for it and I'll lock this!"

CJ couldn't put much weight on her knee and she didn't want Karita to know it. Karita was still an easier target and his attention was starting to slide away from CJ back to the much closer prey.

CJ's hand closed on a mug and she did Lucy proud with that one, catching him on the shoulder. His grin was feral as he decided she made better sport.

"Come on, big man." CJ let all her hate for him and his type show in her voice. "I'm not afraid of you. You think I haven't seen people die? I pulled the trigger myself once, so come on, big man. Show me what you got. I've got an aunt who would have grand-slammed you out of the park by now. You going to let some woman hurt you and get away with it?"

She backed slowly toward the rear entrance, thinking about the shelves there she might be able to pull over to give her time to escape in spite of her throbbing knee.

"You cunts are all alike," he snarled.

"Oh, you think like that—no wonder you can't satisfy a woman."

"I'll take care of you, cunt, and you'll feel like one before I'm done."

Without warning, CJ was seized from behind and pulled to the floor. Something sharp stabbed into her hip. She struggled against the binding arms.

A commanding voice yelled, "Police! Freeze!"

Emily said in her ear, "Get down. Shit! Stop fighting me."

CJ went limp. A real live policewoman, in a real live uniform, with a very real gun, went on shouting orders and in only a few seconds their assailant was face down on the floor and the baseball bat kicked into a corner.

The officer barked something into the radio on her shoulder. CJ stayed where she was, pretty sure her head was on a particularly cushy part of Emily's body. Sirens got louder, then abruptly stopped.

"Is anyone injured? Where's the blood from?"

Karita, sounding a great deal more shaky, said, "It's mine. I whacked myself on the door. It's just a scrape."

CJ decided it was time to sit up. Her wrist and elbow screamed at her, then she felt that sharp pain in her hip again. Shifting in place she saw that she'd landed on a garden claw that had fallen out of the little basket where Emily kept clippers and a pair of worn gloves. It could have been worse. The clippers had quite a point on them. The tines on the claw had put a hole in her jeans, damn it.

Authoritative pounding began on the front door and Emily tiptoed across the kitchen to let in the other police officers. Handcuffs were produced, and the jerk was finally dragged off the kitchen floor.

Officer Lopez—Emily hastily corrected herself after calling her Anita—re-holstered her gun. "I have to do ten pages of paperwork now, just for drawing my weapon."

"You could have just shot him," Emily said drily.

"Would have saved time. You shoot somebody and they give you a stenographer and you don't have to write a single thing." Anita's ferocious stare had already softened to concern as she turned to Karita. "Are you sure that's just a scrape?"

"Yes." From where CJ sat on the floor she could see Karita showing her arm to Emily. "It's not too bad."

"Baby, baby, you're supposed to get to a safe place. What were you thinking?" Emily put her arms around Karita and squeezed her tight. CJ could have hated Emily right then, but she was too shocked for anything more than envy to get through.

Karita gave a wheezy laugh and CJ realized she was crying with the release of tension. "I was thinking that you'd never leave here again because look what happened when you left me in charge."

Everybody, including a couple of the newly arrived cops, laughed. It got even more raucous when Ulli indignantly pronounced, "That man should have to clean all this up!"

"How did he know to come here?" Anita had a notebook out and was already scrawling in it.

"His wife called him. She hid her cell phone, got settled, then called him up to needle him." CJ felt something wet on her sore hip. "They were screaming at each other on the phone when he busted down the window."

"So much for the impact resistant safety glass." Emily finally let go of Karita. "I need to check on the clients and then I've got to find them another place to go. We're not secure with that window all knocked out."

Anita frowned. "Do you have a handyperson who can put up some plywood?"

"You're talking to her."

Anita and Emily disappeared in the direction of the stairs. CJ considered if she ought to try to stand up. Karita was setting chairs upright and making sure Ulli sat down. "I'll make tea."

When Karita's back was turned CJ dragged herself into a chair. It got absurdly quiet for a moment, then Karita finally looked at her.

"He was going to kill you."

"No." CJ hoped she sounded cocky. She didn't want to look down at her hip. "He was going to try. There's a difference."

"You should have run for it."

"That would have meant leaving you." There was way too much truth in her voice, she realized too late.

Karita's eyes shimmered like sunlight on snow. "I couldn't go either."

Aunt Bitty was still in the room, or at least it felt like she was to CJ. Aunt Bitty, throwing one of the little knives she liked, whispering in her ear, "But CJ, isn't that what you're going to do as soon as you can get out of here? Run for it?"

Only if she's safe, CJ answered. She comes first. *I'm such a fool.* "I couldn't leave you alone with a homicidal maniac. You or Ulli," she added.

Karita just looked at her with those incredible blue eyes. Time did that strange thing again, seeming to slow, but not really. They were the only two people alive until the kettle whistled.

CJ watched Karita make up a milky blend for Ulli, delivered with a heartfelt hug. "I'm so sorry this happened while you were here."

Ulli sipped before saying, "You see scenes like that in movies and it isn't real at all."

CJ said quietly, "No, it really isn't."

196

Karita gave her another of those searching looks, all blue and icy fire. "You'd know, wouldn't you?" She set down a sugared mug of tea. "Drink up—oh my God, CJ, you're bleeding."

"It's nothing. I'll patch it up at home." She sipped the tea automatically and her brain started working again. Any minute Officer Lopez would come back and want statements. She'd want CJ to press charges too, and sooner or later someone would want her testimony and she did not intend to be around when they did. That loser could actually end up with a decent lawyer who'd happily go looking for reasons to call CJ Roshe a liar. For all she knew, fingerprints of juveniles, even those with sealed records, could be in the law enforcement databases. Her fingerprints would turn up a match to a young woman who'd gone missing from the hospitality of the great State of Kentucky. "I need to be going, actually."

"I'll get Em."

"No, Karita, please." CJ caught her hand. "Please. I can't talk to the cops. I can't be involved in this. I have to go."

"You're not accused of anything here, he is—" Karita paled. "You weren't making it up, were you? What you told him."

"I said a lot of things, and it wasn't all true." CJ knew she sounded desperate. "I never meant you to know. It's not important. I can't talk to the police."

"They'll just find you tomorrow or the next day for your statement."

CJ burned her mouth on a last gulp of the tea, and pushed herself to her feet. Her wrist and elbow yelped at her to sit down again, but it was her knee that really screamed. Her hip she didn't really feel much beyond the sticky trickle of blood. "I have to go."

Using the chairs and wall she made it to the back door.

"CJ, wait!"

She kept going. Selfish to the core, she thought. She didn't want to spare Karita anything. She was running away because she didn't want to see the look on Karita's face when she put all the

197

pieces together. Every word she'd used to goad that creep had been true.

"CJ!" Karita was beside her, trying to get her to stop.

"That's not my name." But it was—she wanted it to be. She felt woozy.

"I don't care. You can't drive. Where are you going?"

"Canada."

"I'll go with you."

"Karita, you can't." In the dark alongside the house it was easier to find the right words to make Karita go back inside. "I'm not a cause of the week. I'm not a dark spot that a little bit of laughter and light will clear up. I'm a fucking black hole and you don't have that much to give me."

The deepening twilight robbed Karita's eyes of some of their light. "Let me help."

"What would you know about it?" CJ desperately searched for harsher words, knowing that Karita had to walk away, had to hate her, otherwise she would give into the weakness and throw herself into Karita's arms. She'd bloody and dirty the Madonna and lose the woman anyway. "I don't need the kind of Band-Aids you give out so easily. This week it's me. Last week some depressed lawyer. Before that Emily."

"Don't."

"I'm not saying it's wrong. It's who you are. You're like a hummingbird, defying reality, a beautiful mystery, spreading your sweetness to all the needy flowers. Well, I'm no pretty garden blossom and I don't need your brand of sugar."

"You're being an idiot, CJ." Karita made a little gulping sound that almost broke CJ's resolve.

"I'm not just some wounded puppy you can nurse back to wholeness. I'm the bad girl you were warned about."

"No, you're not. You might think you're bad, but you do good things."

A wave of dizziness reminded CJ that she didn't have much time. "You only think there's a heart of gold in here because I wanted you to think that."

"Stop it—"

"Don't you get it? *I killed somebody.*"

Karita gasped and put her hands to her mouth.

CJ limped away, her last salvo fired. At least it had been dark and she could blame the dimming of Karita's eyes on the absence of the moon.

Chapter 13

Fortunately, the police cruiser with the suspect had already left and the one that remained wasn't blocking CJ in. She used the remote to unlock the car, but the street was sloped and gravity worked against her as she struggled with the driver's door.

The door was abruptly propped open and CJ leaned on the car frame, fighting back tears.

"Please, Karita." She didn't even know what she was asking for anymore.

"Get in the other side. I'll drive you wherever you're going."

"I can't send you away again. I'm not strong enough."

"You tried." Karita almost sounded like she was laughing. "You really gave it your all."

"It was the truth."

Karita slipped an arm around her. "Only part of the truth. I have the feeling you left out some things."

She was warm and strong and CJ really didn't want to be weak, but it was hard not to lean on her. They hobbled around to the passenger door and Karita helped her get settled. Her hip and leg felt soaked and her knee was on fire.

Once in the driver's seat, Karita said, "You're right. It's easier for me to love a lot of things. It spares me getting in too deeply with anything that might hurt."

"You're in the wrong car to stick with that philosophy."

"I know that."

CJ gestured weakly. "Under your seat. I need my purse."

Karita fished it out. "Where do you need to go? Please tell me an emergency room."

"No. If I get treatment they can make me testify. Someone will find out who I am."

"You're not thinking clearly," Karita said. "They can't make you testify against your will. They're not even going to need your testimony. That guy is on his way to jail for a while, just for breaking into the shelter, and I fully intend to testify he swung that bat at me with all his strength."

"They'll tell me it's the right thing to do, and I'll have to do it because if I don't then I'm...then I'm really...no good."

"I don't understand," Karita said softly. She started the car. "But give me some time, would you?"

CJ flipped open her cell phone. The number was still on speed dial. She waited three rings, prepared to hang up if she got voice mail. Instead, a sleepy voice answered.

"I need your help, Abby," she said without preamble. "Will you be home for a while?"

"Yes, and I was sleeping, thank you. Can't it wait? I'm—great, you woke her up too."

"I'm sorry, it can't wait. I need a little...patching up."

Abby said a very bad word but the phone wasn't near CJ's ear anymore. The lifeline of Karita's voice grew distant. It wasn't anything like fainting, but more like someone was holding her under black water and she was too weak to struggle.

"How long will she be out?" Karita's gaze kept straying to CJ, who looked lifeless on Abby's sofa.

Abby looked up from scrubbing her hands at the sink in the

small kitchen. "Not long. She told me once she had low blood pressure which is probably why the blood loss hit her so hard. It looked like a lot more blood than it was."

"Those punctures were deep." Val, Abby's girlfriend, still had a disapproving crease between her eyebrows. Both women wore tees and jeans. A twin case of bed head was an unmistakable sign of having been woken from sleep.

"And could fester, though I think she bled freely long enough to flush the wound." Abby dried her hands and sat down at the little dinette with Karita. "Basic RICE treatment for her knee and wrist, though if I know CJ, she's not going to rest, compress or elevate it. Right now is the only ice she'll put on it, too. She's lucky I was home. We both just finished seventy-two hour shifts."

"And we woke you. I'm sorry about that." Karita's memory of the woman CJ had been seducing at Gracie's hadn't been inaccurate; Abby was attractive, not to mention smart enough to be a doctor. She was nothing like a hummingbird—was that CJ's euphemism for *flake*? The more she thought about the remark, the more it hurt.

"I can't say I ever expected CJ to call. It was never her strong suit." Abby's lips twisted in a half-bitter, half-resigned expression.

"How long were you together?" Karita had been wanting to ask that since the moment she'd seen the fleeting look of sorrow on Abby's face when CJ had collapsed onto the sofa.

"Together—that's really not the right word for it."

Val, looking uncomfortable, put a hand on Abby's shoulder. "I'm going back to bed."

"I'm really sorry," Karita repeated, once the bedroom door was closed. She lowered her voice. "Not that it would have changed my mind. CJ was insistent."

"She can be very persuasive."

"She's a keen observer of people." Inwardly, Karita mused that CJ had never tried to talk her into anything except leaving her alone as they left the shelter. Very likely she could have gotten just about anything she wanted. Maybe—and the fact was as hard to face as some of the things CJ had said to her—CJ just didn't want her 'brand of sugar.' "If 'together' isn't the right word for your relationship with CJ, what is?"

"Convenient. We dated at her convenience for the last two years. Not all her fault—I didn't have time for more until recently. And she's not a 'more' kind of woman." Abby's eyes held a warning.

Actually, Karita wanted to say, she thought CJ was definitely a more kind of woman. The problem was that she didn't think she could have more, and possibly didn't think she deserved more. Maybe her reluctance wasn't about Karita's brand of sugar at all. CJ resisted any brand of sugar that could tie her down. She might have said as much to Abby but CJ stirred on the sofa.

"Jesus, Abby, what did you give me?"

"A half a valium and a whole bunch of ibuprofen."

CJ turned her head and blinked a couple of times. "Who took my pants off?"

Abby smirked. "We all did, and you slept through it."

"I'll take you home when you're ready," Karita said. "You're going to be black and blue in a couple of places, and you've got three sets of two stitches on your hip."

"I can't go home."

"You can't stay here," Abby said firmly.

Karita decided Abby's tone was effective. She matched it as she said, "I'm taking you home, and I don't want to hear any more of that bad-person-gotta-run-for-it garbage."

"Huh?" Abby gave CJ a quizzical look. "What's she talking about?"

"Things nobody needs to know about." CJ moved the ice pack off her knee and swung her legs around to put her feet on the floor.

"I wouldn't stand up quickly if I were you." Abby spoke as if she was certain her advice wouldn't be heeded.

Karita wanted in the worst way to go to CJ and help, but

the hummingbird comment stung. The idea that CJ could see love, affection, caring, her desire to make people's live better as somehow shallow felt like Mandy, all over again. Was Emily's commitment to one thing doing more good? Nann—now there was obsession in a nutshell. Nann and Emily were peas in a pod. Women with a vision. What was wrong with being part of their visions if it gave her joy? She paid her way in this world.

CJ had ignored Abby, of course, and she wobbled in place.

"Oh, for Pete's sake." Karita got up to give CJ something solid to lean on while she got her bearings. "There's a difference between stubborn and pigheaded, you know."

Abby snorted.

CJ clamped one hand on Karita's arm. "This is my dream come true, that's for sure. You psychoanalyzing me with my ex."

Karita wasn't all that gentle as she lowered CJ to the chair she had vacated. "You'd better be nice to the woman who cleaned you up in the middle of the night. Plus you need something to wear so you still need her generosity."

"I've got another pair of pants in the car—in the back. There's a suitcase."

Karita made her way out to the parking lot to CJ's Trailblazer and found herself staring in surprise. There really was a suitcase, stuffed to the max, including a laptop. CJ had been that scared. Where had she been intending to go?

After selecting a soft pair of jeans she zipped everything closed again, slammed the rear hatch and went back to the apartment at a slow walk. CJ was right about one thing—simple wishes weren't going to get rid of whatever it was that had her scared enough to run. Had she really killed someone? Was she wanted for murder? It seemed impossible. There had to be an explanation. CJ wasn't a cruel person—maybe it had been self-defense. There was no doubt in Karita's mind that CJ had at some point been battered. She'd presumed it was a childhood scar, but maybe there was a more recent wound.

She handed over the pants and CJ looked relieved.

"Everything's there? Fine?"

"Yes, everything's there. I locked it all up again."

"Great, thank you." CJ moved very slowly, especially her knee and wrist, neatly wrapped in support bandages. "You missed my elbow," she muttered.

"You don't have to be cranky about it." Abby pushed back from the table. "I'll get another roll."

"No—I'm sorry. You've been great and believe me, I won't trespass again." CJ had her pants up to her hips and she carefully got to her feet again, waving away Karita's help. "I can't explain everything. But I never got the chance to say—are you sure it was just a *half* a valium?"

"Yes, I'm sure." Abby stood with her hands on her hips. "You never got the chance to say what?"

Karita couldn't help but think that if CJ had brought her heart to the relationship with Abby they would probably be content as partners—two strong-willed women with similar drive and focus. Not that she had any intention of mentioning it. She'd stood there and let Lucy ask CJ out, risked CJ maybe kissing someone else. She wasn't going to be stupid again.

"If I ever hurt you, I'm sorry. I never lied to you, but even so, I never told you the truth."

Abby's smile finally reached her eyes as she said, "I should have given you a whole valium. There's no telling what you'd say then."

CJ had limited experience with substances like valium. She was perfectly capable of expressing her opinion but simply couldn't find the energy to be alarmed when Karita ignored her.

"It's okay, Em, we're both fine," Karita was saying. For a woman who hadn't known how to turn on the cell phone, Karita was doing well driving and talking at the same time. "She does? Can't I give a statement in the morning? Because she's hurt. I know what I'm doing. Em—I'll give a statement tomorrow. I don't know if she will. I don't know. It's her decision. Co-dependent,

I know. Em, thank you. I know what I'm doing and I know why I'm doing it, too."

Even without the sedative in her system CJ wasn't sure what she was hearing would make sense.

"I'm really not a child."

It took a moment to realize that Karita was talking to her. She answered, "No, I don't think of you as a child."

"Just a hummingbird." The hurt in Karita's voice was palpable.

"That was—I was trying to get you to leave me alone. You don't want any part of my life." Karita turned a corner and CJ recognized her apartment complex.

"You keep saying things like that. I understand you have some kind of issue with law enforcement—"

"To put it mildly."

"But it's not like they're coming for you tonight. Home is the best place for you. Things will seem better in the morning."

"You don't understand." She tried to spur her mind into a faster speed. Karita was adamant that she recuperate at home. Maybe if she appeared to agree, Karita would tuck her in and leave. Then she could head for Canada.

"You're right, I don't understand," Karita said. "You don't have to tell me either. It's not like you owe me anything. All we did was kiss."

Yeah, CJ wanted to agree. All we did was kiss, and it changed my life. I want desperately to be on a path toward you and I have to go the other direction. "What I've told you is true."

"I believe you. Like I said, though, there's more truth. You're not a killer, CJ. And I don't think you should tell me more now because your defenses are down."

"What if I want to tell you?"

"Then tomorrow is soon enough. You'll have to call in sick, I think."

There was no point in saying that she had been planning to quit by long distance and tell Jerry to give all her unpaid

206

commissions to Burnett. "Fine. Whatever."

Karita gave her a suspicious look. "So where do I park?"

CJ pointed out the reserved spot. She was supposed to be in Cheyenne by now. She peered into the decently lit walkway and was relieved to see that no one was lurking. Even if Daria was savvy enough to hit the Internet after seeing CJ's picture, it wasn't easy to come up with a home address unless you paid a fee. Why do that when CJ's workplace was already known? They'd look for her there first.

Getting out of the car proved a challenge, but she gave it her best effort since she hoped to convince Karita she could be left alone. Her knee was stiff, but less painful. The stitches in her hip were really sore.

"Are you doing okay?"

"Yes." She got the door unlocked and herself inside, switching on the lights as she went. It didn't look as if anyone had been there since she'd left that morning. There were no unusual aromas of cigarettes or cologne.

A thump behind her made her turn too sharply and she felt the resulting stab of pain all through her leg. Karita was rolling the suitcase along with her.

She closed the door and leaned on the case, her stance defiant. "So, okay, wishful thinking. If you want to leave, you have to get it back out there all by yourself."

CJ wanted to laugh but the situation was too surreal. What was left of her rationality went up in smoke because Karita was in her apartment. Karita was looking around her, taking it in. Abby's place was a shoebox, but modern. CJ saw the faded Formica and antique kitchen appliances through Karita's eyes. It was safe and clean, but surprise was plain on Karita's face.

"What you expected?"

"No." Karita hauled the suitcase into the bedroom. "I couldn't tell you what it was I did expect, though. My grandmother had the same countertops in the house where I grew up."

She wanted in the worst way to sit down, lay down, but she

didn't want to show Karita how weak she felt.

Karita came out of the bedroom, took one look at her, and said, "Remember what I said about pigheaded?"

CJ hobbled to the kitchen, trying to make it look as if she was after a glass of water, not the counter to lean on. "I'll be fine."

"I'm not leaving." Karita took the glass out of CJ's hand.

She didn't know if her knees were weak because of her injuries or because Karita was so close. "You have to go."

"I've got it sorted out, my own thoughts at least," Karita said softly. "You're hurt and half high and my usual deal is to nurture and cuddle, get you fed and into a safe, warm bed. But that's not what's on my mind, not what being alone with you has me thinking about."

"You have to go." CJ desperately told herself not to touch Karita's hair. "You have to…go." She couldn't let Karita do this. She didn't want to be another charity case. If a kiss had changed her, what would passion do? There was nothing simple about how she felt, nothing light or easy. Of all the things she'd suffered, the next few minutes of her life were the ones that could hurt the most.

"Make me leave tomorrow, then," Karita whispered. Her lips feathered softly across CJ's. "If this is all the time we get, then why not have what we can?"

CJ captured Karita's wandering hand against her stomach. "Because this isn't all we'll want. I won't be able to send you away tomorrow, and you know it. Then my life becomes your life."

It was unreal that those incredible blue eyes were gazing at her with no shadows, no secrets. "I'm free to make that choice."

The heat from Karita's hand was melting away the last of her defenses. "What if I can't handle the guilt if anything happens to you?"

"Anything that happens to me is because of my choices, and not because I love you."

Dear God, CJ thought. She doesn't know anything. Who I am, where I come from. She didn't think that maniac with the baseball bat would hurt her either.

Then, with a sensation in her heart so sharp it was painful, she realized what Karita had said.

She loves me.

I feel magic when I touch her, Karita thought. I know I'm not an elf, and I know I can't wiggle my nose and fix the world, but this is a kind of magic we *can* make. But it takes her, too, it takes her belief and her trying, too.

"I'm not doing this for your sake." Karita untangled her hand from CJ's. "Not even for mine. I want this for the sake of what we could have."

"You have to go," CJ said again. "You're not Abby. I'm not Emily. This isn't casual."

"I know that." Karita trembled as CJ's fingers slipped through her hair. She knew how she could feel when a woman touched her. She knew how it felt to be bathed in affection and tenderness. None of that seemed to have anything to do with the powerful emotions CJ roused—love better than she deserved, and longing more than she could believe.

She stopped telling herself CJ was just another Mandy—she no longer believed it. It wasn't a frog or a princess, no Assassin of Magic, gazing at her with fear and desire. A woman, that was all. And that was everything.

Wishful thinking that fate was granting all her wishes had blinded Karita to Mandy's flaws. She'd loved without reservation and been discarded like an empty champagne bottle. Only now did she realize there was more to risk in loving someone than casual passion, because only now was it clear that she could get hurt all the way to her core.

"I'm afraid I'll make your injuries worse," Karita said. Electricity seemed to dance from CJ's fingertips and along the nerves on Karita's neck. Her skin tightened in reflex. She wanted to be naked so CJ could cover her.

One corner of CJ's mouth lifted in a crooked smile. "My knee is about to give out."

"Then you decide." Karita brushed her cheek along CJ's, then lightly tugged CJ's earlobe with her teeth. "Do I help you get to the sofa or the bed?"

Heat seemed to rise off CJ's body. Another revelation—sex in her past had been about the magic of women, the beauty of their bodies and what they could experience through them. Any hands and mouths touching with affection and knowledge could create the same response. Sex was that simple. With CJ, for the first time, Karita felt as if she knew things no one else did, and her touch would open doors no one else had known even existed.

"You're making it impossible for me to think clearly." CJ shivered against Karita.

"Don't think. Do what you want." CJ's chest rose and fell against her own in an uneven rhythm that Karita understood. Emotions overloaded her senses and it felt as if there wasn't room inside her for anything so ordinary as air.

"Take me to bed, then." CJ gave a little moan. Karita pulled back enough to look at her. "Don't ask me if I'm sure. Just take me to bed."

Arms around waists, they awkwardly crossed the thin carpet to the bedroom. Part of Karita was glad it was a small place while part of her wondered that CJ lived so simply. The furniture was more functional than stylish. Given the money she made, a person might expect an array of electronics, but only a simple stereo system was apparent. The other bedroom held only a small desk, a filing cabinet and a workout bench. CJ's room was just as simple, with curtains and linens that could have come from any of the kinds of stores where Karita shopped out of necessity. CJ wore designer clothes that suited her career, but her home didn't reflect those tastes.

She wasn't Mandy, Karita told herself again. She wouldn't want Karita because she made a nice accessory.

Karita pulled back the covers and helped CJ sit down. "Do you need help with your clothes?"

CJ cleared her throat. "Need it? No."

Her bones suddenly turned to liquid, Karita decided it best to kneel. With care she eased CJ's injured wrist free of the shirt sleeve and with equal care freed the other arm.

"I'm not a child," CJ said.

"No…" Karita brushed her teeth across the front of CJ's bra, finding and capturing a nipple beneath the fabric. CJ shuddered. "No, you're not, but you are fragile. At least at the moment."

CJ squirmed as Karita pulled the shirt over her head. "I just want—I just want you to know that I would usually be more aggressive."

"There's nothing usual about this for me, either." Karita gazed into CJ's eyes. The pupils were lost in the dark depths, but deep down there was that persistent golden light that beckoned to her. The color of her soul, Karita thought, and she kissed CJ, kissed her as if that first kiss had never ended.

The fire that had been kindled that night began to dance along her nerves all over again and only then did she fully admit it had never stopped. It wasn't the ephemeral flash of fireworks or the quick flare of shooting stars. Lost in the welcome warmth of CJ's mouth, Karita pushed away the fear of burning from this pervasive heat. There wasn't another choice because CJ had put her hands in her hair again, and she felt opened from the inside.

It was almost impossible to break the kiss. She didn't want it to stop but there were still clothes in the way and CJ's knee to consider. "We shouldn't do this," Karita said. She briefly touched CJ's swollen knee.

"Now you say that."

"I'm scared. And you're in no condition to…"

"If we stop now, I'll be in no condition for anything." CJ's hands moved slowly to the buttons on her jeans. She didn't resist when Karita pushed her gently back on the bed and slipped the buttons free herself.

Making sure to avoid the three small bandages on CJ's hip, she pulled down the jeans, taking shoes and socks with them. The

211

long, smooth legs were warm against her hands. She wanted to bury her face into the heat of the yielding inner thighs, and use her mouth to pull aside the hi-cut panties. There was time, she thought, time enough to savor her.

Smiling down at CJ, Karita reached for one of the pillows. "You get comfortable and I'll put this under your knee."

CJ bit her lower lip as she repositioned herself. She closed her eyes as her body finally relaxed into the bed. "Thank you."

She looks absolutely wiped out, Karita thought. How can I be thinking about doing what I want to do when she can't keep her eyes open?

Her eyes still closed, CJ reached up with one hand. "Don't go."

"I won't." Karita kicked off her clogs. Her clothes joined CJ's on the floor.

Their fingertips touched and CJ opened her eyes again. "I might not be up for sex, but I want to make love." She laughed. "Okay, that's the drugs talking. I'm not usually so sappy."

Karita grinned as she joined CJ on the bed. "I don't mind sappy."

CJ's olive skin didn't easily show a blush, but it did now. "There are things inside me that I never knew were there."

"I know what you mean." Karita caught back a gasp as she slid her body the length of CJ's, coming to a gentle rest along her uninjured side.

She didn't know how long they kissed. She didn't care. It felt as if their bodies were losing their separateness. When Karita touched the palm of her hand to the softness of CJ's belly their moans were breathlessly mutual. Every sensation reflected back to her. She knew CJ's breasts had tightened when her own did as well. She knew what she would find when she touched CJ lower, because that heat swam between her own legs, too.

Discarded lingerie ended up on the floor. Taking care to avoid CJ's knee, Karita moved half on top of her, and they were skin to skin for the first time.

Kisses. Shared air. Brushes of eyelashes against noses. Karita's hair falling across CJ's face. Each moment was separated with a long kiss that fed the rising fire.

"Can you?"

"Yes."

"Darling..."

They were both shaking. There was no laughter to ease the tension.

Struggling for words, for reassurance when she felt as if something inside her was strained to the breaking point, Karita whispered, "I don't feel like a hummingbird."

"I didn't mean—"

"You were right. It's easy to float. It's easy to let you touch me. I've never done the hard part before—feeling your touch and letting it push me up so high that I can see how far it will be if I fall."

"Karita." It sounded like an endearment the way CJ said it now. "I'll catch you."

"Please, CJ." Karita buried her face in CJ's shoulder. The tears began when CJ's fingers finally touched her. She was scared because there was no magic to protect her. She had to trust CJ now while it felt as if her soul was breaking into shards and she might never be whole again.

They moved faster. Karita was aware of the little noises she couldn't hold back, so different from the lusty groans, heated words and earthy encouragement of her past. Maybe someday it could be that simple with CJ, but right now there seemed no end to the layers of feelings, inside and out, aroused by the swirling and teasing of CJ's fingers. Her heart danced among clouds and stars, between light and dark.

"Karita."

"Don't stop."

"I won't let you fall."

She cried out in disbelief when her frenzy peaked. She seized the pillow to either side of CJ's head and held on while her body shook into a star shower of light that illuminated CJ's eyes. Deep down, on the other side of their midnight depths, Karita saw the truth. "You love me."

"Yes."

Her head was spinning, but she knew it wasn't the altitude. Or maybe it was. She'd never been this high up before, so high that mountains were at her feet.

She could fall, Karita knew that. She could resist it, cling to safety. She didn't wait to fall—instead, she jumped. Spreading herself on CJ's hands, she gave herself to wherever their feelings would lead them.

CJ's arms tightened around her, gathering all of her up, safe, close, treasured. Karita regained her reason, and was glad of the solidity of the bed, of CJ. She hadn't fallen anywhere. She smiled into CJ's shoulder. She hadn't fallen—she'd flown. "Say that again."

"Yes, I love you."

They weren't supposed to be hard words to say. Maybe with practice it would be easier. CJ tightened her arms around Karita, quietly shushing the tears. She wanted to say she didn't know what had just happened between them, but the truth was she didn't want to believe it.

She had thought she would need to lie, scam and cheat her way into bed with a woman like Karita. Instead, she'd told her the truth and she was wrapped in a grace that still seemed to belong to someone else.

She had walked away from the Gathering but she knew it was still inside her. It was difficult to let go of the idea that love didn't exist, and trust was only an exploitable vulnerability. She did not have to deceive someone who loved her, but it was hard to put any more truths into words.

She tried. "I've never said that to anyone before."

Karita stilled.

"It's the only thing I have to give you, Karita. There's been no one else, ever. Not any kind of love. I guess that could be scary."

Karita raised her head. "You don't scare me."

"I should. I'm not—"

"Ssh. Not now. God, not now." Karita kissed her.

Every nerve in CJ's body wanted Karita to touch her, love her, so why was she working so hard to get Karita to stop? Karita couldn't possibly understand or believe her.

"It was all the truth, Karita. I've done really horrible things."

Karita nuzzled just under CJ's jawline. "Do you regret them?"

"Every day. Sometimes I don't trust myself, why I do something, but I do regret hurting people."

"That's all that matters."

The blue eyes of a Madonna gleamed at her. She's just a woman, CJ reminded herself. Just a woman who could touch her in intimate, carnal ways and yet do so with such goodness and grace that she felt loved by a goddess. Just a woman—all of that, inside her. Maybe Abby had it too. Maybe all women did. They just needed the right person to let it shine.

Long fingers stroked the length of her torso. It was nothing like the explosive waves of passion that had swept her away with other women. The feelings started deeper, in places beyond touch. She had no way to discover where these feelings led except to yield, to feel the truth of her words to Karita and let herself be changed.

She caught Karita when she might have moved lower. "No, kiss me. Kiss me, and—" Her breath caught in her throat at the first sure touch of Karita's fingers between her legs. Her legs parted farther in response and she barely felt her knee's protest.

It was nothing she could have planned for, or lied to get, nothing she could have set out to achieve or carefully plotted to create. From Karita's touch something flowed so powerfully, so unrestrained that it could only be given, not stolen. Light flooded every dark place, and even when the pleasure peaked and faded, the light stayed. *I earned this*, CJ thought, and the certainty flooded her senses and opened doors to all the parts of her she denied could exist.

The slick, welcome motion of Karita's fingers finally stopped. In spite of her body's now audible reminders about its various hurts, she felt an undeniable pang. More…she wanted more. She wasn't sure she could ever get enough.

Karita whispered, "I don't know what this is, but it's not sex."

CJ smiled into her kiss. "Then I think we'll just have to keep doing it until we get it figured out." She grazed Karita's breast with her fingers and felt the responsive tingle shiver back and forth between them all over again.

This time they spoke more, whispered love, encouragement, needy things. Some of the emotion was slaked and now their bodies woke in familiar ways. *There*, *more* and *yes* flowed between them, even when words were impossible.

All of it was true, CJ thought. Even after they finally grew too tired to move, the sleepy kisses, the murmurs of love, were true.

CJ's head lost to her heart. She gathered the sleeping woman in her arms, breathed her in, and closed her eyes.

There would be no more running away.

Chapter 14

CJ couldn't shake the feeling that she was in a dream. There was a Madonna seated at her little dining room table, eating toast and drinking coffee.

She'd woken to the warmth of Karita and the distant awareness that she ought to get them both out of the apartment before her family showed up. They would, too. They wouldn't find her at work, so they'd locate her home address, even if it meant paying for it on the Internet. They were as inevitable as ants.

"There's still time," CJ said.

"Time for what?" Karita's arched eyebrow suggested what she had in mind.

CJ fought back a blush. "Time for you to get out."

Karita put down her mug. "What do you take me for?"

"I just meant that—"

"That I didn't mean the things I said last night? That I should flit along to my next flower?"

"No, that's not what I meant."

"I've been thinking about what you said, CJ. You were right. I go to the animal rescue and collect kisses and wagging tails from a dozen puppies, and that's not a bad thing. But it does mean I don't have to take care of any of their other needs. I don't have to see any of the women at the shelter through their entire journey. I get to experience the easiest part."

"What you do isn't easy."

"No, it's hard to do sometimes. But it's not as hard a job as a nurse's when she takes down the details of the sexual battery that went along with the beating. It's not as hard a job as Emily's, who has to listen to the horrific details and decide how this woman can best be helped. And if it gets too hard, I can not show up. I get to take a break."

"I don't believe that. You didn't run from the moron with the baseball bat."

"He nearly killed me. His eyes fooled me. I didn't think he'd swing." Karita waved an elegant hand. "I don't know what I was thinking."

"That he couldn't be that evil."

"No, that's not it." Karita's smile tipped to one side in chagrin. "I was thinking that I was an elf and could use my magic on him."

"I believe you." How like Karita to simply trust that wishing could make something better. "If anyone could do that, it would be you."

CJ guessed she'd said the right thing, because grateful tears shimmered in the vivid blue eyes. "I was trying to use my magic to save you," Karita added quietly.

"Ah, but you didn't know I was beyond saving."

"Stop it." Karita's tone sharpened. "Stop staying things like that, like you believe them."

"I do believe them," CJ said.

Last night in Karita's arms, she had stopped believing for a while. In the light of day, expecting a knock from her past on the door any minute, it was another matter. "Look, I really need a shower."

"Let me help you."

"No, I can manage. My knee is better, and I don't even need this support on my wrist. I'll be fine."

She escaped to the bathroom. Her heart was so weak. She just couldn't resist that unfaltering glow in Karita's eyes. What do you do when your deepest truths turn out to be lies, which ought to be a good thing but you can't stop doubting? Her head remained deeply suspicious of her heart, and she didn't know how to stop it.

Karita listened to the sound of running water. Toast and coffee seemed banal after a night that had emptied her completely. With each tick of the day she began to fill up again, this time, with the knowledge that CJ loved her.

Loved her, yet would not believe in any kind of future.

She realized it was nearly time for work. Calling in so late wasn't very considerate, but she rarely took sick days. She dialed in through the back door so she could leave a voice mail for Marty, hoping she didn't sound as guilty as she felt. Then she called the shelter to let Emily know she was still okay, and was surprised to hear Lucy's voice on the phone.

"I sent her home, the nut. She was up all day and then all night and still saying she wasn't tired. The glazier's here and a specialty cleaner is on the way to deal with the glass in the carpet. A police officer left a business card for you and you're supposed to call no later than tomorrow afternoon. Pauline is going to spell me in a while, so I'll be headed home too. Do you need anything? How's CJ? Emily said she got knocked around."

"She fell on the garden claw—got a few stitches. She'll be fine." Her voice softened on the last word and perceptive Lucy didn't miss it.

"So you had a, um, interesting evening after you left here?"

"You could say that." Karita wondered if Lucy could tell from her voice she was blushing.

"I wondered—we had a nice date but she did pump me for information about you. She was about as subtle as a ten-year-old."

Karita wanted to giggle. Lucy's depiction was at such odds with the darkly pessimistic woman who didn't think she could ever overcome her own past. "I left my purse, my keys, everything, in my locker. I wasn't exactly thinking clearly. CJ's place isn't that far—I don't suppose you could drop them by on your way home? Off of Colfax. You'll be going right past."

Lucy agreed, and Karita hung up, pretty sure Lucy would be as puzzled as she was by the modest location of CJ's home. Given the article in the paper, anyone would expect CJ to own her own home, at a minimum. Mandy had lived in a five-bedroom plus den and bonus room model home.

"Karita? Can you bring me some undies?"

"I'd love to." Not sure where to look, she chose the easier option of the suitcase, where she'd glimpsed some the night before. As she pulled a lovely pair of skimpy pink panties free she dislodged a file folder and its contents spilled across the floor.

"Here." She handed them unceremoniously through the crack in the door. "It's not like I haven't seen you naked, you know."

CJ peered out at her. "I'm just feeling shy right now."

Karita couldn't help but smile. "We'll see about that later."

Kneeling on the carpet, Karita gathered printouts and newspaper clippings, some looking very old. A handwritten list of crossed out names, in a childish script and marred by lines across most of them, had drifted almost under the bed, and she put it on top of the ungainly pile. She carried everything to the table to put it back in order.

The newspaper clippings were dated nearly twenty years ago. A few were from old microfiche and printed on fading thermal paper. She had three in date order when she realized they all bore similar headlines. After that, she couldn't stop reading.

A crime gone wrong…Reverend Paul M. Carter only wanted to spare an elderly parishioner's hard earned funds from a home improvement scam when the crime turned deadly. Assailants at large…a family affair…father and daughter arrested…

A few articles briefly covered the trial, and the father, Callomikea James Rochambeau, had been convicted of second-degree murder and sent to prison, in part due to the testimony of his fourteen-year old daughter, name withheld.

Oh, CJ, Karita thought. You were just a kid. What else were you supposed to do?

She couldn't find any articles at all in a gap of nearly fourteen years. The next item was a page from a church newsletter. The Lord provides…Phoebe Carter reports that her daughter was notified of a scholarship covering her entire tuition and materials at Holyoke Bible College. "I despaired of her being able to go to college at all. The Lord couldn't give her father back to us, but God is kind and merciful…"

Another article, from *The Lexington Gazette*, two years later. Found treasure…Mary Champlain didn't even know what bearer bonds were, but when the stack appeared on the seat of her car she took them to her best friend who works for a local bank…

There were more of the same. People finding valuable coins, sudden windfalls or, in one case, even a pile of cash delivered by a confused messenger who couldn't identify the woman who'd paid him very nicely for the job.

Her gaze traveled from the articles to the list. Mary Champlain, thirty-five thousand; Jimmy Tallarude, thirty-eight thousand; Sarah Benchford, nineteen thousand—name after name, crossed off. At the top of the list was Paul Carter Family, sixty thousand, also crossed off.

Karita's heart was beating so painfully it felt as if it would break.

A little noise from the bathroom doorway made her look up. CJ was wrapped in a towel, looking as if she would faint.

"I spilled it and didn't mean to pry." Karita pushed the handwritten list across the table toward CJ. "That bad reputation you've been working on is really ruined now."

CJ sank into the other chair at the table, her lips pale. "It doesn't make me a good person."

"Yes, CJ, it does."

"It's not all there. I couldn't remember everyone."

"You've done what you can."

"No. Because I'm hiding from the law, I didn't look those people in the eye and apologize. I had to do it all in secret."

"I don't understand." Karita fished out the brief article about the sentencing of the man who killed the little town's minister. "You told what happened. Why are you still a fugitive?"

CJ leaned heavily on her arms. Her eyes were shadowed. "Two separate things. I'm still a fugitive because I left prison before my sentence was up. Three months early."

Okay, Karita thought, that was serious. No matter how long ago, as far as she knew, CJ would still be wanted. But surely it wasn't insurmountable. "You said they were two separate things."

"I didn't tell what happened. I lied in court. I sent my father to prison to escape him. I said he made me pull the trigger, but the truth is I don't know if it was him, or me, or both of us."

Karita took a deep breath. "Why?"

"I don't think I meant to pull it. I'm not sure if that's just wishful thinking." She closed her eyes and held her head in her hands. "My father had the gun. He always had the gun at the final drop, just in case. The minister showed up. I don't know if the guy thought God wouldn't let anything bad happen or what."

She gave Karita a bleak stare. "I guess he was like you. He didn't believe in evil, and yet there we were, about to take twenty grand from an old woman to fix a fake radiation leak in her basement. Daddy would have blown the money on a big-screen TV that Aunt Bitty would have thrown a chair through two days later. If the man had just let us leave it wouldn't have happened. It wasn't his fault, but if he'd just let us leave…"

Karita ached to hold the frightened teenager close, but she knew that CJ didn't want to be told it was all okay. She knew full well that it wasn't all okay. "So what happened?"

"Daddy gave me the gun. Said it was time I learned. A Smith and Wesson .38 not big, but it seemed so heavy. It was hard to hold up. I told the minister I would shoot the old lady. I figured that was what he needed to hear. He told me I couldn't be so bad, and Daddy started yelling at me to pull the trigger, yelling it in my ear. The minister came across the basement at us, and Daddy put his hand on mine, on the gun, helping me aim. It went off and we ran. The old lady was screaming. I know she called for help but it wasn't in time." Her memory-darkened gaze stared into a place Karita couldn't see.

"My father wiped the gun down and stashed it in an irrigation drain. The coroner said in court that it was a lucky shot. Went through his neck and the slug flattened into the brick wall behind the guy. He bled to death in minutes. There was no murder weapon but the witness —the old lady—she said she didn't know which of us fired, but we had both been holding the gun. I told the jury my father pulled the trigger, forcing me to pull it as well. It wasn't quite like that. I don't know if I meant to do it. But when I told the story in court I wasn't trying to get out of jail. I wanted to be sure *he* went to jail. I was trying to get away from my aunt and from him. From home."

Karita extended a hand across the small table and after a moment, CJ took hold. "It was so long ago."

"I wanted him to pay for my mother. He never even would say she was dead. My aunt, Aunt Bitty, she told people my mother ran off. She said the same thing about her husband. That's how I knew that guy would kill you if he could. He swung that bat the way she swung a crowbar."

"Your father's sister?" Violent to their very core, Karita thought, and CJ had overcome it, broken the cycle.

CJ shivered. "Oh yeah. Yeah, same DNA. He could be savage and then sometimes so smart. He taught me I was good for something. He cared when I did good and for a long time all I wanted was to please him. I didn't want him to think I was a waste of space, like my mother. If I pleased him he sometimes told Aunt

Bitty to lay off me. She was a slow poison, like something ate at her all the time and she could only forget it was there when she was angry."

Karita squeezed CJ's fingers. "Have you ever hit anyone?"

"No." CJ's red-rimmed eyes flashed with outrage. "Never, never once."

"You're not like them, CJ. You've truly escaped."

CJ let go of Karita's hand to wipe her eyes with a corner of the towel. "I don't want to talk about them anymore. Not right now."

Karita watched her limp to the bedroom. Trying for something like a normal tone, she called, "I don't suppose I could borrow a pair of panties and a T-shirt?"

"Sure. My pants are going to be too short, though. I thought we were the same height until last night."

Karita leaned in the bedroom doorway, watching CJ's slow but successful attempt to pull a simple top on over her own head. "We are the same height."

CJ wouldn't meet her gaze. "Your legs are longer. I'm usually in heels and you're not."

Karita watched CJ rifle through a dresser drawer, and took the offered underwear and shirt. "Shower time for me."

With hot water pouring over her head, Karita allowed herself to feel the relief of finally knowing what it was that frightened CJ so much. The specter of prison was very scary and very real. Fourteen, fifteen years of thinking any day there could be a knock on the door… CJ had made a small fortune and tried to get right with her own conscience.

She used the dryer long enough to reduce her hair from wet to damp. CJ, looking fragile in jeans and a long-sleeved sweater, was at the table again when she opened the bathroom door. The file folder was filled neatly and closed. About to ask if CJ would like more coffee, she instead went to respond to a knock at the door.

"No, wait!" CJ tried to rise too quickly and faltered with a

224

gasp. "Don't open the door."

Her hand on the knob, Karita said, "It's probably Lucy with my stuff. I told her where to find me."

"Look, at least."

After a glance through the peephole, Karita reported, "It's Lucy and a guy."

"What guy?"

"I don't know him. About my age—he looks like a kid though."

"Big Bambi eyes? That's Burnett—I work with him. You can let them in." CJ sounded relieved.

Karita looked over her shoulder. CJ was still too pale and obviously very much on edge. Suppressing a worried sigh, she opened the door, gave Lucy a brief hug, and introduced herself to the shy young man.

Lucy handed over Karita's purse with a huge sigh of relief. "I hate these things. I was afraid people would think it was mine."

"Burnett," CJ said, still seated at the table, "what brings you here?"

Karita closed the door and wondered if CJ would mind if she offered coffee.

"It wasn't like you to call in sick," he said tentatively. "I didn't realize you had company."

"We met almost on your doorstep, CJ." Lucy dug in her pocket. "Your car keys, Karita. I moved it to the street in front of the shelter to avoid the street cleaners."

"Oh, thank you so much! Like I needed another ticket."

"It's okay," CJ said to Burnett. "I got a little banged up last night is all."

"Well, yeah." Burnett glanced nervously at Karita and she hoped the smile she gave him was reassuring. "Listen, um, I got in early this morning because I was dropping off a revision for Cray. When I got to the office there was this really scary old lady outside the door asking for you."

CJ froze.

Karita asked, "How do you mean scary?"

"Like Bette Davis and Joan Crawford put together in *Whatever Happened to Baby Jane?* Totally off their meds kind of scary. Thing is, she was with the woman from the Rocky Mountain Diner, CJ. The one who said she knew you and kind of freaked you out. I told them you were on vacation."

CJ looked as if she wasn't breathing.

There was a knock on the door and Karita, out of pure reflex, opened it.

It was too late to tell Karita to keep the door closed. It was just plain too late. The nightmares of her past had shown up in the daylight.

The others naturally stepped back from a large puff of cigarette smoke. It was an old trick, and Daria had no trouble getting all the way inside the apartment. Then she stepped back as if to usher in royalty.

CJ had imagined Aunt Bitty older. Had imagined her dead, for that matter. But aside from the gray in her hair, Aunt Bitty hadn't changed. Her face was carved with disdain. CJ thought that every cruelty the woman had ever committed showed in that face and in her eyes.

"You led us right to her, sissy boy." Daria blew smoke again, then slammed the door shut once Aunt Bitty was all the way inside. She flung herself onto the sofa, knocking a cushion to the ground. Another long drag let her blow smoke rings toward Burnett. "So, Cassie June, aren't you glad to see Aunt Bitty again?"

Karita bit back a gasp and Daria gave her an annoyed look. Lucy crossed her arms over her chest and flexed while Burnett waved away the smoke.

CJ stood up, hiding her hurt knee. The stitches in her hip pulled slightly, but she ignored the discomfort. "No, I'm not."

"Is that any way to talk to the woman who fed you and wiped your ass when you were a baby?" Aunt Bitty had a cane, but CJ was sure she leaned on it for dramatic effect when she wanted sympathy, and swung it when she got mad. A glorified crowbar, that's what it was.

"And beat her, and raised her to be a criminal?" Karita's voice shook with outrage. "Who stood by and let her mother be—"

"Karita, please." CJ took a step forward and was relieved she didn't limp. "I want both of you to leave."

Aunt Bitty's grimace showed her amusement at Karita's defiance. CJ cringed when her grip tightened on the cane. "Looks like you've got a white tiger here fighting for you, Cassie June. Is she that ferocious in bed, too?"

"Now, listen here," Lucy began.

"Lucy, please. Everybody, please." CJ had to take two more steps to make herself the closest person to Aunt Bitty and her cane. "One more time. I want you both to leave."

"Or what? You'll call the cops?"

"Yes, I will." Believe it, old woman, she said with her eyes.

"See you in Fayette, then. Every so often someone comes around to find out if we've heard from Cassie June, who is still on the run." The way Aunt Bitty's hands gripped and twisted the cane made CJ's heart skip beats.

"What a pack of—"

"Burnett, please!"

Aunt Bitty included them all with the same gesture of dismissal. "Daria, honey, we're in the company of a bunch of queers."

For a long moment, all CJ could hear was the sound of Aunt Bitty's hand smacking some part of her body and the cackle when Cassie June flinched after a little knife suddenly embedded itself into the wall next to her hand.

A dozen insults a day, a hundred lectures about her worthless, useless existence—they all welled up inside her. She could see the ghost-like face of the old memory of Aunt Bitty standing over Uncle Vaughn, except the apparition she faced now had eyes, eyes like her father's, eyes just like the ones that looked back at her from the mirror every day.

She wanted to crawl away to a safe place. She couldn't find her voice.

Daria's laugh grated down CJ's spine. She took one last puff on her cigarette, then began to stub it out on the arm of the sofa.

Burnett was a blur. He instantly snatched the butt out of Daria's hand. "Well, it's not hard to tell who raised you."

Daria opened her mouth to retort, but Burnett held the smoldering cigarette under her nose.

"I know people who would put this out on your tonsils, and make you like it." He whirled around to face Aunt Bitty, one irate finger pointed at her chest. "As for you, you are rude, crude and thoroughly without class. This woman is my big sister, you shrew, and nobody talks about my family that way."

Lucy drawled, "At least not so unimaginatively. *Queer* is the best they can do?"

Burnett put a hand to his chest. "I could have at least gotten *faggot*, but *sissy boy*? Please."

Karita, radiating her beautiful calm, said simply, "We're not afraid of you."

But you should be, CJ wanted to say. She felt Karita take her hand and she glanced at her.

Those incredible eyes were deep, like lakes fed directly from blue heavens. "I begin to understand what you faced." She squeezed CJ's hand. "You were young and you were alone. Now you're not."

CJ took a deep breath and let go of Karita's hand. Lucy and Burnett were still discussing the lack of appropriate insults when CJ looked directly at Aunt Bitty.

"Are all the men in prison? Is that why it's you who's going to try to fetch me home? Nothing left of the Rochambeaus but you for a matriarch?"

"Your family has been waiting a long time to settle with you, Cassie June." Aunt Bitty leaned on her cane with pure menace. "Your father is still sitting in Big Sandy, waiting for you. You saved your own skin when you said it was him that pulled the trigger. You owe us. You're one of us."

CJ's voice was shaking, but there was nothing she could do about it. "Listen to me, old woman. I got no deal for saying he did it. There was no plea bargain. His hand was on the gun, too. He deserves to rot in prison."

"All you had to say is that he never touched it. You were a minor. Instead of twenty-five to life, he'd be out by now. You wouldn't have done more than five. You turned on him."

"He turned on me by telling me to lie to save *his* skin. A lighter sentence for him, a longer one for me, that was his proposal. No matter how much I did what he said, I was still disposable." CJ pulled herself up short. There was no point in arguing with Aunt Bitty. "So I lied, just a little. Don't it make you proud?"

Burnett, from behind her, said quietly, "You can't have regrets if you're dead, CJ. Remember?"

Out of the mouths of babes, CJ wanted to say, but she heard the siren at the same time Aunt Bitty and Daria did. The three of them cocked their heads, evaluating if it was coming closer. The shared blood, the long history, must be plain to everyone else now.

Lucy brought her cell phone out from behind her back. "Yes, they're coming here. Gotta love text messaging."

CJ didn't know if it was a bluff but the siren was definitely getting louder. Aunt Bitty and Daria had to be thinking about the code of the Gathering. When the cops were on the way, all fights stopped. They'd resume again when the cops left. In front of cops, social workers, any outsider, they were one big happy family. CJ knew if she played by those rules she was back dancing to Aunt Bitty's tune. Never again—she had sworn it her second night in Fayette. Never again.

But what had changed? How could she fight them? What did she have now that she hadn't had then?

"Time's running out." Karita was as calm as she had been last night facing the berserker with the baseball bat, but she'd learned that people like that really would hurt her if they could. Yet she stood her ground, just the same.

"Run along, now," Burnett said. "Shoo."

Lucy and Burnett hardly knew her, and yet they were defending her. CJ heard the echoes of the kind things Juliya and Tre had said, the offers of friendship and introductions to nice women from Raisa and Devon. Maybe they saw someone that she didn't, but she had her whole life to learn to see herself the way they did. Lord knows, she ached to be who they thought she was. She wanted to be the woman Karita loved.

She took one more step, well within range of Aunt Bitty's cane.

"The same blood may flow in our veins, but you are not my family." She spread her arms. "*This* is my family, the one I choose. And to keep my family I will go back to jail if I have to. I will never go back to you."

Daria got to her feet, all swagger. "Such a pretty speech. The tipline pays ten grand for escapees. Double it and we'll leave. For a while."

"She doesn't have any money," Karita said. "She's spent it all paying back the people you taught her to steal from. She put that minister's daughter through college."

CJ, abruptly aware of the cash-stuffed backpack just around the corner in the bedroom, began to shush Karita, but Aunt Bitty actually recoiled. Her disdain of CJ transformed to incomprehension.

Karita, whom Aunt Bitty would see as truthful, honest, trusting—the perfect mark—smiled with something like pity. "She's useless to you. She's raising money for a battered women's shelter. She worries so much about lying that she can't do anything but tell the truth."

The sirens stopped nearby.

Feeling like a helpless spectator, CJ watched Karita's limitless shining light negate Aunt Bitty's darkness. It was no contest, even, but it wasn't Karita's battle to fight.

If a woman like that can love me, CJ thought, then I can fight for myself.

She stood her ground, too, and found the truth. "I'm not afraid of you. If you want to hit me, go ahead. I survived you once, and I can do it again. But I'm not a child anymore. I will fight back, but not in ways you expect." She took a deep breath to steady her voice. "I'm not afraid of the police, and neither are my friends." She swung around to the back door, unlocked it and threw it open. "If you don't want to meet up with the cops you'd better run now."

Daria plucked at Aunt Bitty's sleeve. The haughty, stiff face was the same mask of contempt, but there was something in those eyes CJ didn't recognize. Then Aunt Bitty did something CJ had never seen before.

She stepped back.

CJ took a step toward her and she stepped back again.

In full retreat, circling toward the back door, Aunt Bitty turned at the threshold with a sneer for all of them and spat.

Karita was a crazy woman, a beautiful, darling, Madonna-goddess-elf creature, CJ thought, because she said, "Even a llama spits better than that."

CJ wanted to cry or laugh or both. She wasn't sure. She really didn't know what had just happened except that Burnett was giggling about something and Lucy admitted the siren was a helpful coincidence.

"Suckers! They bought it." Burnett and Lucy shared high fives.

She sat at the table, arms shaking, while they laughed and chatted and drank coffee. She found the wherewithal to make a few offhand remarks, but her head was spinning. What could they be all so happy about? Did other people really laugh when confronted with that kind of threat? Finally, Karita shooed Lucy and Burnett out the door.

With a loving smile, Karita crossed the room to wrap her

arms around CJ's shoulders from behind. The warmth of her body was instantly soothing and the scent of her, blended with familiar shampoo and soap, steadied CJ's reeling senses. "Do I need to make you tea with sugar?"

"Please, no, anything but that." She loved the way Karita's laughter sounded in her ear. "I'd love some water though."

"It's going to be okay. It's really going to be okay." Karita set a glass in front of her and pulled the other chair close. One hand soothingly stroked CJ's forearm.

"Those people…" CJ sipped to clear her throat. "Those people terrorized my life, thirty-five years of it. You all laughed at them and I was scared. Which of us is crazy?"

"Sweetheart," Karita said, "you were raised to fear them. They are scary, bad people, and I know some of what they did to you. There are things they did that I don't know about, too, and so maybe I wasn't as scared as I should have been. But I was still frightened. Mostly by what you thought they could do to you. But no way were they taking you away from me."

"I'm going to have to go back to jail, Karita."

"You don't know that for sure."

Goodness, but she loved this woman. Her endless optimism was unrealistic, but the flicker of hope that maybe, just maybe, Karita might be right, was welcome. She never hoped for good things to happen and so was rarely disappointed. In this case, however, maybe hope, combined with Karita to support her, wasn't completely foolhardy. "On their best days, those people are merely spiteful. Don't doubt it, they will call the tipline and turn me in."

"Then maybe you should do it first."

"Or you should do it, and make the ten grand."

Karita appeared to think it over. "My house needs weatherproofing, real bad."

CJ's laugh turned weepy and she let Karita pull her close. "I'm so afraid that if I go back to Fayette some of them will be waiting for me."

Karita kissed her forehead. "You stay right here."

CJ watched Karita fetch the phone. She was practically humming as she pressed the buttons.

"Where the heck are you? Do I hear puppies barking? You just happened to be in the neighborhood with extra muffins?" Karita listened for a moment, a smile of delight curving her lips. "You were still in the neighborhood after your date last night. I see."

She listened to Karita make plans to meet after lunch with the person on the other end of the line. When she hung up, CJ asked her, "Where are you going?"

"*We* are going to an animal rescue facility."

"Why?"

Karita grinned, looking very much as if she'd just successfully spun straw into gold. "To meet with a lawyer, of course."

Chapter 15

CJ stared out the window of the animal rescue's back room, watching cars go by on the curving, narrow highway that connected the small mountain communities with Denver. The September afternoon was cool, and wind-stirred leaves flashed red and orange in the clear yellow light.

She didn't think Karita's friend could have useful advice, but getting out of her apartment had helped to settle her nerves. Though she hadn't really been worried, it also helped to see that Pam was completely enamored with the dynamic Nann. Whatever feelings had led to Pam and Karita going out on a date, they were clearly based in friendship now.

"I'm sorry you drove up here for nothing, Karita." Pam was busy shoveling chow to kittens. "I took the basic classes in criminal law, but I've never practiced it. I wouldn't be qualified to help you on a matter that was exclusively based in Colorado, let alone a matter in Kentucky."

"Do you know someone in Kentucky?" At Karita's question, CJ couldn't help but turn her gaze to drink in the lovely vision Karita made idly stroking the euphoric kitten draped over her arm. She knew just how that kitten felt.

Pam gave CJ another curious look. "No. Nearly everybody I went to school with headed for the big money firms on the East Coast. I'd be happy to scan the list of people in my graduating class to see if anybody enrolled in the Kentucky Bar, but it's a long shot. I'm curious—why don't you ask Marty?"

"Marty's my boss," Karita explained to CJ. To Pam she said, "I sort of called in sick today, and I didn't want him to know I wasn't."

Pam grinned. Turning to scoop out more chow to the next cage of cats, she said, "The man calls you princess and would adopt you if you weren't too old. He's not going to hold helping out a friend against you. Besides, Marty spent his first five years out of law school as an assistant DA in Jefferson County. It's not Kentucky, but he's got to have some basic advice. He's likely to know somebody who knows somebody."

CJ cleared her throat. "I don't want to cause any more trouble for Karita."

"I can appreciate that," Pam said. "I'd love to tell you that all will be forgiven, but I don't know enough…"

About you remained unspoken between them. CJ understood the protective flare in Pam's eyes. She could only imagine what Emily was going to say.

Fervently, Karita explained, "She's paid back nearly all the people she can remember helping her father to steal from. That's got to count for something."

"It should," Pam admitted.

Nann bustled into the room with a leash. "The owners of that Husky are here." She gave CJ another skeptical look, obviously on the growing list of people who hadn't a clue what Karita could see in her.

"Goodie," Karita said. "Another happy ending. You've gotten so many of them back to their owners already." She signaled for CJ to follow her. "You won't believe how many marmots there are in the back, and half of them got away."

CJ had never been up close and personal with a marmot. She drank in the sight of Karita walking ahead of her and knew in her heart that watching her was far more fun than anything marmots could ever do for her.

Karita opened the door to an outdoor area. "See? Couple dozen of the poor refugees. It'll probably be safe enough to release them tomorrow or the day after."

CJ didn't look at the marmots. She looked at the llama. She looked at Karita. There was really nothing more to say except the truth.

"You amaze me. And I love you."

Feeling exceedingly shy, Karita said, "And this is my little house."

"You have all this land, too?"

"Yeah. A half-acre. If I hike up that way I can see Kenny Peak from the mesa. That's Mt. Evans—a fourteener." Karita pointed at her favorite mountain, all blues and grays capped with white.

"The house is adorable." CJ turned off the engine and quiet fell. High overhead, wind stirred the trees. "What a beautiful spot."

"It is. I like it here. I think my grandmother stayed in Minnesota for me. If I'd known this was here, I'd have moved us in a heartbeat. There's not very much humidity in Norway, so she'd have liked this climate. I know I do."

CJ inhaled deeply and Karita didn't avert her gaze from the lovely parts of CJ that rose and fell. "It's very you—all the trees and the sound of the creek. Fresh. Natural." She bit her bottom lip, slightly flushed. "What a quaint little cottage."

"Quaint is one word for it. Come on, I'll give you the tour."

CJ followed Karita into the house. "It's hardly bigger than my apartment."

"Easy to clean, that's for sure." Karita explained about the weatherproofing and the age of the building, but couldn't help but notice that the kitchen floor was not entirely level anymore, and the living room's exterior walls showed signs of strain. "You think I should probably pull it all down, don't you?"

CJ looked as if she wanted to protest, then she gave it up. "Yes, you probably should. The foundation and the house are going two different directions and I'm pretty sure dry rot is the least of your worries. With the land to mortgage you could build a very nice, modern home. Start with a core structure and plan to expand if you need to."

"I'm not sure I can afford the payments. The law office pays well enough to keep me volunteering for things I care about," Karita said. She gave CJ a furtive glance and was reassured by the nod of understanding. "Here, sit down at the table and rest your knee. I might not be much of a cook, but I make very good coffee."

"That sounds heavenly." CJ dutifully propped up her knee while Karita bustled around the tiny kitchen.

Once they were both at the table, aromatic brews giving off steam, CJ linked her fingers with Karita's. "I can't make you any promises, so it doesn't seem right to ask you for any."

CJ's warm hand caused a riot of goose bumps all along Karita's back. "What do you mean?"

"All I can say is that I'm going to try, try as hard as I know how, to at least give us a chance. And if you'll say the same—"

"Yes."

"I didn't finish."

"Yes."

CJ lifted Karita's hand to kiss the back. "I might be gone for a while."

"Now you know where I live. The only promise I need right now is that you're coming back."

"If you promise me you won't let the roof fall in on you."

Karita laughed. "It's not that bad. Besides, the only danger of that would be if you were here all the time. When I'm with you I think the world could stop turning and I wouldn't notice."

"It does stop turning," CJ said. "I noticed, but when I'm with you I don't care."

"Sweet talker." Karita didn't care that she was blushing. She was glad to see CJ's color had returned and the lines of stress around her mouth had eased. "My boss always has fifteen minutes free after staff meetings on Thursday afternoons. I can get you in to talk to him then."

"Okay." CJ sampled her coffee and made an appreciative noise. "You make Gracie's taste like peat moss."

"Thank you." Karita described Marty and the office, hoping to put CJ at ease. It couldn't be easy talking about her long-held secrets to perfect strangers.

CJ, looking momentarily wan, admitted, "Part of me keeps thinking they'll come back. Any minute they'll knock on the door."

"You'll send them away again, CJ. They're bullies, and they run from anything stronger than they are. They have no hold on you."

"I'm trying so hard to believe it."

They held hands and talked about the mountains, the house, the shelter, anything but the future. When the coffee was nearly done, she drew CJ up from the table. "I didn't show you my favorite room."

CJ laughed when Karita opened the bedroom door. "That was subtle."

"Wasn't it? I'm quite pleased with myself."

CJ helped pull Karita's T-shirt out of her pants. "Why is this your favorite room? You bring all your girlfriends here?"

"No, silly. You're the first."

"Oh."

"I've said I love you to a lot of people. There was even someone who I thought was special and wasn't. I really did think that was love but then…" Karita saw no reason to hold back now. "Then I kissed you. Then I got to know you and every new thing I learn about you ripens the way I feel about you. You don't scare me. My feelings don't scare me. Okay, maybe a little, but only

238

because this is an adventure I haven't been on."

CJ swallowed audibly before saying, "And you really want to go on that kind of journey with me?"

"It wouldn't be a journey I could take, not without you. Taking the risks, living the life *with* you, that's the point."

CJ's eyes shimmered. "And I'm the sweet talker?"

"Must be rubbing off on me." Karita slipped her T-shirt over her head and pulled CJ's arms around her waist. "I love the light in this room. It changes throughout the afternoon and I've always wondered what it would be like to spend an afternoon in bed, just watching the light shift."

"And you want to find out today?"

"Yes."

"That," CJ whispered against Karita's mouth, "is a wonderful idea."

Though CJ still moved stiffly at times, she explored the curves and lines of Karita's body with pleasing thoroughness as the white light of early afternoon eased to a honey glow, then deepened to golden shadows.

Karita knew all about lust and fun, and she had had her share, but every time they kissed, touched, strained together, the layers of sensation were so much more complicated. She explored CJ like a treasure box, stopping to savor each layer, then exposing a deeper one until the most precious jewel of all, CJ's heart, was open to her. The vestiges of the bars separating them melted away and she finally understood what *naked* meant. CJ rose in the circle of her arms with choked cries, and Karita's heart answered from a joyous place inside her she'd never given voice before.

Tears of tension and happiness melted into laughter. It wasn't the same easy, affectionate laughter she'd always known with Emily. This laughter sprang from a deeper well, a well, Karita hoped, that would never run dry.

CJ gathered her close. "I love watching you do that. It's like you're flying and I get to go along."

Karita flushed with pleasure. She felt claimed in ways that she had never thought possible before. Feeling as if she had melted from the inside out, she stroked the loose tumble of curls turned to topaz in the waning light. "The sun is nearly down."

CJ's hands molded Karita's hips. "I want to do this all night."

With just the tips of her fingers Karita found which places were warmer, and cooler, which curves of skin would smooth at her touch, and which would roughen to beg for more. CJ's almost inaudible whimper when Karita went inside her was a shout of joy to Karita. The look of wonder in CJ's eyes intoxicated her all over again.

A lifetime in an afternoon—it was not enough. When CJ dozed, Karita held her close and said every charm her grandmother had ever taught her. This would not be their only afternoon, not if she could help it.

No more frogs, no more princesses, this was a real woman, filled with everyday magic, and she was not going to let her go.

Telling some of her story to one of Karita's friends as she fed dogs and cats was one thing. Doing so at the law offices where Karita worked was something else again. CJ paused at the intimidating glass doors. Her reflection showed a well-dressed, chic businesswoman but CJ felt nothing like that on the inside. She was glad she'd had a chance to gather her wits before telling her tale one more time.

The morning had started early, but delightfully, showering with Karita and watching her dress for work. She'd delivered Karita to her car and headed home herself, knee much improved though her stitches itched every time she breathed in too deeply.

She'd surveyed her parking lot and the stairs to her apartment door, the way she had every day since she'd moved in, and found them empty of threat. As she'd showered and dressed she had allowed that maybe someday she would relax, but for now the mere hope that there would never be bogeymen lurking again was enough. Aunt Bitty hit when a target was within reach, and now that she knew there was no profit in CJ, she wouldn't waste her time. At least CJ continued to tell herself.

At work she'd assured everyone, including Burnett, that she was fine, and an intense morning of phone calls and presentation drafts had made up for the lost day. She'd nearly felt like the old CJ when she'd left to keep the appointment with Officer Anita. Karita had been right about that—her corroboration of time and sequence of events was all the police were interested in.

She was just bracing herself to go into the law office when a voice startled her. "Can I get the door for you?"

CJ stepped back to let a vaguely familiar man do the honors. She'd stopped at Gracie's for two skinny mochas, Turkish and capped. Juggling both of them and her backpack had been awkward. Now she had to go in. "Thanks."

"Did you have a good lunch, Brent?" Karita's voice was charming and modulated. CJ wanted to stand over in the corner out of sight and just listen to her.

"I did, thanks."

"Your deliveries, kind sir. I'll let you know if—" Karita caught sight of CJ. "I'll let you know if anything else comes…arrives," she finished absently.

They were alone in the spacious lobby then, or at least it felt that way to CJ. One look at Karita had brought back the new, blushing CJ. She had clung so long to the idea that she was set apart from other women, but here she was as mushy as a dime store greeting card. It was weirdly comforting to know she felt things that millions of other women felt. Comforting to think that in the matter of love she might really be…normal.

"Is that for me?" Karita eyed the coffee cup with positively lusty intent. "Or are you a two-fisted drinker now?"

"For you." CJ knew her blush was visible. "With raw sugar and chocolate sprinkles."

"You are," Karita whispered, "a really good woman." She took the cup and waved CJ to a seat. "It'll be about ten minutes."

For ten wonderful minutes CJ got to watch the woman she

241

loved in a brand new setting. Elegant and poised in a simple suit of dark rose, Karita brought the same feeling of calm and order to this office that she did to the shelter. Certainly, any office could use someone like that, and it paid decently, no question about it. Yet, in her heart, CJ knew it was a waste. Lawyers and real estate brokers would get by without Karita. Frightened women and children, terrified puppies and even llamas, needed her more. They would make a good team, each of them doing what they did best—CJ stopped her thoughts there. Her future was too uncertain to start making plans like that.

The human animals were predictable, though, and CJ watched no less than five messengers drop off packages. Every single one of them—including a very cute baby dyke and a handsome fellow with a wedding ring glinting on his finger—flirted with Karita. She took none of it seriously, always smiled, and briskly sent them on their way again. The dyke got a friendly wink, but CJ could hardly blame Karita for that.

Moments later she got a wink of her own, and it wasn't some good-bye-cutie-pie wink. It was the full-quality wink, complete with reminders of that shower they'd shared and suggestions for later. She winked back and they both blushed.

Karita's fingers flew over the phone board. "Ready? I'll bring her on back. Thank you, kind sir." Another series of taps ensued before she took off her headset. "It'll be okay."

Her nervousness descended again as Karita introduced her to Marty Hammer. Karita had described him well, including the intelligent eyes dwarfed by astonishing eyebrows, and a congenial air. For CJ, it was the impeccably tailored Ralph Lauren suit that asserted that he was good enough at what he did to be paid very well for it. She told herself not to be intimidated. She could sell real estate to a man like this in her sleep. But this was no business deal, she reminded herself. If she couldn't get a sympathetic hearing from him, there was no way she'd get one from a judge in Kentucky.

"So I thought she should talk to a professional," Karita

finished.

"Thank you, prin—Ms. Hanssen. So, Ms. Roshe—"

"CJ, please."

"CJ, then, if you'll call me Marty as well. Why don't you tell me what these mysterious legal matters are?"

CJ opened the backpack. The money was back in the safe. Instead she had brought something else.

Karita made a little noise as CJ put the gun on Marty's desk. The .38 had sat in that pipe the four years she'd been in detention. She'd gone back for it, not because it had a story it could tell, but because it was still loaded. The thought that someone would find it, and someone else might die, had been too hard to run from. The chill of its cold metal had been a constant reminder of that terrible moment.

"I need to know how to dispose of this. That's one thing."

"You could take it in through an amnesty program."

"Or you could, on behalf of a client."

"On behalf of a *client*," he echoed. His next words he chose with care. "Are you telling me it could be evidence in a crime?"

CJ chose her words equally carefully. "To my knowledge, it has no use at all as evidence in any crime." Justice for the crime she knew about had already been meted out. Because the bullet had flattened into brick, the .38 couldn't even be tied to the death of a town minister twenty years ago. She was ready to be free of the reminder the gun had provided all these years.

"Why are you really here, then?"

She knew her color rose, and her voice betrayed her tension. She had spent so long going over the facts in her head that she could deliver them succinctly. She was aware of Karita, sitting quietly, watching her. She had debated asking Karita to leave but wanted her to know she no longer had anything to hide, wanted her to know that she had told Marty the entire, bitter truth. The dull gleam of the .38 was like a silent witness, and it made the past very real.

She finished with, "I was afraid if I ran into anyone from

my family or the Gathering, or even a rival clan, they'd force me to go back. I didn't want to be in that life anymore. Lying constantly to everybody, including myself. Watching my relatives turn someone else's retirement money, or life savings, into empty beer cans. So when they were transferring me I took advantage of a traffic jam and a scuffle to slip away. Cassiopeia Juniper Rochambeau really is dead. But I have to make it official. She skipped out on her sentence, and I want to make it right so I can finally have a life."

Marty was frowning, but CJ couldn't tell if it was a lawyer concentration thing or disapproval. "If Kentucky is anything like Colorado, you have little to worry about if you surrender yourself and allocute. A judge might tack on a symbolic day, but if you complete your original sentence you would be done with it. Of course I can't guarantee that. You did break several new laws and you were an adult when you did so."

"CJ, you left out the important part." Karita turned to Marty. "She's made sizeable reparations, anonymously, for things that happened when she was barely a teenager, including to the poor dead man's family. Wouldn't a judge take that into account?"

"Yes." Marty straightened up in his chair. "It would definitely be of interest to the court."

"I don't see why it would matter to them. It's not about why I took off. The court doesn't even know I was part of those cons."

"CJ, it's a big deal—"

"Princess—sorry, Karita, if you'll allow me."

"Sorry," Karita muttered.

Marty had thawed considerably. CJ wondered if until then he'd seen her as someone taking advantage of Karita's desire to help. She abruptly felt that now he saw her as someone who might, *might*, given time, be good enough for Karita and she shushed the lingering but increasingly distant whisperings of Aunt Bitty trying to tell her that if he really knew who she was, he'd be the first person to turn her in.

"Forget television and movies, CJ. The law isn't like that. No matter how perverted it can be in sensational cases, the law was created to protect people and their property. Sometimes it fails miserably and then it makes headlines. But most of the time, in cases nobody ever hears about, judges really do care about justice, which balances the greater good against the threat of harm. In case after ordinary case, a good judge knows that restitution is more useful and more lasting than punishment." He gave her an encouraging smile. "Let's find you a good attorney who'll get you a hearing with that kind of judge."

Marty made three quick phone calls and wrote down three names as a result. He passed the list to CJ. "Give them all a call, tell them what you told me, and take it from there. If you want some help choosing, I'll be happy to advise you."

"Thank you," CJ said. She rose to her feet, guardedly hopeful. She gestured at the gun. "I took the firing pin out. I don't want to take it back. I don't need it in my life anymore."

"Are you my client?"

CJ smiled. "I have three deliveries of substantial sums of money that I no longer need to handle anonymously. I would like a legal agent to do that for me from now on."

Karita hopped to her feet. "I'll get a retainer deposit form." She paused for a second to touch Marty's hand. "Thank you."

To CJ's intense relief, Marty picked up the gun. "I'll lock this up until I can see it disposed of safely."

CJ watched the lump of metal, and all that it represented of her mistakes and regrets, go out of her life. She hoped with all her heart that it was a harbinger of things to come.

Chapter 16

"Four weeks sabbatical, eh? Starting tomorrow?"

CJ gave Jerry a reassuring smile to hide her irritation. He'd interrupted her last few minutes in the office to rehash her request for leave. "It's a once-in-a-lifetime thing, Jerry. I have to take care of it now."

"And your deals in progress really are covered?" His boyish charm was marred by a deep scowl.

"As I said, I've farmed them out to the people with the best chance of closing them. I saved this one for you. Last-minute gift." It hurt to hand Jerry the largest client she had, one interested in an entire floor in the Prospector Building. She had been planning to give it to Burnett, but had held back just in case Jerry did exactly what he was doing now. It was a bribe, plain and simple, and she hoped the lucrative possibility would keep her in his good graces. Though she knew any agency in town would be happy to bring her on, starting over would be an energy drain she didn't want to juggle right now.

"Well, it's highly unusual." He looked slightly mollified when he saw the name of the client on the folder. "I still wish you'd given more notice."

"I know, but I seriously doubt I'll ever be in this situation again." CJ could say that with almost absolute certainty. After the initially tempestuous conversation with Emily, dealing with Jerry was a picnic.

"You are so on probation," Emily had declared. "Hurt her and I'll probably have to kill you."

Karita had laughed and kissed Emily with a hug, but CJ had taken the threat seriously. She wouldn't forget the bond between Karita and Emily and had no intention of giving Emily any reason to be alarmed. If she hurt Karita, she was perfectly aware that Emily would have to get in a long line for the honor of killing her. Nann and Pam could feed her to a mountain lion. Lucy could bury her somewhere no one would ever find. She hoped that making Karita deliriously happy *and* raising a bunch of money for the shelter would get her in good with all of Karita's friends. It was a con, oh yes it was, but she was up front about it, and the rewards were worth it.

She left Jerry salivating over the possible deal and took care of the last detail of her day.

Nate Summerfield was expecting her call.

"So, CJ, my favorite real estate broker, are you calling to take me out for a wonderful lunch, or do you want a favor?"

"If we go to Elway's again, you're buying. You're right, though, it's a favor I'm after. I need something only you can give me," she finished in a breathy contralto.

He chuckled. "Who do I make the check payable to?"

"Not so fast, it's actually something else."

Nate laughed. "Is my wife going to object?"

"Your wife may kiss you."

"I am thoroughly intrigued."

CJ took a deep breath, but kept her tone casual. "Here's the deal. There's a new program called After the Big Game. We're hoping to have Marguerite Brownell, or someone equally prominent, be our lead cheerleader. It pays for the extra staff in a local shelter on the nights after big sporting events. More kids and their mothers end up in shelters on nights like that. What would be really neat is if some of the men like you, who know that sports give a lot to the community in terms of economy and pride, also supported something that helps with the downside."

Nate didn't sound quite as enthusiastic as he had, but he said, "Okay, you've twisted my arm. Why don't I write you a check?"

"We're thinking of a way to thank the men who donate big dollars, give them something that would really put a smile on their face without costing any money from the program. None of you guys needs another tie clip. You've got three minutes of DiamondVision ad time because you're a sponsor of the University of Colorado's big rivalry match. What you can give me, which nobody else on the planet can, is thirty seconds up on the scoreboard to plug the program and thank the big guys who give us some real dinero."

"Thirty seconds? Do you know what that space costs for every ten seconds?"

"But you already wrote that check, Nate." CJ knew he was going to say yes and tried to keep the glee out of her voice. "I'm not asking you to write another one. Once Cheri knows what you're doing, she will kiss you. And so will your daughters and so will all the women who work for you. So will I, if that's worth anything to you."

Nate laughed. "You could sell exhaust fumes at a NASCAR rally, you know that?"

CJ ginned so hard her cheeks hurt. "So I've been told. I try to use my powers for good, though. Listen, one more thing. I'm going out of town for a few weeks, so I'm dropping a big packet of information in the mail. Do me a favor, don't treat it like other stuff from me—read it, okay? The name and number of the shelter director is in there if you have questions. When I get back I'll approach Brownell. Your support already in hand will make a big difference."

She put the phone down and glanced at the clock. Sure

enough, she heard Karita's voice asking for her, then Burnett giving her a hearty hello.

With a nervous shiver, she picked up her small suitcase, knowing she wouldn't be back for a while. The sight of Karita's long, silver-gold hair sweeping around her shoulders didn't help the shivers, but the steadfast, loving look in those amazing blue eyes did. "That time already?"

"Yeah."

"Have a good trip, you two." Burnett hugged them both. His boisterous declaration had heads popping up over cubicles.

"Hey! You're not going on vacation by yourself, are you?" Juliya peered curiously at Karita, gaze narrowed.

CJ was shocked, and pleased, to realize Juliya was giving Karita a skeptical once-over. When she got back she'd assure Juliya that Karita was good enough for her, good enough and then some.

Tre came out of his cubicle, saying, "Weird enough you're actually taking a vacation, but with another human being? Since when?"

Grinning, CJ hooked her arm around Karita's. "Since now."

Karita gave Tre a big smile and touched the small framed print of an elegant Vietnamese charcoal drawing and script lettering that he'd hung on his exterior cubicle wall. "I love Nyugen Du. This is such a beautiful poem." To CJ's amazement, Karita traced the first line with her fingertip, reading it aloud in Vietnamese.

Tre laughed, answered rapidly in his native language, then said, "When you get back we'll have to have lunch or something."

"I'd love to hear how things really are faring in the Red River area." Karita turned to CJ. "Ready?"

Just when I thought the llama was the big surprise. It could take years to learn all there was to this amazing woman, years she looked forward to with all her heart. CJ knew she probably had the sappiest look of all time on her face as she answered truthfully, "Yes, I'm ready."

They got on the elevator to a chorus of well wishes. A

person might almost think they were leaving on a honeymoon or something. Burnett's quiet, supportive nod said he suspected the truth and CJ was okay with that. There were things that family ought to know.

"Guess what was in my mailbox this morning?" CJ stole a kiss as the elevator descended.

"I've no idea." Karita kissed her back.

"A notice from the Denver Traffic Court. I forgot to go to traffic school. They're very upset with me and I need to pay a big fine. Turns out going to community service didn't save me a dime."

Karita was still laughing as they boarded the shuttle bus to the airport. Her laughter was a healing balm to CJ's strained nerves. She was going back to Kentucky, back to Fayette, and part of her was terrified. But she also knew, strange as it seemed, that she had an elf by her side.

The distant roar in CJ's ears hadn't subsided. From the moment the judge had said, "Sentence reduced to time served" she'd been lightheaded. Shock, probably. Or she was walking on air because the weights of the past, carried so long, had been knocked off her shoulders by the rap of a gavel.

Getting off the transfer bus in the side yard inside Fayette's walls didn't help reconnect her to her body. She followed the other inmates through the massive barred door and her nose twitched at the strong odor of pine disinfectant mixed with the acrid stink of the grease used to keep the steel door hinges oiled. She stood quietly at the end of the line, already on the guard's radar as the new arrival who was the oldest by twenty years, and who wasn't wearing county-issued orange.

That they hadn't made her change her clothes helped CJ damp down the blind panic that still threatened to overwhelm her. If they were going to incarcerate her, she'd be in a jumpsuit by now.

The girl in front of her started to sniffle again. CJ wished she had a tissue to give her. She couldn't have been more than thirteen, and her dark braids and haunted eyes reminded CJ of herself all those years ago.

"You can survive this place." She hadn't realized she was going to speak to the child. "I did."

The girl gave her a suspicious look and didn't answer.

I don't know her story, CJ thought. I don't know how to make her believe me. "I'm nobody special. Only thing I had in here was my brain. You've got a brain too. I can see it in your eyes."

"No talking in line," a guard called.

One by one the teens in front of her were processed through the large door to the new arrivals' holding room. CJ could see beyond the thick glass and marveled that the off-white walls and falsely cheerful mural of woodland creatures hadn't changed one iota. But she wasn't going through that door, she reminded herself. Today she got to walk in the other direction.

When CJ reached the front of her row she gave her papers to the bored guard and waited as they were examined.

"You were here a long time ago." She fixed CJ with a steady, gray-eyed look. "Sure you don't want to stay?"

"I am *quite* sure." CJ's heartbeat refused to slow, even when the guard gave her a ghost of a smile.

At the bottom of the first page the guard signed her name and then ran a seal over it, adding a layer of luminescent ink that blazoned the date and time. "You are now an inmate of Fayette County Juvenile Detention Center."

CJ caught her breath. The echo of those same words, said more than twenty years ago, was heavy in her ears. "And now?"

The guard turned to the second page, signed and inked again. "Please proceed through the door to your rear." She handed CJ her papers without another glance.

A muffled buzzer sounded as CJ approached the door. After it rolled to the left, she went through it to find herself in a small Plexiglass enclosed space. The door at her back rolled shut, another buzzer sounded, and the opposite door opened.

A disembodied voice said, "Follow the yellow line."

She did as she was told. The yellow line promptly ended at a tiny window. Another guard with another set of dispassionate eyes glanced at her paperwork. She handed the papers behind her and said to CJ, "Follow the red line."

It was only a few steps around the corner, but she was brought up short by one of the broadest-shouldered women she'd ever seen. "Stand on the X," she was ordered.

She did. The woman looked her up and down, then carefully studied the contents of a folder. "Are you Cassiopeia Juniper Rochambeau?"

"Yes," she said firmly. It was the last time she would have to admit it. She didn't mind Cassiopeia so much—no one had ever called her by it. She'd always been Cassie June. Even Cass was better than that.

The guard lifted a photograph taken at the courthouse booking station from the folder and held it next to CJ's face. "It's a match," she called. She put the photograph back in the folder and walked away in the direction CJ had come from. "Follow the green line."

The green line ended at another thick, steel door, which swung open with a soul-chilling screech. A blast of sunlight left her dazzled as she staggered her way to freedom.

"I wasn't even back to the car before she called." Karita switched CJ's cell phone to her other ear as she turned into the visitor's parking lot. "It went even better than the lawyer thought."

Emily still sounded simultaneously protective and disapproving. "So she's not having to spend any time in jail?"

"They took her into custody at the courthouse and she went to the county jail. She stayed there just long enough to get transferred to the facility where she was all those years ago. They'll process her back out to make it official. Approaching it as an extension of her juvenile case let the judge treat her like a juvenile and put the whole thing under her juvenile record. She's agreed to finish making restitution and has to show the proof to a parole officer in Kentucky. Once that's done her record is sealed. She could even legally apply to change her birth name to the one she's been using. She said she'd take out a loan and be done so she could move on with her life." Karita knew her voice went all mushy and soft, but she couldn't help it. "To get on with *our* life."

Emily's voice was drenched with skepticism. "You'll get to have your life, the one you want, even though she's some hotshot businesswoman? I'm so afraid you're going to get lost in *her* life."

Karita sighed happily as she parked near the exit gate. "On the flight here, do you know what we talked about? It was her idea, completely. I told her about the Peace Corps and she thought that if I got a credential, I'd be a lot happier teaching English-as-a-Second-Language courses to Vietnamese immigrants than I am working in a law office. She doesn't think that's flaky at all. I wouldn't make as much money, but I'd be happier and if the lack of money is ever a problem for her, for us, she promised to talk to me about it. She thinks that's a wonderful way for a person to spend her life." She swallowed hard.

"Oh." Emily's tone softened slightly. "She may have a point there. So...she's not a karmically bankrupt yuppie? You're sure?"

"The fundraising thing she's doing for you isn't a fluke, Em. She's a good person, in spite of being raised to be a bad one." She started to add that neither she nor Em had been tested the way CJ had, but she heard a doorbell ring in the background on Emily's end of the line. "Answer the door. I'll call you later."

She snapped CJ's cell phone closed and dashed tears out of her eyes. CJ had held her hand on the plane, pale and worried. But she'd talked about Karita's future with a glow deep down in her dark eyes, and Karita had glimpsed the gold she'd seen during that first astonishing kiss. It was the color of CJ's soul, and she felt blessed to be the one who finally got to be warmed by it.

"All the magic worked, Gran. It all worked. I wished, as hard as I could, and I tried to be brave when I had to be, and everything is going to be okay." She wasn't an elf, but she felt as if magic was all around her, and would continue to be, with CJ in her life.

CJ stepped out into the sweltering, thick afternoon. The humidity threatened to choke her to a standstill but her heart was already over the nearest fence. After a grateful gulp of air that helped clear her head of the lingering smell of disinfectant, she walked across the yard toward a small guardhouse and a chainlink gate.

Karita was looking at her through the gate, wiping away tears.

She took a shuddering breath and addressed herself through more thick Plexiglass to the lone guard. "Rochambeau. I don't have any personal effects."

The woman's dark face was impassive. She retrieved a card from a small printer behind her and pushed it through a thin slot. "Sign here."

CJ did as she was told, then watched the guard sign directly under it, then ink over both their signatures with the date and time. She slapped it on a little copier, then gave CJ the result. "You are now released from the Fayette County Juvenile Detention Center." In a bored tone, she added, "Good luck in your new life."

It didn't seem real. She turned her head to gaze at Karita through the gate and then, yes, it was real. She was free. "Thank you, but I don't think I need luck." She grinned. "I've got magic."

The gate rolled open.

She walked through it, head up. *Good-bye Cassie June.*

Karita swept CJ into her arms, laughing and crying. "I want to take you home, right now, this afternoon. All we have to do is drive west until we see the Rockies."

Karita was squeezing her so hard that she couldn't breathe. "It's at least a thousand miles, crazy woman. It'll take a whole day. Let's just get a flight. If we're lucky we can sleep in your bed tonight."

"What a wonderful thought." Karita pulled her toward the rental car.

"And if we can't get a flight we'll just hole up in an airport motel and pretend we're rabbits. Or marmots. Or llamas." She looked up at the blue-white sky. This is what it felt like to be free. It was like flying, on the inside, in waves of golden light.

"No llamas. Spitting is not my thing."

Laughing, she took Karita's face in her hands. This is what it felt like to be free and in love, she thought, and then she kissed that wonderful mouth, kissed the streaks of tears, kissed the nose, kissed everything. She was free in her soul, finally, and could give her heart completely, at last.

"I like this," Karita said between smooches, "but I would like even more to get far away from here. Soon."

"Can I drive? I want to leave here under my own control."

Karita gave her the keys, tears again shimmering in her eyes.

Once they were in the car, Karita turned up the air-conditioning. "I'm sure areas of Kentucky are lovely but I'll be happy not to visit this particular part of the state again."

"I'm with you, absolutely." CJ pulled out onto the county road. The rental's air-conditioning was still struggling to cool the car. "I should have taken off my jacket."

She squirmed to get her left shoulder free, awkwardly trading hands on the wheel.

"I'll hold it," Karita said as she reached over to keep the steering wheel steady.

CJ finished wiggling out of the suit jacket, aware that she had, without a second thought, put her life in Karita's care. It felt wonderful.

"Thank you." Once she was settled, she clasped her hand to Karita's. They rounded a gentle curve in the road. Easy as that, Fayette disappeared from the rearview mirror. "I gave it some thought, and you can call me Cass if you want."

"I like CJ." Karita drew CJ's hand to her lips. "I always have."

CJ spread her fingertips against the warmth of Karita's mouth. She was going to spend the rest of her life, day in and day out, earning this woman's love. "I never thought I'd say this, but I like her, too."

About the Author

Among Karin Kallmaker's more than twenty-five romance and fantasy-science fiction novels are the award-winning *Just Like That, Maybe Next Time, Sugar* and *18th & Castro* along with the bestselling *Substitute for Love* and the perennial classic *Painted Moon.* Two dozen short stories have appeared in anthologies from publishers like Alyson, Bold Strokes, Circlet and Haworth, as well as novellas and dozens more short stories with Bella Books. She began her writing career with the venerable Naiad Press and continues with Bella. Her novels have been translated into Spanish, French, German and Czech.

She and her partner are the mothers of two and live in the San Francisco Bay Area. She is descended from Lady Godiva, a fact which she'll share with anyone who will listen. She likes her Internet fast, her iPod loud and her chocolate real.

All of Karin's work can now be found at Bella Books. Details and background about her novels, and her other pen name, Laura Adams, are at www.kallmaker.com.

Publications from
Bella Books, Inc.
The best in contemporary lesbian fiction

P.O. Box 10543, Tallahassee, FL 32302
Phone: 800-729-4992
www.bellabooks.com

WITHOUT WARNING: Book one in the Shaken series by KG MacGregor. *Without Warning* is the story of their courageous journey through adversity, and their promise of steadfast love.
ISBN: 978-1-59493-120-8
$13.95

HFRAW KALLM

THE CAN[   ] by [   ] Presidential candidate Jane Kincaid had already expected the road to the White House would exact a high personal toll. She just never knew how [   ] forced to choose between her [   ]
ISBN: 978-1 **KALLMAKER, KARIN,**
$13.95   **THE KISS THAT COUNTED**

FRANK
TALL IN **12/09** by Karin Kallmaker, Barbara Johnson, Therese Szymanski and Julia Watts. The playful quartet that penned the acclaimed *Once Upon A Dyke* and *Stake Through the Heart* are back and are now turning to the Wild (and Very Hot) West to bring you another collection of erotically charged, action-packed, tales.
ISBN: 978-1-59493-106-2
$15.95

IN THE NAME OF THE FATHER by Gerri Hill. In this highly anticipated sequel to *Hunter's Way*, Dallas homicide detectives Tori Hunter and Samantha Kennedy investigate the murder of a Catholic priest who is found naked and strangled to death.
ISBN: 978-1-59493-108-6
$13.95